Divulge

Book two
The Obscured series

C. M. Boers

ISBN: 978-0-9906452-2-1

CONTENTS

Acknowledgements

I would like to thank my kids for being understanding when mommy had to work. My husband for at times doing bedtimes alone and going out of his way to give me time to work. My sister, Kelly, for being the amazing model you see on my the cover. I can't forget our other close friends and family that have encouraged, inquired, reviewed, read, or gave feedback.

Last, but not least, my readers for taking the time to check out my books!

CHAPTER ONE

A deep sense of dread filled me as I gave chase. I can't stop. I have to catch them. I have to. I don't know what I will do if I can't. I gasped for air and cursed myself for not being in better shape.

The vacant streets of this sleepy town lay eerily quiet, sending shivers down my spine. Rain was not far off. The fragrant must of an impending downpour filled my nose. I could see the threatening bolts of lightning in the distance coming so close to the ground that I wondered if something had been struck.

The sound of my footsteps bounced off the red brick walls and echoed around me, giving the effect of countless people surrounding me. I pressed forward toward the figure in front of me. Just ahead I spotted a flash rounding the corner and vanishing from sight. I sprinted faster. The corner seemed to be miles away. My side ached and my steps faltered as the ache intensified, engulfing my entire side in fire, fire that burned unseen deep in my muscles.

Finally I made it there. I peered around the edge of the building…

I jolted from my sleep and was met by Eli's masculine scent. It filled the air, bringing me back to reality. I felt the coolness of sweat on my forehead. I was in Eli's room. It was a surreal feeling, waking up in his bed. But it was the only way I knew the night before had been real. My nightmare, on the other hand, I could only hope was just a dream. I had a sinking feeling that was not the case. After the last nightmare came true, I hoped it had been a fluke one-time thing. The last thing I needed was another complication in my already complicated life. I couldn't keep up.

After my psycho ex-boyfriend Pete kidnapped me and Bailey, he was sentenced to appear before the elders. As it turns out, Pete's family had an axe to grind with Eli's dad, and I guess if you're friends with someone who has enemies you automatically become a target. Unfortunately, the elders asked Eli and Ren to bring Pete to Colorado for the meeting, leaving me behind. The elders had assured Eli that I would be safe, and that was the one and only reason Eli, my assigned Protector and boyfriend, had left me in the first place. But it appeared that one of Pete's buffoons had other plans, and I was kidnapped once again. It was one big fiasco after another. Eli's dad, Vince, came to my rescue that time and brought me back to Eli safely. When Eli and I drove back to Phoenix late that night, I got the privilege of sleeping in Eli's bed. Of course Eli slept on the floor, but his bed smelled of him. It was intoxicating, a scent I couldn't get enough of.

I didn't want to open my eyes. If I did, that would mean this moment here, curled up in his bed, would have to end, and I would once again have to face reality. Reality was uncertain and confusing. I wasn't ready for that. I needed just a few more moments of bliss.

"How long are you going to lay there pretending to sleep?" Eli asked, startling me from my thoughts.

Dang! I had hoped he was still sleeping. I could never pull anything over on him; because of our connection he was able to sense my every emotion, my every feeling, my every desire. I opened my eyes to find him sitting across the room in a chair, watching me with a smirk on his face. He was fully dressed and his jet-black hair was wet like he had just gotten out of the shower.

I gave him a sleepy smile as he made his way over to me. Sitting down on the bed, he laced his hand into mine. It was moments like these that made my heart feel like it would burst. Our love was a breathtaking feeling, unlike anything I had ever experienced before. It made me feel like I was floating on air, like I could do anything.

He leaned down to place a kiss on my forehead. "Good morning. It's getting late. You need to get up."

"I don't want to."

"Come on," he said, pulling up on my hand and throwing the covers off me. "You can't be late for school."

Cool air filter through the sweatpants and a t-shirt Eli had given me to wear late last night. I was so comfy that it was almost painful to get up.

I sat on the edge, giving myself a few more moments of complete relaxation before I rose. Eli pulled me into his arms and held me tight. A girl could get used to waking up to this delightful welcome, in spite of my bed head and morning breath.

"Thank god you're safe. I don't know what I would have done." His hushed voice trembled.

I knew he would blame himself for what happened, but the truth was that nobody could have predicted that Randy, Pete's buffoon, was still a threat, let alone that he would attack me while Eli was gone.

"There was nothing you could have done. No one could have known what was going to happen," I said as I tugged his chin, making him look me in the eye.

The sadness in his icy blue eyes tugged at me. He pulled away and ran his hands through his hair. "Dang it Abby, if I had been there he never would have gotten within five feet of you." He would no longer look at me. "I should never have left you. I won't make that mistake again."

"It's okay, Eli," I said, hoping to convince him it wasn't his fault. "Besides, you can't be with me all the time."

He had already made up his mind, and there was no way I could change it now.

"No, it's not. It's my job to protect you, and last night I didn't do that."

I didn't say more, knowing there was nothing I could say that would make him feel better. He would have to work this one out on his own. Instead, I stared at the floor, unsure of what to do or say next.

"I bought some clothes for you to wear. They're in the bathroom," he said.

I kissed his cheek and wandered through the door of Eli's adjoining bathroom. He occupied the smaller of the two master suites of his parents' large, three-bedroom house.

I showered, toweled off, and looked at the clothes Eli had picked out for me, surprised to find that they were just the right size. The outfit was simple and exactly to my taste. I wondered how Eli knew me so well, but then I felt silly. Of course he knew me well—he could feel everything I felt, everything I liked or disliked.

I slipped into the clothes and combed out my hair with what I assumed was Eli's comb. I found a brand-new toothbrush lying on the counter and smiled, thinking about how good he was at making me feel comfortable and at home here.

I found Eli waiting for me in the same chair as before, reading a magazine. We went into the kitchen and found his mom and dad at the table eating breakfast together. I don't know what I had expected to find, but their coziness surprised me. I guess I figured that since his dad had been gone, his parents were no longer together, but based on what I was seeing pass between them, that wasn't the case. They seemed so happy to be together.

"Good morning guys," Vince said as we sat down at the table.

"Morning," Eli and I said in unison. We looked at each other, surprised, and I felt my cheeks warm.

We each poured our cereal and ate as quickly as we could.

"How are you doing, Abby?" Vince asked me, his voice filled with concern.

"I guess I'm doing okay. It's been a bit of a roller coaster. Being kidnapped once sucks, but twice in less than a week is overwhelming to say the least. But I'm managing," I said, trying to sound lighthearted when that was the last thing I felt.

He looked at me sympathetically but didn't say more.

"I'm glad you're holding up," Eli's mom, Elizabeth, said.

I hadn't noticed before how radiant she was. She glowed. Maybe it was because the love of her life was back home with her. Her straight black hair hung just past her shoulders, and her bright hazel eyes sparkled. I could tell Eli got quite a few of his amazing features from her.

I wondered what life must be like for her. Her husband was a Protector, assigned to protect others at the elders' discretion. She couldn't follow him either, at least not all the time. It was the same life I was inevitably facing with Eli, and I wasn't sure how I could do it. It saddened me to think I would live much of my life without him.

When we met Bailey in the courtyard at school, she swept me up in a whirlwind of Bailey enthusiasm and immediately began firing questions.

"What in the world happened last night?"

"Hello to you too," I said, sticking my tongue out at her.

"Don't laugh at me! I was so worried about you!"

"I'm sorry, Randy kidnapped me." It came out of my mouth as a fact, as if I were detached from it, like we were talking about the weather.

Bailey's eyes grew round and for a moment she was speechless. "Oh my gosh Abby! That's awful. But how did you get away?"

"Well, he drove me to the middle of nowhere. We ended up getting a flat tire, that as it turns out, Eli's dad, Vince, caused." I grinned at Eli. "Then Vince came out of nowhere. Literally, he came out from behind a bush in the middle of the desert to confront Randy and rescue me. Eli, with our connection being what it is, knew something was wrong. He jumped on the first flight he could and drove the rest of the way out to meet us. We got back to Eli's house around one o'clock in the morning. I stayed the night, and here we are." I was breathless when I finished.

Bailey didn't seem to know what to say.

"Wow."

"We have to get to class, we're going to be late," Eli cut in.

The last thing I wanted was to go to class. I had so many questions that needed answers I wouldn't get in class. I couldn't wait to drill Eli when we were alone again.

I pushed all my troubles away for the time being and tried my hardest to focus on school. By lunchtime, I felt like my efforts were just beginning to pay off. I sat there, taking in the surrounding conversations without adding anything of my own.

I felt a little like a double agent living a secret life apart from our friends at school. Their biggest concern was their next test or why their parents were on their case this time. Mine was whether I would make it through the day without yet another person coming out of the woodwork to do Eli or me harm. To top it all off, I was having a new nightmare that had a good chance of coming true. We were worlds apart, yet here we sat, all together as if nothing was separating us at all. I longed to be like my friends again, to lead a normal life with normal problems. But then again, I wouldn't have Eli. Some things were worth the sacrifice.

I continued to push through the day with my curiosity picking and pulling its way through the web of happy thoughts I created, casting dark shadows on even the good.

When the final bell of the day rang, I felt nothing but relief. I meandered my way through the halls to meet Eli, and my heart leapt at the sight of him waiting for me. His striking good looks captivated my attention first; then he flashed a huge smile just for me. It was enough to make me melt.

He drove us to my house and, for the first time in over twenty-four stress-filled hours, I stepped past the threshold. My house waited for us, empty, perfect for our upcoming conversation. I had been both dreading and anticipating it. I grabbed us drinks before plopping down on the couch.

"Okay, what's going on with Pete?" I asked without wasting another second.

"They are proceeding as planned. They held the meeting last night; obviously, I wasn't able to be there. I talked to Ren this morning before you woke up, and the elders decided that Pete will be stripped of his immortality, which in my opinion should have been done long ago, as his dad and uncle were. He has been told to leave the United States and find a new place to live." He paused, "If he doesn't, they will be forced to take further action."

"What does that even mean?"

"I don't know."

I frowned.

"Now what?"

"Ren is holding Pete until they can carry out the punishment, and then they are trusting him to leave on his own."

"And they expect him to just do what they want?"

"I guess."

"I can't believe this! He's just going to walk away like nothing happened!"

"Well, not completely," Eli said.

I shot him a dirty look.

"Okay, okay. I understand why you're angry. I am too. But what choice do we have? There's nothing we can do."

I shrugged.

"He won't be stupid enough to come back here again," Eli said.

"Where did that kind of assumption get us last time?"

He laughed and wrapped his arm around me. We sat with our sides glued to each other, enjoying our time together. As much as I didn't want Pete to walk free, I was glad he was at least being punished. I hoped it would be enough of a deterrent for him to leave us alone. It was about time Eli and I got to relax and just have fun together.

"I should go. I have a lot of homework to catch up on."

I shot him a pouty face.

Reluctantly, I walked him to the door and kissed him goodbye, waiting until he drove away before closing the door. I already missed him. I had it bad. Really bad.

The next day I felt like an ordinary high school student, enjoying my day at school with my boyfriend by my side. We didn't discuss anything other than school and weekend plans. After so much craziness, it was nice to feel the same as everyone else. I never thought I would crave normalcy so much.

Today was the day our troubles would end, the day we had waited for: Pete would be stripped of his immunity to peril and sent packing.

Eli was talking to Ren as we walked to lunch. From the sound of it, everything was progressing on schedule. He would take Pete to the elders at 1 p.m., just a short two hours away. I couldn't wait for the call that the deed was done.

When I met with Eli after school, he informed me that Ren still hadn't called. He seemed more worried than I expected him to be. It had been nearly two hours since the meeting had been set to begin.

I dialed Ren from my phone, and the call went straight to voicemail. A sick feeling bubbled up in my stomach. *What could have happened?*

Instead of wasting time waiting for him to call back, we went straight to Vince.

CHAPTER TWO

By the time we found Vince, he was on the phone making call after call. Ren seemed to have gone AWOL; he hadn't made contact with anyone. I knew there must be something wrong.

When Vince finished making calls, he strode to his bedroom without so much as an explanation. I looked at Eli, but he only said that when his dad was ready to explain, he would. That didn't calm my nerves at all. I could feel the anxiety in my chest tightening in on me. *Was this what a panic attack felt like?* All at once, Vince emerged from his bedroom and sat us down.

"Ren and Pete never showed up to the meeting." Vince let that hang in the air for a moment before continuing. "The elders are afraid that Pete may have gotten the upper hand. There is no telling what he could do. I'm going to Colorado to see if I can find them. The elders let me in on the few leads that they had, but they honestly don't sound very promising. I am hoping that they can start investigating while they're waiting for me to arrive."

I hated Pete now more than ever. Ren wasn't just my friend; he was one of the most noble people I knew. He didn't deserve this. Today marked the second time Pete had taken someone I cared about away from me, leaving us scrambling in his wake.

My dream suddenly came to mind. It took place somewhere I had never been before; maybe Colorado. *Oh no.* Perhaps ignoring it hadn't been the best idea.

"Ah...Eli, can I talk to you for a minute?"

His confused expression wouldn't begin to cover the way he was going to feel after our talk. My hands shook as he led me up the stairs to his bedroom. I clasped them so my nerves wouldn't show. I had to hold myself together.

"Is everything okay?"

"Well, no, not really, and Ren's disappearance doesn't help either. I'm not even sure where to start." My fingers fidgeted in my lap until Eli claimed them in his. I took a deep breath before pressing on. *I can do this. I'm not crazy.* "Six months before I moved here, right about the time I found out we were moving here, in fact, I began having nightmares; one nightmare in particular. It began with me running in the desert and ended in a clearing. In the dream, I was running from something or someone. It felt so real. The heat. The dust. Everything. I even woke up sometimes, screaming or sweating as if I were actually there." I waited to see if he was following.

He nodded for me to keep going. "Well, that night in the desert with Pete, it came true. Every sight, every smell, every detail. The only thing that had been missing the whole time was Pete."

"So you're telling me that you think you saw the future?"

"Yes."

"You should have told me before now, Abby," he said. "Has this ever happened before?"

"No."

"You're sure?"

"Yes, I think I would remember."

"Ok."

He sat lost in thought, his face twisted in deep thought.

I took a deep breath. "That's not all."

"What?"

"I haven't had the dream again since that night."

"Well, that's good, right?" he asked.

"Yeah, except last night I had a new dream, and it felt real in all of the same ways."

He nodded. "You think it might come true too?" He stood and began pacing the room.

"I don't know. Last night I had a dream that I was chasing after somebody. I don't know where I was, but it seemed like a small, deserted town. I've never been there before. There were brick walls all around me, and I was scared...scared of losing you, I think. I tried so hard to catch up, but I think I fell behind and that's when I woke up covered in sweat."

"And you do think it may come true? Is that why you're telling me?"

"I tried to push it from my mind, hoping it wasn't true, but now that Ren is missing, I'm even more afraid."

He blew out a large breath of air and reached out with both his hands and rubbed my arms up and down as if to soothe me. "It's okay. We'll figure this out." He sounded confident, but deep down I knew he felt worried too. Stress had etched itself in the lines on his face.

"What are we going to do?" I asked.

"Well, let's keep your dream to ourselves for now, at least until we figure out what's going on."

I was relieved he didn't want to tell anyone. The last thing I wanted was for people to think I was crazy. I already felt a little crazy for thinking I possessed some kind of psychic dream power.

A deep sigh escaped my lips, and Eli put his arm around me. "Come on, it will be all right," he said.

He led me back downstairs to bid his dad goodbye when he left for the airport. They didn't know when he would return, and I was sad to see him go, not just for Eli and his mom, but for me as well. I couldn't say that I had any right to feel that way, seeing as I had just met him, but I already deeply respected him. He was like my dad in so many ways and more. He had been there for me when I needed him, and I would always be grateful.

Eli took me home shortly after his dad left. I set out to work on my homework straightaway, but the chaos in my mind drew me into a blank stare more often than I wanted to admit. I couldn't seem to get past my dream, not now that things had changed. I chastised myself for not saying something sooner; perhaps I could have prevented all this. Maybe we were all worked up for nothing and Ren was fine, but until that was proven, I couldn't help but fear the worst.

Just as my mom walked in the door, I headed out for work. I had told Eli I would walk today since he was off, but in truth I needed the time alone to clear my head. Surely fresh air would help me sort through the thoughts bouncing around in there; I hadn't breathed without feeling a heavy weight on my chest in what felt like a long time. When Eli offered to calm me, I declined. Because of our connection, Eli could change my emotions to help me, but at that moment I felt fully capable of calming myself. But even out in the warm breeze, I failed over and over to convince myself that Ren would be all right, and my worries remained.

When my head hit the pillow that night, I fell fast asleep in minutes. A chaotic day sure could tire me out.

There are three of them. My chest is burning; my quickened breathing continues. They are getting further and further out of sight. The musty smell of rain filled the air. The brick walls around me feel as if they are closing in on me, and I run faster. I can no longer see two of the figures in front of me, giving me only one focal point to follow.

Sweat pours down my forehead into my eyes, and I had to blink to clear them, blurring my vision. The last figure disappears.

I sat straight up in bed. These night terrors filled me with anxiety about what was to come and what I might be capable of. Eli's gifted nature put him through so much; now I might be set to face the same fate. I just wanted to be normal. The same normal I once detested.

I couldn't wait to find out if Eli had heard from his dad. The instant I heard his horn outside, I raced out the door and into his car faster than I had ever run before.

"Wow, you must be happy to see me," he teased.

"Did you hear from your dad?" I asked, breathless.

"Good morning to you, too."

"Sorry."

"And, no I haven't," he said.

The unknown was killing me, and I dreaded another day at school. At least spring break was next week—I could sure use it.

My day went by in a blur while worries occupied every nerve in my brain. My mind seemed to multitask subconsciously because I still managed to complete my work with little effort.

Seeing Bailey at lunch was the highlight of the day. I could tell she was trying to hide her worry for Ren. She seemed to be overcompensating by dialing up her normal exuberant personality around our other friends. I still hadn't filled her in on my dreams. I felt bad keeping her in the dark about them, but I didn't want anyone else to know about them until I understood for certain what they meant. I had to be fair to myself.

"Hey Bailey, do you want to come over after school?" I asked as we walked out of the cafeteria.

"Sure. I'll check with my dad, but I'm sure it'll be fine. Got anything particular in mind?"

"No, just figured we could hang out. It seems like it's been forever and I'm in need of some veg out time."

"Sounds good to me! See you after school," she called over her shoulder as she dashed to her next class.

A visit from Bailey was exactly the distraction I needed. It felt good to be excited about something, even if it was overshadowed by Ren's disappearance. Even if things were bad, we could still eat junk food, watch bad TV, and paint our nails.

When the final bell rang, I hurried out of class, escaping to Eli's car. He dropped Bailey and I off at my house, and I kissed him goodbye.

"So how are things going with you and him anyway?" Bailey asked once we were alone in my living room.

I sighed.

"That good huh?"

"No, things are fine," I said.

"Fine?"

"Yeah, it's just that we haven't had a chance to enjoy being together without all this chaos around us. I feel guilty for wanting to just be a couple right now. Ren is who-knows-where, and all I can think about is wanting to be with my boyfriend. I'm such a terrible friend."

"You're not a terrible friend! You rescued me, didn't you? Of course you want to be with your boyfriend! That's only natural. You need to cheer up!" she said, throwing me a bag of gummy worms. "Eat. Sugar makes everyone feel better." She slurped a worm into her mouth.

We painted our nails hot pink and danced around the living room awkwardly on our heels till the paint dried to the radio, singing too loud and off-key. It felt great to be carefree. I hadn't realized how reserved I had become since moving here: This was the first time I had really let loose and the first time I felt like me again in a while. I didn't want it to end, but when my mom walked in the front door, I knew our fun was over for the time being, Bailey wouldn't be as inhabited with her in the next room.

Bailey stayed for dinner, and we brought her home afterwards. I was so grateful to have Bailey as my best friend. I promised myself I would make room for more girl time with her from now on.

My phone rang as soon as I stepped into my bedroom.

Eli's smooth voice filled my ear. "Hey sweetie."

"Hey," I said, a smile spreading across my face, and I sprawled out on my bed. "I just got back from taking Bailey home."

"I figured."

"What?" I asked.

"I just mean it seemed like you might be getting settled in," he said.

"Right…my feelings," I grumbled.

"Well don't say it like that."

"Sorry, I didn't mean it like that."

"I'm glad that you and Bailey got to hang out. I haven't sensed your mood that carefree since you got here," he said.

"It felt good to forget for a little while."

"You shouldn't have to worry about any of it," he said, and I felt our joyful conversation slipping away.

"Don't think like that. If it weren't for all this trouble, we wouldn't have what we do. It's brought us closer than ever. Don't think I'm not grateful for that."

"Well, I hope that's the way you feel after I tell you what I've just learned. I hate to end such a good day on a bad note…" He paused. "But I heard from my dad."

My heart rate peaked, and I rolled onto my stomach, at full attention. "What did he say?"

"He's positive that Pete took Ren hostage."

My heart sank.

"The elders handed over all their leads, but he said it's not looking very promising so far."

"Why?" I asked.

"He's looked into five of them already and they haven't gotten him anywhere."

"We should be there helping him," I said.

"I wish I could be."

"You mean *we*."

"No, I don't want you in the middle of this. You've already experienced more problems than I could have ever imagined. There is no way I would willingly put you in harm's way by involving you," he said.

But the more I thought about it, the more I felt compelled to go. I just had to convince him.

"We have to go," I said with more certainty than before.

"No."

"Eli…"

"We can't."

I could tell he felt backed into a corner. I did too, but I was ready to fight my way out. Was he? I heard a rustling over the phone, and I pictured him pacing his bedroom in frustration.

"What would we tell your mom?" he asked.

I had thought of this too, but good ideas were evading me for the moment. That wouldn't stop me though.

"I'll think of something."

"You shouldn't have to. This isn't your fight," he said.

"It is my fight. I've been in the center of this since it started." I knew he couldn't argue with that, and his silence told me he couldn't think of anything more to say.

I gave up trying to convince him for now, but this conversation wasn't over, and he knew that just as well as I did.

CHAPTER THREE

The idea came to me while I was putting the finishing touches on my makeup for the day. A class trip excuse would be just the ticket and with Spring break beginning tomorrow it was the perfect timing. I decided to tell my parents that the trip was optional and was reserved for students with at least a 3.0 grade point average. They would be proud of me for earning something not everyone else had, throwing them off their game.

I was thrilled with myself and spent the next fifteen minutes devising all of the little details that would make it seem real. I just hoped that my parents wouldn't question why I was asking so late, but if they did, I had a plan for that too. I was becoming good at lying, not that I should brag about that.

I couldn't help myself when Eli walked through the front door to pick me up for school. I blabbed my whole plan in such an overwhelming rush that I got winded.

"Sounds like you've thought of everything, except one thing," he said.

My smile turned to a frown as I frantically tried to think of something I had missed. "What?" I asked.

"We're not going." He didn't even glance in my direction.

"Eli, come on. You know we have to help. Ren is missing."

He ignored me and headed for the door. "Let's go."

Why did he have to be so difficult? I got in his car and didn't say another word, giving him the silent treatment he deserved.

At school, my mute protest continued throughout the morning. I was so frustrated with his stubbornness. We had to help find Ren—we just had to. Ren would have done the same for us in a heartbeat.

"Hey Abby," Bailey said.

"Hey," I grumbled.

"Wow, you're in a great mood. Why so glum?" she asked as we walked to lunch.

I let out my breath in a long, dramatic growl. "I'm so frustrated."

"About Ren?" she asked.

"I should be there! We should be there! Helping Vince find him. Eli is so stubborn. He refuses to go. I even came up with the perfect cover story for my parents, but he still won't even consider it."

"Oh," she said.

"Oh? That's it? Oh?"

"Well, I…I sort of understand where you're coming from, but…I can also see Eli's side of things. I mean, I don't want to see anything happen to you. Pete has already done so much to wrong you…us."

Great! Not even Bailey was on my side. As we approached the lunch table, our private conversation ended and, despite the chattering voices around me, I sat in silence. Between Eli and Bailey I felt helpless. Eli kept looking in my direction with puppy dog eyes. *Did he really think that would make things better?* I stopped making eye contact halfway through lunch out of self-preservation. I wanted to scream.

As soon as I finished my lunch, I got up alone and headed out of the room. I needed some time to myself. The second my foot left the threshold, someone put a hand on my shoulder to stop me.

"Wait."

I whirled around, ready to pounce, but Eli put his hands up in the air to surrender, and I stopped myself.

"You win," he said so quietly I thought I misunderstood him.

"What?"

"We can go," he said as he stared at the floor.

"Really?"

"Yeah," he said. His eyes met mine, and I could see fear in them, but then he looked away, and when his gaze made its way back to me, the apprehension was gone.

I understood how he felt. After all, the whole thing terrified me too, but I knew it was something I had to do. We had to help Ren. I knew he would have helped us; it was just what friends did for each other.

I threw my arms around him. "Thanks Eli."

He pulled me in for a kiss that left me grateful we were alone in the hallway. He dipped me like we were dancing before pulling away, and I gasped for air. I giggled when he righted me and set me back on my feet. We walked down the hallway, enjoying our alone time.

"When do we leave?" I asked.

"*If* your parents say yes, you mean?"

"Yeah," I said, rolling my eyes.

"Tomorrow."

He kissed me goodbye for the time being, and I went to class.

My mind raced through plans for the trip to Colorado. I mentally prepared my to-do list that I would have to start on as soon as I got home if I wanted to be able to leave in the morning.

On my way out of school, Bailey bounded up to me.

"Eli told me the news," she said.

I beamed at her, knowing I had gotten my way, as if I were a spoiled child gloating.

"I can't say I won't be worried about you, but I'm glad that there will be more people searching for Ren. I really hope he's okay," Bailey said, biting her lip.

"We'll be fine," I said, smiling. "So will Ren."

"You'd better call me to let me know what your parents say."

"I will. I'd better go. I have a lot of work to do. See ya!"

"Bye," she called after me.

Eli dropped me off at home so I could pack and talk to my mom by myself. I felt uneasy about asking her about this trip. She had always been accommodating about the things that I wanted, and since she rarely got upset I shouldn't have been so worried, but we had been so distant lately that I wondered if things would still be the same. I felt terrible that I hadn't had the time for our usual mother-daughter chats, but I hoped to change that once this whole fiasco faded into the rearview mirror.

Then it hit me: Even though Eli and I were off the whole weekend, I was sure we would have to work the following week.

I grabbed the phone and dialed his number. "Hey Eli, you have to call to get off work."

"I already did," he said.

"Oh, ok."

I breathed a sigh of relief. Now I hoped I would be able to get off as well.

"I'll call you later," I said.

"Okay, I love you."

"I love you too." I blushed.

It took me a minute to come down from my cloud. Hearing that someone—especially someone as amazing as Eli—loved me felt surreal.

I picked up the phone once again and called work. "Hey Laurie, it's Abby. I was wondering if I could get off work from tomorrow through next Sunday?"

"Oh! Abby, I just gave Eli the whole week off. I can't lose both of you the same week," she said.

Dang it! How could I have been so naïve? Maybe Eli had been counting on this when he said yes. He knew Laurie wouldn't let us both off, and he didn't want to be the bad guy.

"Oh, okay. If there's any way, please let me know," I said, trying not to be too pushy.

"I'll see what I can do."

"Okay, bye."

I hung up, feeling defeated all over again. One step forward and two steps back. I slid down the wall to the floor and hoped that someday things wouldn't be so difficult. When the knock at the door came, it startled me, but I should have known Eli would come to see what was wrong with me. The second my mood plummeted, he knew.

He walked right in, not waiting for me to get to the door.

"Abby?" he called.

"In here."

"What's going on? Did your mom say no?" he asked.

"I haven't asked her yet."

"Well then what's all this…this…frustration? Is that right— frustration?"

I nodded.

"What's wrong?" he asked.

"I can't get off work." I wouldn't look at him as I said it. I couldn't handle his 'I told you so.'

"I'm sorry," he said.

"No you aren't. You don't even want to go," I said.

He fell quiet for a minute before speaking. So quiet that I almost caved and snuck a glance at him.

"I want to go," he said, startling me. "I just don't want *you* to go. You know I'm just worried about you, but I'm putting what I want aside. I will keep you safe, and we will go. I promise."

"How? I can't get off work."

"I'll figure something out. You just worry about the two P's."

"The two P's?" I asked.

"Packing and parents," he said with a grin.

"Okay!" It felt good to laugh.

I hugged him with a renewed sense of hope, though doubts still remained in my mind. How did he plan to convince Laurie? I couldn't let my thoughts linger on that, so I pushed it aside and tried my best to focus on the task at hand: the two P's.

"I'm going to go, you take care of your things and call me after you talk to your mom, okay?"

"Alright."

He kissed me goodbye and walked out the front door. I made my way to my bedroom and pulled my duffle bag out from under the bed. As I set to work laying out all of my clothes, I hoped the duffle would be big enough.

I tried to imagine how the conversation with my mom would go, but I just couldn't come up with any reasonable scenarios. Nothing came close to being realistic. I could only discern one reason for why my mind was set on unrealistic expectations: I couldn't fail. There was no telling what Pete was doing with Ren, or if he had done anything terrible already. Pete had already allowed someone to die, after all. Ren didn't deserve this. It wasn't his fight to begin with. To be fair, it hadn't been mine either, but I should have stayed away from Pete from the start. I should have known better. When something appears too good to be true, it usually is.

My bag filled quickly, and when I was finished, I stowed back where it came from, under my bed, hidden from view in case my mom came into my room before I could ask her.

I sat back on my bed and fiddled with my hands, hoping that the conversation would go well.

I tried reading to take my mind off of it, but that didn't help. After reading the same sentence ten times, I gave up. Rolling onto my back, I sighed as I studied the texture of the ceiling, looking for pictures in the protrusions. A tiger. A lopsided face.

When I heard the front door close, I knew it was show time. I took a deep breath, rolled out of bed and marched down the stairs. Here went nothing.

CHAPTER FOUR

"Hey Bailey," I said into the phone.

I had decided to wait until we were driving to call her, since I would have plenty of down time in the car.

"Abby! Are you in the car?" she asked before even saying hello.

"Yep! We're driving to Colorado! My parents said yes!" I beamed.

"I'm so glad you got to go," she said, but her voice sounded distant and unsure.

"What's wrong?"

"I'm just worried about you, that's all. Call me every day?"

"Sure."

"Okay, well I should go. I'll talk to you later, okay?"

"All right, bye," I said.

I sighed and leaned back against the seat. We had a week to find Ren and bring him home safe. I hoped it would be enough.

After the sixteen-hour drive from Arizona, we arrived at our destination in Denver, Colorado right on time for dinner. Spring was well on its way in, and the weather was glorious for the whole trip up. With the convertible top down, the drive took my breath away. Flowers blooming in a rainbow of purples, yellows, oranges, pinks, and blues gave the air an enchanting fragrance.

I had never been to Colorado before, but the mountainous atmosphere made me want to go camping. I could almost smell the campfire and pine trees.

I couldn't have imagined a better way for things to work out. Eli had worked his magic and gotten Laurie to give both of us the time off we needed, but he wouldn't divulge how he had made it happen. I had a sneaking suspicion that he had used his wit and charm. He had a certain way with words.

My made-up class trip excuse had gone over wonderfully with both of my parents. My mom didn't question a bit of it. I had made sure to add that Eli's dad, Vince, would be chaperoning, in hopes that they would feel more comfortable since it was someone close to me, even if they had never met him.

We pulled around the valet loop at an impeccably landscaped hotel in the heart of Denver, and I knew the money my mom had given me wouldn't even begin to cover the cost.

"Don't worry about it. Protectors have all the funds we need provided for us," Eli said.

It was almost as if he could read my mind, but I was sure he had only sensed my uncertainty.

The valet driver appeared at Eli's door in seconds. He seemed to be my age and looked thrilled at the opportunity to drive Eli's car. I couldn't blame him. Most guys would kill to drive his car.

We walked into the building hand-in-hand, leaving our bags in the car to be unloaded by the bellhop. Vince met us in the lobby and steered us straight into the hotel restaurant. It smelled amazing, and I was starving. My stomach grumbled when we sat down at our table. The ambiance screamed ritzy sophistication. I had never stayed at a hotel this nice before.

"How was the drive?" asked Vince.

"Good," Eli answered from behind the large menu.

"What about you Abby? How are you?" Vince asked with a smile in my direction.

His concern for me touched me deep within my heart. "I'm doing fine, thanks."

Silence set in as we awaited our food. I wasn't sure how much more waiting I could take, so when the waitress arrived, I felt even more grateful than usual.

"The trail seems to have gone cold, but I have a few hunches. I suspect someone is feeding the elders garbage to throw them off the trail," Vince said.

"A mole?" Eli asked.

Vince nodded, his face was grim.

"So we haven't gotten any closer to finding them?" I asked.

"Well, I've managed to get some leads on my own. It seems that Pete made a lot of enemies along the way, and they are more than willing to roll over on him. Just a few minutes before you arrived, I got a couple good leads."

"What's the plan?" Eli asked.

"After we eat, we go."

We didn't disclose to Vince that I might have insight into an event that could happen somewhere on our journey. The whole idea was far too vague. It made me nervous, being in a strange place, knowing that the dream took place somewhere I had never been before. I wasn't ready to admit it to anyone except Eli. I still hoped it was just a coincidence, though I knew the chances of that were slim. Besides, unlike the last dream, where everything felt so vivid, the details in the new dream had been vague and didn't really give us much of a clue as to what would happen.

When the food came, I was unimpressed with the quality for such an extravagant dining room. I ate the rest of my mediocre meal as my mind wandered elsewhere. My eyes roamed the fancy restaurant but didn't land on anything that stood out.

"Abby?"

"Huh?"

"Are you okay?" Eli asked.

"What? Oh. Yeah, I'm fine. Why?"

"Well, I was talking to you, but you were off somewhere else."

"I guess I was daydreaming. Sorry. What did you say?"

"Don't worry about it. You have enough on your mind," he whispered in my ear and kissed my forehead.

He made me feel like I was the most important person in the world in one small gesture. I could have melted right there in my seat, but I saw Vince out of the corner of my eye. Even though he was looking away to give us privacy, my cheeks still flushed in embarrassment.

Eli and I had been a couple for almost a month now, but it still felt strange when someone watched us together, especially our parents. It was so easy to get lost in the moment with him. I had never felt the way I did for anyone before I met him. I knew the connection we shared would last, and I think Vince knew it too.

"Are you ready for this?" Eli whispered in my ear.

"With you by my side, I'm ready for anything."

When we got to our rooms, our bags had already been brought up. Vince had gotten Eli and I adjoining rooms. There were two beds, one in each room, but thinking about sleeping one room over from Eli gave me butterflies.

I glanced around the room before heading for the bathroom. When I emerged, Eli was standing by the door, looking concerned.

"What?" I asked.

"Are you sure you're up for this?"

I didn't hesitate. "Of course."

"All right, let's go," he said.

I took his hand, and off we went.

Vince's rental car was squeaky clean and brand-spanking-new, but it couldn't be compared to Eli's beautiful car. The new-car smell almost overwhelmed me as I sat in the back seat watching the Colorado landscape go by. I wasn't sure where we were headed or what our lead was, but I didn't need to be. We were here, and we were going to find Ren. That was all that mattered.

CHAPTER FIVE

What kind of a lead could have brought us here? Our first stop landed us at another hotel. Ahead of us, Vince crept up to a side entrance that seemed to be only for employees. I pressed myself into Eli's arm. The door was so well-hidden by the faux-brick paint job camouflaging it with the building that I wondered how Vince could have found it. He had to have been here before.

Walking in, I immediately felt out of place as we were pushed back and forth by the waitstaff bustling about the kitchen. Vince whizzed his way through the crowd as if he had been there a hundred times before. We tried our best to follow but couldn't manage to stay right on his tail. I ended up colliding with a busboy carrying a bucket full of dirty dishes. The whole thing crashed to the floor, and pieces of broken plates and bowls went flying in all directions leaving glass landmines strewn about the floor.

"Good job!" the busboy said, rolling his eyes.

"I'm so sorry," I said as I bent to help clean up the disaster I had caused.

"Abby, come on, they'll take care of that," said Eli.

"Hold on, just let me help," I said.

Eli hoisted me up by one arm and dragged me forward. "We have to go."

I stumbled as he pulled me out of the kitchen, and looked up just in time to see Vince jog around a corner far ahead of us. *Oops.*

"I'm sorry," I called behind me to the busboy as we ran after Vince.

"Yeah, right," I heard him mutter under his breath.

I felt bad about it, but he didn't have to be so rude. We sprinted down the corridor, trying to catch up, but by the time we rounded the corner, we came upon a long, empty hallway filled with doors. Vince was nowhere in sight. After the bustling kitchen, the empty hallway was eerie to say the least. I could feel the hair rise on my arms and legs. Something about this place unsettled me.

"Now what?"

"I don't know. Come on," Eli said with uncertainty.

We ventured down the quiet corridor, listening at each door we came to and hoping for a clue. We had to find out which way Vince had gone, but each and every time we stopped, we were met with the deadliest quiet imaginable. When we reached the end, we still hadn't heard a thing. The corridor came to a halt at a T before a large window. Two more empty hallways filled with doors stretched out in opposite directions.

"I'm sorry," I said. "It's all my fault."

All I seemed to do was throw a wrench in things. *Ugh!*

"It's not your fault. It was an accident, and you were trying to help."

"Yeah, but I made us lose Vince. I mean, the whole reason we came here was to help Vince follow a lead. How are we going to help him get information if we aren't with him? If it weren't for me, you'd be right where you're supposed to be—with him."

"Hey, calm down. So we won't be there for this one. It's no big deal. He will find us when he's done, and we will hope for good news. In the meantime, let's go back to the car so my dad knows where to find us."

"Okay," I said.

We stood by the car, and while we waited for Vince we watched the happenings of the street, most of which seemed mundane. However, once in a while someone would walk by who just didn't seem to fit. It seemed I wasn't the only one to notice; Eli tensed each time one of the oddballs passed by. I couldn't help but notice that those peculiar ones all slipped into that same side door through which we had entered. It was strange; I had to be missing something.

Eli picked up on my confusion right away. "What is it?"

"There are people that have been coming up the street. They seem out of place. Each and every one of them has gone through there," I said, pointing at the faux-brick door. "It's strange, right?"

"What do you mean, 'they seem out of place'?" he asked.

"I don't know; something about them just seems off. They don't look any different. I can't explain it."

"Hmm...That's amazing."

"What?" I asked. I stared right at Eli.

"Most of the people that work here in this hotel are 'special,'" he said.

"Special?"

"Yeah, like Pete, ex-Protectors, or maybe even something else. When Protectors refuse to do their duties and protect their assignments, they are stripped of their title, but most of the time their immortality is left intact, leaving them to live on while hardly ageing. That can create a problem with mortals. Specials flock together out of necessity to avoid detection. There are lots of places around like this."

"So they're outcasts?" I asked.

"Exactly," he said. "What surprised me was that you noticed them at all. They don't look any different."

"They do to me," I said.

"That much I gathered. But the only thing that differentiates them is their aura, and most people don't even pick up on that."

"Great! Another thing that makes me different." I sighed.

"Hey, that's not a bad thing. That's just another thing that makes you the incredible person you are. I love uncovering all these blossoming talents. Besides, it gives us an upper hand."

I raised my eyebrows. "How so?"

"You will be able to see if there is someone that could be working with Pete even if I'm not around. It will make you put up your guard."

When everything seemed to be going wrong, Eli always knew just what to say to make me feel better. I couldn't disagree with him. I rested my head on his muscular chest and relaxed as much as I could.

"What happened in there?" Vince's harsh voice made me jump out of Eli's arms.

"S-s-sorry," I stuttered.

"We fell behind so we came out here to wait so you could find us," Eli said, interrupting my stammering. "Did you find out anything?"

"Yeah, the guy is lying."

Eli laughed. "Well, that isn't surprising. We knew that any lead would lie, but did you get any usable information?"

"We're going to follow him."

"Let's go," Eli said as he moved toward the car.

"He's not off for another two hours," Vince said, his voice drifting back to its usual calm.

"Great!" Eli said. He ran his hands through his hair, and I could almost feel his frustration coursing through my own veins.

"Eli, why don't we go for a walk?" I said.

If he could calm me down when I needed it, I had to do what I could to help him in turn.

His angry eyes darted to me as if he was ready to go off on me for even suggesting it, and my reflexes made me take a step back. My heart raced as I glanced at Vince, then back to Eli. When he saw and, I was certain, felt the effect he was having on me, his face softened. It was another moment before he succumbed and took my outstretched hand and we walked away slowly.

We strolled up the street until the building ended and the sidewalk curved around it. The moment we were out of view of Vince I stopped, turned him to face me, and kissed him. He was hesitant at first to return it, but within seconds, his kiss answered mine, deeper and hungrier. I felt some of his tension melt away as I held him my arms wrapped around his shoulders. My body hummed to life as his kiss swept me away. When he pulled away, I was left panting, and I looked up at him with dazed eyes. I don't know what I had hoped to find in his, but the connection I felt took my breath away once more. So much lay behind his gaze that was impossible to describe. Love. Longing. Gratitude. The intensity in his eyes made me look away, blushing and breathless. The goal had been to make him feel better, not for me to get carried away, but I could hardly help it.

"Do you feel better now?" I asked shakily.

He grinned at me, and I went weak in the knees. "What do you think?" he asked as he lifted me up off my feet and brought me to his mouth to kiss me one more time. My feet dangled over the sidewalk. I couldn't help but giggle.

He set me back on my feet again, and we walked for another block or two before Eli suggested we go back. "We don't want to miss anything...again."

We meandered back, his hand warming mine. I paid closer attention to our surroundings on our return trip. This ritzy neighborhood gave me the willies—the dogs carried in purses that I could only imagine were filled with urine and feces, the fake-looking owners that looked as if they had never lifted a finger to clean anything in their entire lives. It made me sick to think of the amounts of money they expended on unnecessary extravagance. It was hard to imagine outcasts like Pete hanging around in such an area. They were polar opposites.

Eli and I arrived back at the rental car in what felt like seconds, and Vince smiled as he saw us approach. We all piled into the car and waited. And waited. And waited. It felt like we waited forever for this unknown person to exit the building. I had been staring at the hidden door for so long I felt like my eyes might burn a hole through it. My eyelids began to feel heavy, and I felt myself dozing off. Eli's intuition was right on key as usual—he slipped his arm around me and kissed my forehead.

"It's okay. Take a nap. You won't miss anything," he whispered into my hair.

I smiled up at him and let my head rest on his solid chest, my hand on his abdomen. I could feel his six-pack underneath his shirt. My fingers traced the craters and bulges until I fell asleep.

My dreams claimed me quickly.

Running. I am running. My sense of urgency spikes, filling me with adrenaline. Someone is behind me, but that isn't the reason I am running. Who is behind me? I push myself to catch up. My lungs are burning, aching for more air. I stumble, catching myself just before I go down. Bending over and resting my hands on my knees, I gasp for a good breath of air. It fills my lungs, but the burning doesn't subside. I press on. A rogue lightning bolt streaks the sky in the distance. I can't help but wonder if it struck something on the ground. The streets seem empty and void of character. Brick walls surround me on all sides. Windows glisten high above my head as the lightning strikes again, miles away. The figures ahead of me disappear around a corner. I am alone with the person behind me. I stop. I failed to keep up. I lost them.

"Abby. Abby! Wake up."

A hand brushed across my face. I thrashed back from it, batting it away with my arm.

"Don't," I mumbled. "I failed."

"Abby, it's okay. Wake up. It was just a dream."

My eyes shot open. A dream. *Where was I?* I looked around. In the car. Vince's concerned face stared into my wild eyes. Eli and Vince had witnessed me having a nightmare. *Great!* I wanted to crawl into a hole. I buried my head in Eli's chest and hoped it would all go away. Eli stroked my back, comforting me. Slowly, my breathing returned to normal, and my heart slowed.

"There he is!" Vince exclaimed in a hushed voice.

The car roared to life and jolted into drive. I bolted upright to catch a glimpse of our suspect. We were hot on the trail. It was clear that this wasn't Vince's first time following someone. He stayed far enough back to go unnoticed, but not far enough to lose our mark.

I felt Eli's heart racing under my hand at his chest. We were all on the edge of our seats, and my dream hadn't helped.

We rounded the tenth corner and came to an abrupt halt. Vince eased the car into a parking spot five cars back from where our suspect had parked and waited for him to emerge from his vehicle. We slid out one by one and snuck closer to the person-of-interest's car, doing our best to keep silent.

The man disappeared into a house to the right of the car. Vince motioned for us to approach the door, and he rounded the house to the back and vanished from sight.

"What are we supposed to do?" I whispered.

Eli shrugged but moved forward.

I followed Eli's cue and headed up the stairs. He hesitated before knocking on the door. Shuffling sounded from inside. I took a step back, and Eli stepped in front of me, blocking me from whoever would materialize when the door opened, but the door didn't budge. Instead, we heard a commotion in the backyard. Eli took off, almost slamming into me, and disappeared around the house. It only took me seconds to follow suit. I stumbled down the steps as my mind raced ahead of my body.

We arrived just in time to see the man kick Vince to the ground and jump over the fence. We didn't pursue any further. Trying to catch him as he went through backyard after backyard would attract too much attention, which was the last thing we wanted.

"You okay?" Eli asked Vince. He reached down and pulled Vince to his feet.

"Yeah, I'm fine," he said, brushing off his pant legs.

I sat down on the back porch steps with my head in my hands. Everywhere we turned we were presented more problems. I had known it would be difficult—I didn't really expect to find Ren the first evening—but my patience seemed to evade me as effectively as Pete did. And if this lead was connected to him, Pete would now know we were on to him. We might as well have hired a skywriter to announce us.

"Let's check inside and see if he left behind any clues," Vince said, pointing toward the open back door.

We followed him into the dark house. *What is with the Protectors and darkness?* Pete always kept the lights off at the house in Arizona. I couldn't see a thing. I felt along the walls to try to work my way into the house. I knew Vince and Eli had to be close; I could hear their shoes moving along the floor every few seconds. The wall to my right ended abruptly in an open doorway. I tried to see into the room it opened into, but it was even darker than the spot I stood. I hoped neither of them had gone in there, because I wouldn't.

I couldn't fathom how they accomplished anything in such darkness. Even at night, one would think that light from streetlamps would flood through the windows; there must have been blackout curtains on them, preventing even a sliver of light from entering. I held my arms out to my sides, but they came up empty: I was on my own now, with no walls to guide me. I shuffled my feet back and forth as I slowly propelled myself further. I could hear my pulse in my ears, then papers shuffling in a room up ahead. I focused my direction on a faint glow that looked like a night light, but my feet hit something hard, and I toppled forward and landed on my left hip. The crash of my hipbone on the hardwood floor echoed through the house.

"Ow," I whimpered to myself.

I held my elbow and tried to rub away the pain, but the throbbing in my hip was sure to bruise. It ached as I brought myself to a sitting position and leaned against the wall.

The floor underneath me vibrated with approaching footsteps. I pulled my legs in toward my body, curling into the fetal position. The last thing I wanted was to be stepped on.

"Are you okay?" Eli and Vince asked in unison.

How could they see me?

"I'm fine," I groaned.

"What happened?" Eli asked.

"I tripped on something. I can't see a thing in here."

"Oh, I didn't realize. I'm sorry."

"It's fine, just help me up."

Eli's arms guided me to a standing position, and I could feel the pain in my left side as I put my weight on my left leg.

"I'm going to wait in the car," I said. The last thing I wanted to do was try to go through the rest of the house in utter darkness. I turned to leave, and Eli caught my arm.

"I'll come with you," he said.

"No," I said. "I'm fine. Stay here and find the information we need."

Eli ignored me. "Dad, we'll be outside. Call me on my cell if you need me to come back in."

"Okay," Vince said.

I didn't want to stand in the way of finding Ren, but Eli wasn't changing his mind, that much was clear.

We waited in the car. It felt like that's all we had done so far. I felt terrible—I had stopped us from helping Vince again. It hadn't been on purpose, but I still wanted to curl up under a blanket and hide.

It wasn't long before Vince emerged, empty-handed. I hoped he had learned something inside that would lead us to Ren. I tried to read his expression, but it was set in stone, unchanged.

"Find anything?" Eli asked when we were back on the road.

"Nothing," he said.

The tension in the car made me feel claustrophobic. Tomorrow would be better, I tried to tell myself, but convincing myself was a different story. Maybe Eli was right; maybe I shouldn't have come.

*   *   *   *

It was a bit overwhelming, climbing into bed in a strange place.

"I can sleep on the floor in here if it makes you feel better," Eli said for the tenth time.

"No, it's fine," I assured him.

Truthfully, all I wanted was to have him right next to me, but I insisted he sleep in his own bed. I turned out the light and rolled onto my side, facing the doorway to his room. Taking a deep breath, I closed my eyes and tried to push all my thoughts aside. It took me a while to fall asleep.

The next thing I knew, sunbeams spilled from the crack in the curtains, shining right onto my face. I stretched lazily and rolled onto my back. My arm dropped to my side and landed on an empty, cold sheet instead of dangling off the bed like it would have at home. Here, I was alone in a huge bed. I sat up and looked around the room, trying to remember where I was.

I climbed out of the fluffy white blankets and walked to the bathroom, peering in before I walked inside. Having an entire hotel room to myself was weird. A girl sure could get used to it, though. I decided it was a good opportunity to shower. I unloaded my essentials and hopped in. I didn't know what time we would be back at the hotel tonight.

I was drying my hair when I walked out of the bathroom and saw Eli waiting in the corner, with breakfast laid out for me. The smell of maple syrup filled the room, provoking a growl of protest from my stomach.

"I brought you pancakes. I hope that's okay." He was smiling at me.

30

"They smell delicious! Thanks!"

I devoured the food he placed in front of me at an alarming rate. He looked at me in surprise.

"Hungry?" he teased.

"Shut up!" I mumbled through mashed-up pancake.

"My dad left to follow up on something else, so we have the morning to ourselves," he said. "Want to check out the hotel?"

"Sure."

We wandered down the long corridors lined with doors, our arms brushing every so often, sending jolts of electricity through my body. At the end of the last passage, the elevator chimed to announce its arrival, and we coasted down to the lobby. I seized the moment alone in the elevator to corner Eli. I pushed my body into his and he pulled me closer, kissing me deeply. My heartbeat quickened. When the elevator began to slow, he pulled back and nuzzled his nose against mine, letting us catch our breath before anyone saw us. When the double doors slid open, no one stood in view. We shared a guilty grin before heading toward the pool and workout room.

We ambled along, gazing at the vacationers who were having the time of their lives splashing in the indoor pool. Next, we came to a window that overlooked the golf course at the back of the hotel. The lush green grass beckoned me to roll down the hills like a child on a hot summer day, and for a moment, I felt the carefree whimsy that I had last known back home on the beach in California surging up again. But Eli squeezed my hand, and we were on our way again, passing through the doors to the patio. The second the mountains came into full view, I stopped in my tracks. I could see why people paid an arm and a leg to stay at a place like this.

We sat down at a table and watched the minutes slip by, enjoying the beautiful spring weather while gazing at the forest in the distance. I almost forgot the anxiety that clawed at me. Almost.

"I'm sorry I've been so unhelpful. Your dad must be really frustrated," I said at last.

"What?" he said. "My dad isn't frustrated with you, and neither am I. Accidents happen, and none of them were your fault."

"Yes, they were."

"It was a dead-end lead. It's not a big deal."

I disagreed, but arguing seemed pointless, so I zipped my lips and tried to lose myself in beauty of the mountainside in front of me.

"Excuse me, are you Abby?" asked a plain man I had never seen before.

He seemed to have come out of nowhere, and I looked around, as if to find the path he had taken illuminated for me to see. I shook my head to dismiss the thought.

"Uh, yeah," I said.

Eli stiffened and leaned toward me. He was on high alert.

"This is for you," the man said, tossing a note on the table in front of me. He turned and walked around the corner, out of sight just as quickly as he had come.

I snatched the paper off the table as if it might run away if I didn't grab it quickly enough.

Go home, you have no business here.

It was short but not sweet, and it provoked a wave of nausea in my stomach. Eli snatched the note from my hand, and his jaw tightened as his gaze trailed over the words. We had told no one where we were staying, yet our enemies had found us.

"We should go," Eli said, rising out of his chair.

"Where?"

"I don't know. Anywhere but here."

I rose, and we headed straight to the valet to get Eli's car. It only took a few moments for the men to pull it around.

We were already on our way out of the parking lot when I noticed a piece of paper hanging out of the glove box.

"What's this? Did you leave this here?" I asked Eli, pointing to the ominous white sheet.

"No, I didn't," he said. His hands gripped the wheel tighter. "What does it say?"

The cathedral on 5th and Harbor. Ten minutes.

This note had been scribbled in the same handwriting as the first. I couldn't say what worried me more, that he hadn't come to us face-to-face or that the note was placed inside Eli's car, a car that should have been locked. Whoever did this was bold.

CHAPTER SIX

Using the map on my phone I directed Eli where to go. Ten minutes barely gave us time to get there, and we couldn't miss whoever had left the notes. We should have called Vince first, but there hadn't been time. Eli's car came to an abrupt stop in front of what looked like an abandoned cathedral, jolting my head forward. The cathedral looked as if it hadn't been used for quite some time. I scanned the street before glancing up at the tall gray building and its long, blackened windows. A large black crow sat on one of the steeples. The sight gave me the chills.

We walked up the front steps and pushed the doors open. The chamber within was the picture of a classic Catholic Church, boasting a dimly-lit cross hanging on the wall above the sanctuary. On one side of the room sat rows of candles, only half of them lit. Despite its outward appearance, this church was well-used and properly maintained inside.

"Hellooo," Eli called out to the seemingly empty church. His voice echoed around us eerily. I stepped closer to him, my arm pressed against his.

"Back here," called a man's voice from the far end of the church.

We followed the aisle to the altar and turned left, heading in the direction of the voice. In the next room we found a man scrubbing the stone floor on his hands and knees. His worn face scowled at us, as if our interruption was an inconvenience.

"How can I help you?" he asked as we came into view.

"We're looking for Pete," I said.

He stopped scrubbing, and I realized we were on the right track. Every other time, Pete had been one step ahead of us. I felt my stomach drop with excitement, hoping maybe, just maybe, we had come a step closer.

"What makes you think I know anything about...who did you say?" he asked in a snide tone.

"Pete," I said.

"Yeah, Pete."

Eli smirked. "A very reliable source."

"Is that so?" the man asked.

Eli nodded once.

"Well, I'm sorry to say that you have been misinformed. I have nothing to tell you."

"I think it's time you start telling the truth," Eli said in a voice that made even me want to step away from him.

I stayed put, watching the exchange in front of me. Eli seemed to be handling things just fine. The man dropped his scrubbing brush with a thud and stood. He was taller than I would have guessed, and his angry stance intimidated me enough to make me finally take a step back. But instead of going backwards, Eli took a step forward, challenging him. I began to worry about where this was headed if the man didn't back down. But I knew Eli could handle himself in a fight. No matter how big this person was, he didn't stand a chance.

"I think it's time for you to leave," the man said.

"Not until we get the information we came for," Eli said, holding his ground.

The man took two long strides toward Eli, and I heard myself gasp. But before the man got any closer, he fell to his knees, grasping his head and yelling out in pain. "Oww! Stop! Stop! Please stop! I'll talk, I'll talk, stop!" he pleaded.

"Now that's better. Where is Pete?"

"Who are you?"

"Let's not beat around the bush any longer. Where is Pete?" Eli asked again, a little more impatiently.

"I don't know."

"I am going to ask one last time. Where is Pete?"

"I don't know. Ow! Wait, stop! He was here, but he left!" the man blurted out.

"Where did he go?" This time, I asked the question hoping to alleviate some of the tension in the room.

"I don't know. He said something about too many familiar faces around here, and that he had to get out of town."

"What else can you tell us?" Eli asked.

"He was staying around here, somewhere close, but I don't know where."

"How long ago did he say he needed to leave town?"

"Two hours."

At that, we turned and rushed toward the door, but we stopped when we heard the man's voice once more.

"I don't know who you are, but Pete isn't someone you want to mess around with. You would be best to leave him to run off. Everyone is better off in his rearview."

"Thanks, but I think I'm capable of handling myself against Pete, wouldn't you agree?" Eli threw back, grinning as we walked into the night.

We got back into Eli's car, unsure of where to go next. Strange clues left in mysterious ways had led us this far, yet here was another dead end. Had it all been a ruse to throw us off the trail while Pete made his getaway? Or was someone really trying to help us? It seemed that the person we had met couldn't shed as much light about Pete's whereabouts as we had hoped. We sat in the dark, deserted street in silence, like we were both lost. Failure rested on the tips of our tongues, and it was bitter.

Suddenly, a figure emerged from between the cathedral and the building next to it. The person seemed to ensure nobody was watching before slinking into the pools of darkness along the building fronts as he made his way down the street. It seemed a little strange, even for this seedy neighborhood. Eli and I looked at each other to see if we were on the same page, as if even in the confines of his car we might be overheard if we spoke.

With great caution, we emerged from the car as silently as possible. We shut our doors together on the count of three. Eli darted across the street and started to make his way down the opposite side of the street, following the figure. He sunk into the shadows against the buildings. I fell into step behind him with my pulse drumming in my ears. I was so worried I would misstep and blow our cover, ruining our mission once again. My track record so far hadn't been very impressive.

The mystery person slipped around a corner. Eli picked up his pace to a jog, and I had to run to keep up. I tried my best not to let my footfalls echo around us, but my efforts were futile at such a fast pace. Eli beat me to the corner and disappeared almost immediately. I was alone on this spooky street, and even though Eli was only a few feet ahead of me, it seemed like much more. I looked behind me as a sneaking sensation of being followed filled my gut, but I couldn't see a soul. When I rounded the corner, Eli was already halfway down the street. I needed to step up the pace.

I sprinted in his direction, not caring how loud I was anymore. I had run a third of the way down the street when I realized where I was. It hit me with violent force, like I had just struck an invisible wall. I crashed to my knees as dizzying spell of déjà vu overtook me. The brick walls. The dark, empty street. The echoing of my footsteps. My second nightmare was coming true. I tried to catch my breath. I knelt on the ground, gasping and wheezing with each struggling breath.

No, no, no! This cannot be happening. It was like I replayed the dream in slow motion, and there was nothing I could do about it. I had to get out of there. I scrambled to my feet, only to stumble as I picked up speed. The flash rounding the corner ahead of me was Eli.

"Eli!" I shrieked, but I knew he could no longer hear me.

Right on cue, the streak of lightning and distant rumble of thunder arrived. I was almost to the corner. I can do this, I tried to tell myself. What I might find around the corner terrified me, but what choice did I have? I took a deep breath and looked around the bend. I saw no one. The next street was barren. I stood there a moment and debated what to do. I couldn't let myself get too far behind, so I braced myself to sprint forward, but before I could take off, I toppled over. I had been struck from behind, hard, and knocked to the ground. Panic threatened to seize me, but I took charge of myself and sprang to my feet. I had to prove I could take care of myself, and this was my chance. I could no longer burden Eli with my shortcomings. This time, I wouldn't screw up our mission.

I spun around, fists ready. My first blow landed on his face, but the moment before my knuckles collided with his cheekbone, I recognized him. I had seen him before, but where? He stumbled backwards before catching his balance and coming toward me again. This time my foot delivered a swift kick to his groin. Now it was he who dropped to his knees. He crawled away and tried to scramble to his feet as I closed in on him. I kicked him once more in the stomach, and he collapsed to the ground.

"Next time think twice about messing with me!" I shouted at him as loudly and forcefully as I could.

He clambered to his feet, holding his stomach, and took one last look at me before hobbling off in the opposite direction. I slumped against the wall, and slid down to the ground. My adrenaline caught up with me, and the shakes engulfed my body. I could barely keep my head in my hands. But I had done it. I had defended myself.

CHAPTER SEVEN

Eli raced around the corner. The instant he saw me safe, slumped on the ground, he doubled over and grabbed his knees, his rapid breathing made him look unstable on his feet. Once he had caught his breath a little, he jogged over to me and dropped to the ground in front of me.

"What happened?" he asked.

"A man attacked me," I said.

"Who?"

"I don't know. I think I've seen him before but...I can't place where. I don't understand how he got behind me. I never saw him coming. Did you see where the other guy went?" I asked.

He looked at me with a bewildered expression "You didn't see?"

I shook my head. "I couldn't keep up...again." My eyes plummeted to the ground.

"The guy we were following went into a house. Just as I was nearing it, Pete emerged. The other guy was with him. Pete made sure he looked around before coming out, but I was hidden, so he didn't see me. I followed them."

"What happened?" I sat up straighter.

We had been on the right track! Excitement filled me, and I hoped desperately for good news. One step closer to saving Ren.

"I caught Pete, but the other guy kept running," Eli said.

My heart thumped in my chest.

"Great! Where is he?" I felt victorious that I hadn't messed things up for us, for once.

"He got away."

"What! How?" My voice turned shrill, and my eyes searched his. When he didn't answer right away, my stomach sank. "He got away because of me, didn't he?"

He wouldn't look at me.

"Eli," I said.

"I felt your fear. Something was wrong. I had to get to you. I didn't have another choice. I let him go."

Great! Would my interference ever end? Here I was, celebrating the small victory that I had defended myself, and I had cost us our ultimate goal: Pete.

Eli sat down next to me and leaned against the wall, his breathing still rapid and uneven. He thrust his hands into his hair, resting his elbows at his knees.

"Now what?" I asked.

He threw his arms up in the air. It was pretty much how I felt too. You can only get backed in a corner so many times before wondering if it's all for nothing.

"We should have waited for your dad," I said.

"Yeah, we should have."

"Will he be mad at us?" I asked.

"Would you be?"

I didn't have to answer; it was a given. Now it was time to face the music and ask for help.

Eli pulled out his phone and called his dad.

"Hey Dad, I have some bad news..."

I couldn't hear Vince, but whatever he had said had cut Eli off.

"Someone tipped us off at the hotel, so we followed the trail. Eventually it led us to Pete, but we were ambushed, and he got away." Eli paused again and listened for a moment.

Eli didn't blame me, at least not to Vince, and I wondered if he would ever tell him what had really happened.

"He was going south on Charleston..."

Eli paused here and there without finishing his sentences.

"We're three blocks away..." He nodded. "Okay...He couldn't have gotten very far..." He paused once again. "I'm sorry."

He hung up and let it sink in.

"What did he say?" I asked.

"He's five minutes away. He's going to try to head off Pete."

I was relieved we would have another shot at catching him. We sat quietly, letting our breathing even out. I rested my head against the wall, tilting it back to see the sky above. The stars that poked out between the clouds seemed brighter than they did in Phoenix. Maybe it was the darkness; the street lights here seemed dimmer to me. Of course, it might have just been my imagination. Either way, it was gorgeous.

"Well, let's go," Eli said, pulling me to my feet.

"Where are we going?" I asked.

"We'll try to meet up with my dad, to help him catch Pete. There could be another ambush," he said.

He was right. We ought to be right in the middle of the action, as far as Pete was concerned. But after all my failures, that was the last place I wanted to be. We hustled down two streets before finally approaching our destination. I gazed up at the large street sign that read "Charleston" in big white letters.

Suddenly, Eli came to a halt, so quickly I almost crashed right into him. He pulled out his buzzing phone. "Hello?"

I waited, listening for a clue about who it was, but before I got one, Eli took off running. I guessed I was supposed to follow, so without skipping a beat I was racing after him. He ran three streets further before disappearing around a turn. *Dang it!* I needed to get in better shape. I couldn't seem to keep up with him. I lifted my feet higher, lengthening my stride in hopes it would grant me the extra speed I needed.

When I caught up and rounded the corner, Vince and Eli stood under a lone street light on the otherwise dark road, with Pete sitting on the ground in front of them, his hands tied together and nestled in his lap. *Yes! We got him!*

The guys were already discussing our next move. From what I could gather on my walk up to them, Pete wasn't talking—not that I was surprised.

I sat down on the curb far from Pete and tried to catch my breath while attempting to follow Vince and Eli's conversation.

"Okay. Abby and I will go check it out now," Eli said. "We will catch you back at the hotel. You sure you can handle him by yourself?"

"I've got it." Vince assured him.

My breathing was just beginning to even out and the stitch in my side subsiding when they broke off their discussion.

"Well, let's go," Eli said, walking over to me.

Already? Ugh!

"Where are we going now?" I asked, wishing I could just sit there for a little while longer.

"To the house Pete came out of. I doubt Ren is there, but maybe we'll find something that could lead us to him."

"Okay, but what is Vince going to do?" I asked as we turned to leave Vince and Pete behind.

"He'll take Pete back to the hotel," he said, as if it was a silly question.

I could tell he wasn't as happy as he should have been after catching Pete. I would be willing to bet that his dad had been upset with him, and it was partly my fault. I felt bad. Since his dad had been away for so long, disappointing him had to be much harder. And when you hold someone's life in your hands and you screw up, that's a tough blow. Even though it wasn't all his fault, Vince didn't know that. Eli was going to beat himself up about this.

When we arrived at the enormous house, I was surprised to find that I had run by it already and hadn't noticed it. Looking at it now, it stood out like a sore thumb, not matching the size, coloring, or shape of any other house on the street.

I sat down on the curb in front of it. "I'll wait here," I said.

"Why?" Eli asked.

I raised my eyebrows.

He threw up his arms. "I'll be right back."

The street was quiet, so quiet that I jumped when a cat pounced on a leaf that tumbled through the yard. The leaf crackled beneath its quick paws. The cat toyed with it for a moment until it realized it wasn't alone. Its eyes darted toward me, and its tail flicked back and forth.

I put my hand out and called, "Here kitty-kitty!"

It spooked and ran in the opposite direction the second it heard my voice. I dropped my hand to the ground behind me and leaned back. I understood why the cat was so afraid. This eerie street made my skin crawl. My eyes flicked back and forth down the road, following every movement I saw. Leaves. Branches blowing in the wind. A plastic bag billowing in a gutter.

"Abby, come here!" Eli shouted from inside the house. "Hurry!"

I jumped up and vaulted the steps in three strides. I didn't even know I could do that.

"What?" I asked as I stumbled through the door.

"Hey Abby."

Ren stood in front of me with a lopsided grin on his pale, bruised face. Eli beamed beside him.

"I found him!" Eli said.

I threw myself at Ren and gave him the biggest hug I could manage. I was so relieved he was safe.

Eli was already on the phone with his dad before I could say another word.

"How are you?" I asked Ren. I tried to look him over, but the house was too dark. It frustrated me that I couldn't see him well.

"A few bangs here and there, but I'm fine," he said.

"I'm so sorry. Pete is such a dirtbag."

"Yes, he is," Ren agreed.

"Let's go," Eli said, as he put his cell back in his pocket. "We'll take Pete to the elders in the morning and let them deal with him," he said. "Then we'll go home."

CHAPTER EIGHT

"Hey Bailey," I said into the phone. "Sorry I didn't call sooner."

"I've been worried sick! How are you?"

"I'm fine. We found Pete, and Ren is safe."

"Oh my gosh. I've been a wreck!"

"How are you?" I asked, wanting to take my mind off of my life for a few minutes.

"Great, now that I don't have to worry about you anymore. Ryan is taking me on a date tonight. He said it would be a really special one!" she squealed.

"Ooh, that sounds amazing! I hope you have fun," I said.

"I can't wait!" She paused a moment before continuing. "How is staying in the hotel with Eli?"

Her voice was so over-the-top I couldn't help but laugh.

"Uh...it's...nice," I answered, unsure of what else to say.

"Nice? That's all? Nice?" she asked, sounding disappointed that I wasn't dishing out more details.

I laughed. "Well it's not like we're sharing a room!"

"Yeah, yeah, yeah," she teased. "When do you come back?"

"I don't know."

We hadn't discussed if we would go home earlier now that we had accomplished our task, so I didn't know when we would be back. I hoped to stay and enjoy a couple days' vacation. True vacation. Now that would be nice.

"Well, I should go," I said.

"Okay, but don't forget to call me. I want updates!" she said.

"All right, I will." I smiled, imagining how crazy she must be going without me calling to keep her tuned in. After missing five calls from her since the last time we had spoken, I felt bad I hadn't called her sooner. It just never felt like the right time, when I didn't have any good news, but I could breathe easier now that Pete was back where he should be, captive. I walked around the empty hotel room, enjoying the little bit of time to myself.

The view was beautiful, even from my room's window, overlooking the city. I could see what seemed like thousands of pine trees intermingling with hundreds of houses. Seeing so many pines within the neighborhoods made me feel like I was in the woods and all those houses were cabins. It made ache for my dad and our many trips to the forests in California.

I grabbed for my phone and pushed the number two in my favorites. He picked up on the first ring.

"Hey Dad."

I swallowed the lump that had formed in my throat.

"Hey honey! How's your trip?" he asked.

"It's great. I'm having a lot of fun. You would love it here. There's an awesome view of the mountains on the back patio of the hotel. I could sit out there all day. And the stars—it's like being in the forest in the middle of town."

"I bet. What are you going to do today?" he asked.

"Umm…" I thought for a moment. "I'm going down to the pool."

"Oh, that sounds relaxing."

"I hope so."

"Well, I should let you get to it. I don't want to take any time away from your vacation," he said. "Have a blast! I'm glad you called. I'll talk to you soon. I love you."

"I love you too," I said, just before the line went dead.

I tossed my phone into my purse and headed to the bathroom to change into my swimsuit. I hadn't planned on going to the pool, but I might as well do as I said. A little time poolside might ease some of the leftover tension I felt. I jotted a note on a piece of paper and set it on the desk for Eli before I left.

Eli,
Went down to the pool. See you soon!
Love,

Abby

I felt so ready to enjoy this gorgeous weather on the patio by the large heated pool. As I walked into the pool area, I grabbed two of the hotel towels, which were far too small for anyone over the age of two. I haphazardly draped both of them over a lounge chair.

As paranoid as I was now, I surveyed the area, being extra cautious of the darkened corners. I wasn't alone at the pool: Two older women sunbathed, and a man swam laps on the opposite side of the pool, but none of them seemed to be a threat. I threw my cover-up on top of the towels and walked to the steps to ease into the water. I hadn't swam for pleasure since moving away from California. I plunged my feet into the water, and the water felt foreign against my skin. I rested my hand on the surface, testing its buoyancy under my fingertips. The water was like gelatin under my hands. I thrust my fingers downwards and pushed my them back, so that it rippled away from me. My fingers cut through the water like knives, and I relished the feeling of water flowing between my fingers. I slid my body deeper into the pool and began swimming laps, using the large strokes I had relied on in the ocean to fight my way through the strong undertow.

I swam laps until I grew tired, which took far less time than it used to. I rested on the steps for a while before getting out to soak up some sun. I tossed my cover-up off my towels and was about to plop down onto the lounge chair when I noticed something resting on it. A small piece of paper had been slipped into the crease of one of the towels. My heart picked up speed as adrenaline filled my body. I reached for the paper with shaking hands and looked around at the other pool-goers who were absentmindedly relaxing and none the wiser.

Slowly, I unfolded the page, trying to keep it hidden in case someone was watching me. My hands shook as I held it open in my palm.

Gotcha.

It only took one word to make me come unhinged. I sat with my knees pressed up against my chest, sucking in deep breaths to stave off hyperventilation. My arms quivered as I wrapped them around my legs. Whoever was working with Pete had made it clear that he could get to me wherever I was. I hadn't seen anyone come or go while I was swimming, and the thought made my skin crawl. Someone could still be watching me.

I crumpled up the note and threw it to the ground. I would not let myself look as rattled as I felt. I was going to be strong. Taking in a deep, cleansing breath, I tried to steady myself and hoped it would slow my heart, which seemed to be trying to pound its way out of my chest. Gradually, I inched my feet out in front of me and laid my head back on the chair. I refused to close my eyelids, but my sunglasses hid my ever-searching eyes. I scarcely blinked. When one of the ladies across the pool stood up, I sat up a little straighter and adjusted my body for a better view, watching her every move as she made her way to the door and back into the hotel. I relaxed a little when only two others remained in the pool area with me. I found myself staring down these two people, wondering if either was watching me. I debated going back up to my room but decided against it when I envisioned someone ambushing me once I was alone in the hallway. At least here there would be witnesses.

I jumped out of my chair knocking it over when someone put a hand on my shoulder. Landing on the ground, I clambered to my feet and turned, ready to strike. Looking up, I came face to face with a very surprised Eli.

"Did I scare you?" he asked.

"Oh my gosh, I'm so happy to see you." I stepped over the overturned chair and threw my arms around him. I stood up on my tiptoes and whispered in his ear. "I was swimming. When I came back to my chair, someone had slipped a note into my towel. I never saw anyone come or go. I swear, it could have been anyone. I didn't know what to do, so I stayed here where there were other people."

His face had blanched when I leaned back to look at him. "What did the note say?"

"Gotcha."

"What?"

"It said 'gotcha,' and that's it," I said.

He looked around one last time, his face grim. "Let's go."

We strode back to the hotel room where Ren was waiting. Eli didn't waste any time and motioned for him to follow us. The three of us headed straight for Vince's room, where he still babysat Pete.

"We need to move to a different hotel," Eli said the minute we were all in the same room.

"Why?" Vince asked, on high alert.

"People are watching us here. Abby's gotten two notes since we arrived. Today someone was bold enough to leave it in her towel while she was swimming. She never saw anyone come or go," Eli answered in a rush. He was disturbed by the idea of someone who was so close, who could have done something worse than leave a note. They were taunting him—or all of us, I suppose—boasting of how much damage they could do, and that we would never see it coming.

"Okay, how about we separate?" Vince said.

"Separate? Why would we separate?" I asked.

"Well, I would assume they're working with Pete. If they're trying to help him, we can split up to make things harder and more confusing for them."

"I think that's the best idea," Ren said.

"Eli, you can take Abby and Ren to Aurora and find a hotel there. Don't tell me where." Vince motioned to the bathroom where Pete was being held. "I'll take Pete to a different hotel here in Denver."

"Okay," Eli said.

Eli turned to leave, and Ren followed. Vince looked at me just before I turned to step in line behind them. "Take care, and don't trust anyone."

His words chilled me. If he was this serious, serious enough to separate us, I knew this was more dangerous than I had thought.

I started packing my bags and began helping Eli with some of his things. Ren knocked on the door just as I put the last item in my bag.

"All set," he said.

"Me too."

Eli zipped up his bag, threw it over his shoulder, and hoisted my duffle on his arm before heading out the door without a word. He hadn't relaxed since learning about the note. It had put us all on edge.

"After you," Ren said, motioning to the door.

I smiled at his sweet and benignly simple gesture. He never forgot his gentlemanly side.

Aurora was only a short drive from the heart of Denver. When we entered the city limits, Eli got off the highway, making a few random and unexpected turns that threw off my balance in the back seat.

Suddenly I realized that, amidst all the chaos since the pool, I had never asked the most important question. "What happened at the meeting this morning?"

"A bunch of crap," Eli said without looking away from the road ahead. His hands released the steering wheel and then gripped it again so tightly that his fingers turned white.

I didn't know how to respond; with his foul mood, we clearly weren't going to have a conversation at the moment. I looked at Ren, his demeanor welcoming and calm, and I hoped he would answer so I didn't have to wait until Eli's mood turned around.

"What Eli is trying to say is that they're calling in another Protector with the gift of past sight so they can establish the slimy things Pete has done and is capable of," Ren said. "At the moment, they don't believe that he is as terrible as we're saying he is. It's almost as if Pete has penetrated the counsel and persuaded someone to be on his side."

"What? They don't believe you?" I asked in disbelief.

"Nope," Eli snapped.

I couldn't believe it: Here we were, running from people who had been helping Pete, and the counsel didn't believe us. We were alone in our struggle, with only each other for support and protection; at least until the other Protector came to help. Then they would be sorry. Or maybe they wouldn't. Perhaps they wouldn't even care. Either way, it didn't help us for the time being.

"How long this time?" I asked.

"A week," he said.

"Great! So we're just supposed to put all of our lives on hold waiting around for them to get a clue." I crossed my arms and stared out the window. I was so over this.

We pulled up in front of a hotel with paint chipping in so many places that I wondered if more of the old color showed than the new. No valet stood by the door. We parked the car and walked into the building, Eli and Ren carrying all of our bags.

I couldn't help but notice the pool as we walked up to the door and I cringed at the rusted gate. It didn't look the least bit inviting. We checked into our two rooms, Eli and I in one and Ren in the other. Eli refused to let me out of his sight now that we knew someone had been following us, and I didn't argue.

We spent the next two days hanging out at the run-down pool, shopping, and sightseeing—all the things my parents expected me to do on my trip, so I took lots of pictures to show them.

We kept ourselves busy so we didn't dwell on the situation with Pete, though I knew it was in the back of all of our minds, the decaying hotel a constant reminder of why we were here. All the same, it was nice that our problems didn't dominate our existence for a change, and that we could have some fun together. The worry lines even left their faces halfway through the first day, even if it was only for brief period of time.

The second day, we went to Cherry Creek State Park. We rented bicycles, and checked out some of the bike trails the park offered. It was beautiful biking through the trees, listening to the birds chirp in warning as we sped by. I tossed my bike down just before the water and my heart soared at the stunning mountain views from the sandy beach by the creek. The three of us waded into the water up to our knees to cool off when the sun reached its highest point. At sunset, we sat together, watching the bright orange ball descend on the horizon until it slipped behind the hills, leaving a dazzling display of color that lingered until the last patches of light left the sky.

My phone chirped with a voicemail alert when we arrived back at the hotel. I clicked the listen button, and the second Bailey's worried voice bubbled into my ear, I felt terrible. I hadn't called Bailey since we had left the nice hotel, and she had wanted me to keep her posted. I didn't want to ruin my mood by going back into the Pete saga, so instead of calling her back I typed out a quick text.

Sorry I haven't called. We're just fine. Don't worry. I'll call you later.

While I packed my things for the third and final time this trip, I let my mind wander back to my nightmare. It had come true again, and that could only mean one thing: I had a gift. A gift that, to some, would mean a great and exciting new adventure, but for me it just opened doors that I would rather keep closed. Every time one of these new doors opened, I ended up in some kind of danger. Nothing good could come from this.

We loaded up Eli's car, I squeezed into the back seat, and we were on our way home. I leaned my head against the car seat and watched the rain run down the windows. The rain pelted the roof in loud thumps. Trails of water made their way down the closed convertible top to the trunk, each stream taking a different path. I closed my eyes and let the rhythmic sounds of the rain and the cars around us relax me as we jostled back and forth.

CHAPTER NINE

"Hey Mom, I'm home!" I called as I walked through the front door and tossed my duffle to the side.

I hadn't called to say I would be home early, so my mom was surprised to see me home, but I explained that I had gotten the dates wrong and I was in fact home on the right day. I held my breath, waiting for her response, hoping she bought my excuse.

"That's not like you," she said.

I shrugged. "I know, I guess I've been a bit distracted lately. I've been stressing keeping my grades up. I'm going to go to bed, it's been a long day," I said, exhaling and hoping she didn't notice how nervous I was.

"I see. Well, I'm glad you're home. I missed you."

"I missed you too," I said, throwing my arms around her waist and snuggling close.

I climbed the stairs to my room, and when I jumped into my bed, it felt so good to be home. There was nothing better than being in my own bed after a trip, even if it meant being away from Eli. My body molded into the bed and my muscles felt soothed by the familiarity. I was so relieved to be home, and I took comfort in knowing that Pete sat captive sixteen hours away, and Eli was safe and less than ten minutes down the road.

I fell asleep in my clothes and when I woke the next morning, my face was resting on my brush. *Ouch*. The bristles left a spotted design on my cheek that felt like a bruise. I didn't know how I hadn't woken earlier solely from the discomfort of it.

I could hear voices downstairs. I knew one was my mom's, but I couldn't place the other. I threw on my robe and went downstairs, my curiosity propelling me faster than normal.

I caught my mom in mid-laugh when I walked into the room. A strange man sat in my usual chair at the dining room table, but I could only see his back. His jet-black hair was combed straight back.

I cleared my throat.

"Oh, good morning, honey," my mom said. "This is George. George, this is my daughter, Abby."

The man stood and turned to face me while smoothing his clothes. "Hi Abby, it's nice to meet you. I've heard so much about you." He politely extended his hand as he spoke.

"Hi. That's funny. I've heard nothing about you." I glared at my mom before I took his hand and shook it firmly.

I walked around him to the kitchen to get my own plate and dished up what was left on the counter. Afterward, I sat at the breakfast bar, avoiding the whole situation. *Just what was that about anyway? Who was this man, and why was he in my house?*

When I finished eating, I stalked up to my room to get ready. I was not going to deal with another one of my mom's dating debacles. And springing him on me at breakfast? *Not cool, Mom, not cool.* A little warning would have gone a long way.

I tried to waste time in my room, waiting for this mystery George to leave. He had to be leaving soon, right? Every few minutes, I listened for his deep voice to echo through the house, each time getting more and more frustrated when it carried up to me.

When I heard the front door, I felt myself relax. Good, he was leaving. When I heard the door shut again, I decided it was safe and went downstairs. But as my foot landed on the very last step, I heard voices. Stopping, I grumbled to myself. *He's still here?* Another voice had joined in. I peeked my head around the door jamb into the dining room, taking extra care not to be seen, and found Eli sitting among them.

"Hey," I said, stepping around the corner. "What are you doing here?" I walked over to Eli and wrapped my arms around him, but before I let go I whispered in his ear, "Get me out of here." I pulled away, looking innocent.

The look he gave me showed that he had caught on, and he made a disgusted face in George's direction that only I could see. I held back my giggle.

"Mrs. Martin, would it be okay if I took Abby to a movie?" Eli asked.

"Sure," she said, her grin spreading across her face, and as soon as Eli's back was turned, she winked. I couldn't help but roll my eyes as I bolted out of the room.

"Okay, bye Mom!" I called behind me as we rushed out the door.

I waited until we got in the car before I spoke, "Oh my gosh! I couldn't wait to get out of there! I could kiss you!"

He laughed at me. "Then why don't you?"

I grinned, lifted myself to my knees and gave him the biggest kiss of gratitude I could manage. I plopped back on my seat to appraise his reaction, smiling broadly at him.

"Maybe I need to come over unannounced more often, if I'm rewarded like that," he said, a silly grin on his face.

"You don't know how much you saved me. I couldn't handle being there another minute."

"Who was that guy anyway?" he asked.

"I don't even know. My mom's never mentioned him before. Then I came down to breakfast this morning, and he's there. It already feels like the last time she tried dating."

"You think they're dating?" he asked.

"What else would it be? He was there for breakfast!"

"I don't know, but don't you think she would have mentioned him before now?"

"Yes...no...I don't know...My mom dating isn't territory I've been through enough times to know what 'usual' behavior looks like."

He considered this a moment. "I guess."

He didn't say another word about George, and I was glad. I had wanted to escape the house to get away from that junk in the first place, not to have it follow me around all day.

"So, where are we going?" I asked.

"The...movies," his puzzled voice responded. "Is that okay?"

"Oh..." I laughed. "Of course. Sounds great."

My mind was cleared by the time the previews ended and the movie began. Being on a date with Eli felt great. It was still one of our first. We walked around the mall when the movie was over and sat in the courtyard, where a band played and people congregated at tables and on the ground to enjoy the music.

"You hungry?" Eli asked.

"Actually, yeah," I said.

"I'll go get us some food. I'll be right back." He brushed my cheek with his lips before he walked away.

I sat on the grass, watching the band in their element. The courtyard was full of people swaying to the music, just as I was. I leaned back on my hands, letting the sun warm my skin and the band's music carry me away.

"Abby?" a voice called from behind me.

My head whipped around at the sound of my name, my heart racing and eyes searching.

"Bailey!" I exclaimed with relief and surprise.

"Hey, what are you doing here?" she asked. "I didn't even know you were back!" Her gaze swept over me, questioning and perplexed.

"Eli and I are on a date," I said, beaming.

"Oh! How fun!"

"Are you working?" I asked.

"Yeah, I'm on my lunch break so I thought I'd check out the band. They're pretty good, aren't they?"

"I was just thinking the same thing."

"When did you guys get back?" she asked.

"Last night, really late, or I would have called. I literally laid down on my bed and crashed without changing my clothes. I woke up sleeping on my brush," I said, laughing at myself.

"Oh, ouch." She smiled half-heartedly.

"When I got up this morning, there was a man eating breakfast with my mom," I said as I stared off into the distance.

"What?" she asked, looking alarmed.

"Eli showed up and got me out of the house," I said. "Thank goodness."

"So who is he?" she asked.

"I don't know. I didn't get to have that talk with my mom. I'm sort of dreading it." I cringed just thinking about it.

"That royally stinks!" Bailey said.

"Well, look who we have here," Eli said as he approached, his hands occupied with our tray of food.

"Hey Eli!" Bailey said. "I'm glad you guys are back!"

Eli placed a tray with two subs and two drinks on it in front of us. *Yum!*

"I should get back to work, call me later? I need details," Bailey urged me.

"Definitely." I smiled at her.

"Bye Bailey," Eli said.

"That's funny, running into her. Did she know we were back?" Eli asked.

"Nope," I said.

"I hope subs are okay. It sounded good to me," he said.

"Absolutely."

I devoured my sandwich in half the time it took Eli to eat his, and he laughed at me.

"What? I was hungry!"

"Clearly," he said, a huge grin on his face.

We finished eating and decided it was time Eli brought me home. I groaned and dragged my feet on the way back to the car. He placed his hand on the small of my back as he guided me through the crowd of people that had gathered to listen to the music. His touch sent shivers down my legs and made me weak in the knees. I latched my arm around his elbow and tried to hide my wobbliness.

"What are you smiling about?" Eli asked me, rubbing his hand on my back.

I looked at him and blushed.

"What?" he asked with a guilty smirk.

"You know what," I said.

"No, I don't," he said, "but it sure makes you happy."

He certainly enjoyed teasing me when I was embarrassed, so I stayed quiet. I wouldn't admit how he affected me, but I knew I didn't have to. He already knew more about me than I knew myself.

Back at my house, Eli walked me to my door. He pulled me close and wrapped me in his arms. This was home. Right here in his arms. I didn't want to move. I breathed in his glorious, manly scent and let it take me away. Without warning, Eli dipped me back as if we were dancing and kissed me. I giggled like a schoolgirl. He righted me securely on my feet and bowed. I played right along with him and curtsied.

"I should go," he said. He bit his lower lip.

I daydreamed about biting it just like he was, and my body hummed to life. My face flushed as embarrassment rushed through me. Quickly, I looked at the ground, hoping he hadn't seen.

"Okay."

He grinned and whispered in my ear. "You're adorable when you get embarrassed...even if I don't know why you're embarrassed."

My breath hitched in my throat and a shiver shot up my spine as his breath tickled my ear in just the right way. He kissed me one last time, his lips lingering a little longer than normal, and then he turned and walked away, glancing back a couple times as I stood there watching him go. I could still feel the warmth of his arms around me, the caress of his lips on mine. I reached up and touched them once, as if I could capture his kiss in my hand.

Finally, after standing there long after his car had disappeared, I turned to go inside and face my mom. The idea of staying outside the rest of the day tempted me, but I suppressed it.

"Hello," I called out into the quiet house.

"In here," my mom hollered back.

I went into the kitchen to grab a soda first; I needed the sugar to get me through this crash course in everything George.

"Hey," I said.

"How was the movie?" she asked.

"Good."

"That's good," she said.

"Let's cut to the chase. Who was that?" I knew I sounded rude, but for the time being I wasn't about to let my guard down.

"Relax Abby," she said, reprimanding me. Her voice cut me down to size, and I immediately sat down.

I took a deep breath. "So?" A hint of attitude hung on the simple word.

"I didn't expect you to come home last night," she said. "I didn't plan to spring him on you like that. I'm sorry."

I couldn't help but roll my eyes. *So I ruined her plan by coming home early? That was her excuse? Newsflash, I live here too.*

"I met him a few weeks ago, and I've been spending time with him while you were away," she said. "Just to test the waters."

I wasn't sure if she expected me to say something, but I didn't.

"I know last time didn't go so well, but I'd like to know if it would be okay with you if we officially start dating."

I thought about it. *Isn't that what they were already doing?* Honestly, I didn't care, but I didn't want to have to talk about him. Not now. Not later.

"Just keep me and Dad out of it," I said with more vehemence than I had intended.

I stormed out of the room. That was the last I wanted to hear about this George person. I hoped she would keep our encounters to a minimum.

My phone buzzed in my pocket before I even mounted the landing above the stairs.

"Hello?" I said without looking at the screen.

"Hey..." Eli's soothing voice purred in my ear. "Ah...how did it go?"

"Fine," I groaned. "She wants to date him. She asked for my approval."

"Are you okay?" he asked.

"I'm fine."

"All right. Well, I just wanted to check on you. I'll let you go. I'm sure you want some time to think," he said.

"Thanks Eli," I said.

I laid in bed with my laptop in hand. After a little alone time and a movie, I would feel loads better. Or so I hoped. I started a movie, but I don't think I got very far. The next thing I knew someone was sitting on my bed, fingers intertwined in my hair. They glided effortlessly through it and down my back, gently coaxing me awake.

"Good morning sleepyhead," my mom's voice broke the silence around us.

"I don't want to get up," I said, stifling a yawn. "It's spring break."

I rolled onto my back, stretching out across the bed. The morning light shone too brightly, and I snapped my eyes closed again.

I groaned.

"I took the day off. Let's have a girls' day!"

I stretched my arms upward. "All right, I'll get up and get ready," I said, sitting up.

* * * *

Throughout the morning, the tension between us remained pretty thick, but as the day wore on it began to fade. Despite our disagreement, shopping with my mom made for the perfect stress-free day.

We grabbed a quick lunch in the mall food court and headed off to see a movie. Two movies in two days was a record for me.

Early on, Eli texted a few times to see what I was doing, but after I told him I was on a girls' day, I stopped hearing from him. I hoped he was out doing something with Ren. It would be nice for them to catch up without me around. Maybe they would let their guard down a little. Something Eli didn't do with me, ever. Tension always marked his face, written in the worry lines that I wished would fade away, at least for a little while.

We finished the day with some frozen yogurt. It couldn't have been more perfect. I loved choosing exactly how much yogurt I wanted. I could rarely finish off a normal-sized ice cream anyway. I piled mine full of peanut butter cups and topped it off with a cherry. Or three. I tossed a couple into my mom's too, when she wasn't looking, earning me a playful dirty look. I batted my eyes, feigning innocence.

When our yogurt dwindled in our bowls, I realized that it took much longer to make our creations than it did to devour them. I licked my spoon clean while my mom finished her last few bites.

"Would it be okay if I went over to Eli's?" I asked when we were driving home.

"Sure, do you want me to drop you off?" she asked.

"Can you?"

"Sure."

I directed her where to turn and finally where to stop. Eli's car wasn't in the driveway. I guess I should have told him I was coming, but I had hoped to surprise him.

"Thanks Mom," I said as I got out.

She drove away before I knocked on the door. I'm sure she assumed that I had cleared it with Eli first. My hands started to sweat, and I knocked hard. I waited, holding my breath as I listened carefully for movement from the inside, but all I could hear was the drumming of my own heartbeat. I was getting ready to walk away when I heard the door chain moving. It opened slowly, at first only a crack.

"Abby?" Eli's mom said from behind the door.

"Yeah."

She opened the door all the way and stood in front of me. "Did Eli know you were coming?" she asked, looking a little confused.

"No, I just finished a day out with my mom and thought I'd surprise him. Guess I really did, 'cause he's not home," I laughed while wringing my hands.

"He's out with Ren," she said.

"That's okay. I'll just call him later," I said.

I started to walk away, but she stopped me.

"You can wait for him. I'm sure he'll be back soon."

"Okay," I said.

Walking into Eli's house when he wasn't home felt weird. I hadn't had many conversations with his mom in the past, and they had all been very short.

"Do you want anything to drink?" she asked.

"No, I'm fine. Thanks."

She nodded and disappeared a moment later.

I wondered if waiting had been a bad idea as I sat down on the couch in the living room, alone. The house was quiet. So quiet that you could hear everything. His mom was making a drink in the kitchen. First the ice clinked into the glass, then the drizzling liquid splashed through the ice cubes, the ice cracking as it warmed. A moment later, she wandered into the room, drink in hand.

"We haven't had the opportunity to talk very much," she said.

"No we haven't."

My slick hands sat in my lap. I rubbed my palms on my pant legs to dry them, but seconds later they were sweaty again.

"What are you interested in, Abby?" she asked.

I felt put on the spot. Not that it was a hard question—I had just never thought about what I liked in enough depth to answer it.

"Um...I like to read," I said.

She smiled. "I do too."

"What do you like to read?" I asked.

"Mystery. It's the only genre I read. I guess intrigue comes with being a Protector's wife."

"Really? I love mystery, though I don't have a specific favorite," I said. "I honestly could read just about anything fiction."

I sat and tried not to make eye contact. I didn't know what more to say. Small talk wasn't exactly my strong point. I rummaged in my purse and found what I was looking for a little too quickly, applying a thin layer of gloss to my lips, which were far from chapped, and dropping the tube back into my purse.

"How is school?" she asked.

This was clearly difficult for her too.

"Good."

"That's good, I'm sure your parents are proud," she said.

I smiled, and the conversation died once again. A dog barked in the distance. I looked at the window and pointlessly wondered what it was barking at. Then the front door opened suddenly, startling both Elizabeth and myself.

"Mom?" Eli called into the house, his deep voice echoing throughout.

"In here," she said, her voice so quiet and mouse-like that I thought she probably never yelled, ever.

He walked in out of breath, a hand towel hung around his neck, his body covered in sweat from head to toe. Absently, he dabbed drops of sweat from his forehead before they ran down his cheek. "Mom, I'm..." He stopped in his tracks when he saw me sitting across from his mother. "Abby? What are you doing here?" he asked, sounding almost alarmed.

"I thought I'd surprise you." I rose to my feet, my hands fumbling in my pockets.

"You definitely did," he said.

"Is this a bad time?" I asked.

"No. No, of course not. I'm glad you're here," he said with a smile, any hint of hesitation gone like it was never there to begin with.

"Are you sure?" I asked. "I could go..."

"Of course." he said, cutting me off. He leaned over and placed a kiss on my cheek. "I would hug you," he looked down at himself, "but I don't think you want me to touch you right now."

I giggled. "Not exactly." I knew his mom was watching, and doubted I would feel comfortable even if he hadn't been covered in sweat.

"Come on," he said, reaching for my hand.

I smiled at his mom before taking his hand and letting him lead me away to his room. He shut the door behind us.

He pinned me to the door with a hand on each side of my head, resting his sweaty forehead on mine. I could feel his rapid breath on my face. Then he kissed me so passionately it took my breath away. It only lasted a second before he pulled away.

He headed toward the bathroom, looking back at me with a grin. "I'm going to take a shower, do you need anything?"

I shook my head. "I'm okay," I said.

He tossed me the TV remote and rushed into the bathroom. Almost instantly I heard the water running in the next room. I tried to relax, but just being in Eli's bedroom made me jittery. When I thought about him taking a shower one room over, my stomach pooled into a bundle of nerves.

I tried to take my mind off him and let it wander to other things. I couldn't help but consider what his mom thought of me. I had blown my chances to make a good impression, and like a coward, I had gone running with my tail between my legs the minute Eli arrived. I could have waited in the living room with her while he showered. I should have. But who was I kidding? I couldn't wait to get out of there. Not because I didn't like her, but because I didn't have a clue what to talk about with her. I felt bad that I hadn't pushed myself harder for Eli's sake. Next time I would. Maybe.

"Earth to Abby," Eli said, peeking out from the other side of the bathroom door.

I could see his shirtless chest, beads of water still clinging to his skin, his broad shoulders bulged as he moved. My mouth went dry.

"Huh, what?" I said.

"Did you want to go out for dinner?"

Hot, steamy air came rushing out of the bathroom as Eli opened the door wider. He stood in the opening with only a towel covering his unmentionables. I wanted to look away, but I couldn't. My eyes were glued to his large shoulders, his impeccably toned chest, and his rock-hard abs. Every ripple, every bulge, every crevice captivated me. When my eyes finally made it back up to his, I realized my mouth was hanging open. I clamped it shut and tried to recover as if nothing had happened, but the amused grin on his face told me I had been caught taking in all of his manly glory with eager eyes. I blushed and looked at my hands.

"Sure," I said.

"What were you doing?" he asked, playing innocent.

"I guess I was daydreaming," I said, sticking my tongue out at him.

A grin spread across his face as he went back into the bathroom where I couldn't see him and emerged moments later fully dressed.

"Where do you want to go?" I asked.

"There's somewhere I want to take you, but it's a surprise," he said.

He led me downstairs and to the front door, calling out, "Bye Mom." He didn't wait for her to respond as he pulled me out of the house. His excitement was contagious, and I could feel my stomach fill with elation.

"Bye," I tried to say to her, but I doubted she had heard me before the door shut behind us.

Once again, Eli helped me into the car by opening my door for me, and we were off. The sky had already darkened, the sun long out of view. Eli reached over and put his hand on mine. Flutters filled my stomach. The coziness of riding in his car, holding hands as we drove was so simple yet perfect.

"It doesn't take much, does it?" he asked.

"For what?"

"To make you...excited or nervous," he said, testing each word.

I looked at him out of the corner of my eye. He squeezed my hand, reassuring me that he was there either way. I had to get over my shyness with him. I loved him, but there were still things that made me jittery, though I couldn't explain why. Eli had never given me any reason to be so bashful.

I decided I would throw caution to the wind. "You do it to me; your simple touch is...electrifying." The last word came out breathlessly as I thought about how his touch on my skin made me feel.

"You feel it too?" he asked, almost amazed.

I waited to get my bearings before asking, "What do you mean, 'too'?"

"That's how it feels for me. I thought it was just me. My skin tingles. It's electrifying. I hadn't been able to describe it before, but you nailed it," he said.

I should have known he felt it too. Our connection ran deep.

"I didn't say anything before because I thought I was just weird or something," I admitted.

"You aren't weird, and you can tell me anything, no judgment. Besides, I don't think anything would surprise me anymore."

I considered this for a moment and realized he was right. So much in this world was so far out, and I had only just begun to touch the surface. "I'll try," I said.

We pulled into a parking lot with a massive gate at the entrance. It must have been at least twenty feet tall, and the building that stood behind it looked elegant and expensive. I instantly felt underdressed, but thankfully Eli was dressed at about the same level, so I didn't feel completely out of place.

We walked into the dimly-lit restaurant, and it took a moment for my eyes to adjust. Candles in a variety of shapes and sizes were glowing in all the right places. They lit the restaurant with the most romantic ambiance. I had never been anywhere this elegant before.

"Eli, this place is amazing," I whispered as we walked behind the hostess to our table.

"I know, it's great right?" he said, squeezing my hand.

"Aren't I a bit underdressed?" I asked him.

"No, you're beautiful."

I smiled at his compliment, but I wasn't convinced. This was the type of evening every girl dreamed of—the perfect date with the perfect guy. I smiled to myself, knowing I had found the happiness that everyone longs for, that once-in-a-lifetime romance.

It felt as if time outside of our table had stopped, and we were the only two people in the room. After spending so much time in our relationship running, we finally relaxed, just chatting, getting to know each other without any interruptions, except the waitress, that is. I was surprised to learn that Eli had been out of the country several times. In fact, he had lived in Europe for a while. It shouldn't have been a surprise, since his dad must have had to travel a lot throughout his life, and it would be only natural for Eli to have gone along sometimes. I bit my lip with envy. Traveling was something I had always dreamed of doing, but I had never been able to partake in more than a few small vacations here and there with my parents. Now, I hoped I would be able to travel with Eli. There were so many amazing places we could go; we could explore the world together.

When our food came, it was hard to stop talking to enjoy it. I wanted to know everything about him, and I knew our time in this bubble wouldn't last long enough. It was as if the all-about-Eli floodgates had opened, and I wasn't ready for them to close again.

After we finished our steaks and baked potatoes, we split a warm brownie topped with vanilla ice cream. The rich chocolate melted in my mouth and the ice cream slid down after it, the two mixing together beautifully.

"Let's go outside," he said.

Eli paid our bill, and we stood up at the same time. He led me out onto the patio, which also doubled as a skygazing deck. An unlit firepit sat in the center of a cluster of outdoor couches and open-topped cabana beds. We picked one, and Eli laid down first. My heart rate picked up. I hesitated for only a second, staring at his powerful body, before climbing onto the bed next to him and placing my head on his chest. We gazed at the stars for a long time in silence. Eli's breathing grew deep and even. Slowly, I sat up to look at him and found him sound asleep. I laid back on one of the pillows next to him, resting my head in my hand as I watched him sleep so peacefully. He looked so comfortable and at ease. I loved seeing his face soften, so I let him sleep.

I was so engrossed in watching him that when someone tapped my shoulder I jumped in surprise. My heart rate stammered to life, beating wildly, and my head whipped around in alarm. Before I had laid eyes on whoever it was, Eli had woken and leapt in front of me protectively, crouched in an animalistic attack position. It was the waitress. She had backed up about five steps and looked terrified.

"I-I-I..." she stammered.

"Eli, stop," I said. "I'm sorry, did you need something?" I asked as I crawled around Eli and stood up next to the cabana bed.

"I-I was just making sure you guys were okay," she said, her voice trembling.

"I think you startled him, I'm sorry. He had dozed off. Thank you for checking, we were just leaving," I said, taking firm grasp of the out-of-control situation. I gathered my things and walked to the door, feeling mortified.

I didn't know if Eli was following, but I was so mad at him that it didn't matter. I would walk home if I had to. I stormed out to the parking lot and stood at the edge of the pavement, looking out at the cars. As I stood there fuming, I could hear him approach, but I refused to turn around and face him.

"What were you thinking?" I barked, catching even myself off guard.

"I'm sorry," he said. He tried to reach out and touch my shoulder, but I yanked it out of his reach, letting his hand fall back to his side.

"You have no right to come out of the gate swinging every time you think someone might hurt me! It was the waitress for goodness' sake!"

"I know," he said. "It's hard to decipher your emotions sometimes. I fell asleep, it startled me awake, I overreacted. I know that. I'm sorry."

I finally turned to face him. He was looking at the ground, and I could tell he felt bad. His cheeks flamed red.

"Don't let it happen again," I snapped before I turned and walked to the car.

We didn't speak the whole way back to my house. I watched the trees fly past my window as I fumed in the passenger seat. I was so disappointed that our perfect night had ended this way.

He walked me to the front door, and I hugged him goodbye and hurried inside without another glance. I hated that he thought he needed to protect me every moment of the day. That was far from what I needed, but how could I prove that to him?

The next morning I spoke to my dad about my trip. There wasn't much to tell him, but he too was surprised by my early arrival. I couldn't say for sure, but part of me felt as if he didn't believe me when I explained why, though he didn't argue the point. He was glad I'd had fun but equally glad I was home. Deep down, I think he had worried more than my mom, who had seemed to not even notice I was gone. She had seemed almost disturbed that I had returned, now that she had *George* in the picture.

Summer was inching closer, and its excitement was setting in. My dad and I discussed plans for me to come visit during my break. We set a tentative date for one week after school got out, though I hadn't talked to Eli yet. I hoped he would be willing to go with me. I knew my dad would love to see him again. I thought he might even be disappointed if I came alone.

I went downstairs to breakfast in my PJ's after I had said goodbye. Rounding the corner to the kitchen, I came face to face with George once again.

"Hey Abby," he said, greeting me.

I just nodded my head in his direction, grabbed a bowl of cereal, and headed back up to my room. I would rather eat by myself than with my mom and her new boy toy. The whole thing was too awkward. Breakfast was not the meal I would have chosen to get to know him at. Half the time I wasn't even completely awake. I hoped that either it would get easier, or he would just go away and the problem would correct itself, but I doubted I would get so lucky.

I ate while I sat on my bed, and when I was finished I brought my bowl back downstairs, tossed it in the sink, and headed to the living room. I refused to let this George guy make me stay hidden away in my room for the rest of the day. I would go about my day as if he wasn't even there, even though I could hear his voice trailing out of the dining room. I crossed my arms and slumped deeper into the couch, letting the cushions press into the sides of my head, muffling all distant sounds.

I picked up my phone and called Bailey.

"Hey Abby," she said.

"Hey," I grumbled.

"Uh oh, what's wrong?" she asked.

"My mom's boyfriend is here," I whispered into the phone while cupping my hand around my mouth.

"Oh," she said with instant understanding.

"Want to come over?" I asked.

"Sure! I'll have my dad bring me over."

"Okay, see you in a few," I said and hung up.

She arrived twenty minutes later with a pint of ice cream. We went straight to my room and devoured it all.

"This was just what I needed," I said as I licked the last of the ice cream off of my spoon.

"Yep, that," she said, pointing at the empty container, "is my go-to whenever my dad has a date. Though I've been lucky enough that none of them have turned into girlfriends or taken up residence in my kitchen every morning. I'm not sure how I would handle that." She shot a glare toward the stairs.

I giggled at her enthusiasm. *If only I could be that lucky.*

"I hate waking up and seeing him at breakfast." I rolled my eyes. "It's the worst. I ate breakfast in my room this morning just to avoid him."

She laughed. "I don't blame you. I would have probably done the same thing."

A grin spread across my face.

"So what's Eli doing today?"

I hadn't even thought much about him since I was so preoccupied with George. But even if I had thought about him, I wouldn't have wondered what he was doing. I was still angry with him for last night. He had put me in such an uncomfortable position at the restaurant, a position that I wouldn't even have to worry about if things were normal. I sighed.

"Ugh. I don't even know," I said.

"Wow, bad there too? Sheesh. What's going on?" she asked.

"We went on a date last night. Oh Bailey, it was amazing." I sighed, thinking of our perfect little bubble. "The perfect date, you know—the one every girl dreams of. We went to an amazing restaurant that I'm sure I was way underdressed for. After dinner we shared an incredible dessert. They had a stunning patio, too, with cabana beds and lounge chairs. We went out to star gaze from a cabana bed. It was so romantic," I said wistfully, as I recalled the night in my mind.

"Well, that sounds more than perfect," she said.

"It was."

"What am I missing?" she asked. I could see the confusion in her eyes.

"When we were watching the stars, Eli drifted off to sleep." I paused as I thought back.

"That isn't so bad," she offered.

"No it wasn't. He looked so peaceful. I just sat there watching him sleep, but that's not it. A waitress came out to see if we needed anything. I didn't hear her approach, so she startled me." I looked up from the bed to see if Bailey was following.

"Uh-huh," she nodded, urging me to go on.

"I guess Eli sensed that I was startled," I said, "and before I realized what was happening, he jumped over me in an attack position, as if the waitress was going to hurt me. It was so embarrassing! The poor girl was terrified."

"Oh no! What did you do?" she asked.

"I didn't know what to do. So I told her that he had fallen asleep and gotten startled, which wasn't a complete lie. You should have seen her face." I paused, recalling the fear in her eyes. "Once I told her we were fine, I fled. In the parking lot, I let him have it. I didn't even kiss him goodbye, and I haven't spoken to him since. I guess he's giving me space to cool down."

"Oh man." She thought for a moment. "That's rough, but you can't completely blame him; he was just trying to protect you."

"From the *waitress*?" I shrieked before covering my mouth and glancing at the door. I didn't want my mom to overhear this conversation. "What was she going to do, serve me to death?"

"Well, yeah, she wasn't actually a threat, but he didn't know that. He was startled awake, and all he knew was that you were alarmed. It's not surprising he acted the way he did."

I thought about what Bailey was saying; maybe I did overreact a bit. He was new at this, and he was just as embarrassed as I, if not more so.

"Hey, don't worry about it." She nudged me on the shoulder. "Eli loves you, and he knows you love him. You guys will get past this."

"I hope so."

"You have a crazy life, I don't know if I could keep up!" she said, laughing.

"Tell me about it. I don't think I am," I admitted. "Hey, how are things going with your beau?"

"Good, really good. He's amazing! And you know what?"

"What?"

"My dad loves him!"

"Really?"

"Yeah, I was shocked. He never likes anyone I date, ever. Not even Eli!" She chuckled.

"He doesn't like Eli?" I asked.

I recalled Bailey and Eli's brief relationship. They had spent just under three months together, but when neither had developed feelings for each other they decided to end it, remaining good friends.

"Nope."

"That's weird, everyone likes Eli..." I paused, "well, except Pete."

"I know, right?" she said.

I couldn't understand what would have caused Bailey's dad not to like Eli. He was so likeable. He just had one of those personalities. I guess I would never know.

After an hour, Bailey looked at her watch. "Shoot, I've got to go. I have to be at work in an hour."

She called her dad and headed out within ten minutes, leaving me to dwell on my date the night before. Then, a close second, the man that had taken up residence in my kitchen. It was 3 p.m., and I still hadn't spoken to Eli. That was unusual for us, but I wasn't going to be the one to come to him. As far as I was concerned, I didn't care if I talked to him at all today. I spread myself out on my bed and dove headfirst into a book, letting the world come to life in front of me.

The next thing I knew, my mom was calling me down for dinner. My book had worked like a charm, immersing me in a make-believe world that I wanted to be in, momentarily clearing my mind of my troubles. I made my way down the stairs, stretching out the kinks in my neck and yawning. Just as I entered the dining room, I heard the voice that made me want to run back upstairs, and I stopped dead in my tracks. George. *Would he ever leave?*

Then, I listened a little closer, and I heard another voice more distinctly. *Eli?* I rounded the corner and saw Eli setting the last full dish of food on the table, just as Mom and George wandered into the room. Eli's eyes met mine, and I could tell he was uncertain. I had never seen him unsure like this, nervously gripping and ungripping the chair in his hands.

"What are you doing here?" My eyes cut into him like daggers.

"He made us dinner," my mom chimed in. "Isn't that sweet?"

"Very," I said, but my eyes never left Eli's.

Finally, he looked away and stared at the food on the table. This was the first time I wasn't so sure I was happy to see him. Bailey had said I was overreacting, but I still wasn't convinced. George and my mom disappeared once again into the kitchen.

"Hey," he said.

"Hi."

He came around to my side of the table. "I'm sorry. Do you want me to leave?"

I didn't have a chance to respond before my mom returned, with George carrying four drinks. I shook my head and sat down in my seat.

Dinner was...awkward. I refused to look at George, which left either my mom or Eli, so instead of looking around, I stared at my plate. I wanted to gag while I listened to George try to act interested in all things Eli.

By the end of dinner, he knew all about him, from where he went to elementary school to his favorite sport, right down to his favorite color.

It was as if he thought that showing an interest in my boyfriend would make me like him. I had news for him: That would not work, especially tonight.

On the plus side, the food was amazing. One thing was certain: Eli knew his way around the kitchen. I finished my food and took the opportunity to leave the tension that filled the dining room, carrying all of my dishes in one trip and tipping them into the sink. I stood in front of the sink filled with dishes and took a deep breath. Normally, dishes were the last thing I would ever choose to do, but today was another story; the last thing I wanted was to go back into that dining room with Eli and George. I filled the sink with hot, soapy water and plugged in my earbuds to tune out the world around me. Loud bass filled my ears as I plunged my hands into the water, my hips bobbing to the beat.

A sudden tap on my shoulder jolted me from my music-induced bliss. I pulled the headphone out of my right ear and turned around, in one swift move. Eli stood before me, looking unsure of what he should do.

"Do you want me to leave?" he asked.

I stood there and stared at him. I didn't know what to say. If he left, I would be alone with my mom and George. But did I want to be around him? I considered my options, but realized I really didn't want him to leave, and it wasn't because of George.

"Abby?"

I hesitated. "No," I whispered so quietly that I wasn't sure he would hear me. Truthfully, I didn't want him to leave. What I wanted was for things to go back to the way they were, before he overreacted and embarrassed me. I wanted to forget about it all. But my mind held firmly to the image of him pouncing over me like an animal, and I shuddered as it played through my head for the hundredth time.

He reached out to hold my hand in his, and his fingertips brushed the tops of my wet knuckles. "I'm sorry," he said, his voice deep and husky. "I'm so sorry."

I took a deep breath and let it out slowly. "Okay."

His arms were around me before I could develop another thought. I breathed him in and let myself enjoy the comfort his arms provided. My soapy wet hands rested on his shoulders, and it made me laugh that I had soaked him, breaking my anger.

He grinned at me. "Makes you happy to get me all wet, huh?"

I nodded through my laughter.

"I'll have to remember that." He chuckled at me. "Want some help?" he asked, gesturing toward the remaining dishes.

"Sure."

Once we finished the dishes, Eli and I went into the backyard to get away from my mom and George. In the clear Arizona sky, thousands of stars appeared one by one.

Last night's fiasco wasn't brought up again, but I couldn't say it wasn't on my mind, and I could tell it troubled Eli too. As much as it pained me to admit, Bailey was on the right track; I did overreact. Maybe even just as much as he had.

CHAPTER TEN

The week flew by without a single complication, for once. Vince seemed to be the saving grace that we so desperately needed with Pete in Colorado. Not a single problem had arisen. When the time came, the elders took Pete in and jailed him. He was currently performing manual labor doing the elders' laundry for the rest of his life, and I couldn't be happier that he was out of our lives for good.

Vince would arrive home the next day, and I was looking forward to seeing him. He had become family.

The end of the day bell rang, and we all filed out of school. Bailey, Ryan, Eli, and I were going to the movies. It was the first time we were all off work at the same time in what felt like months, and for the first time in nearly as long, things felt 'normal.' *Finally*.

We laughed through the whole movie. My cheeks hurt from smiling, and I went home with sore stomach muscles. We had all needed a comedy desperately.

For once, George wasn't staring me in the face when I arrived home, but unfortunately neither was my mom. Alone again. I stomped up the stairs in protest and, doing my best to forget that nobody was home, went to bed.

I woke the next morning with sunshine in my face. I stretched out on my bed and stared at the window. My eyes screamed out in protest. My mom must be home and awake; I could smell coffee in the air. I hoped and prayed with every fiber in my being that she would be alone. I rolled out of bed and sauntered down the stairs. The kitchen was empty, so I took a deep breath and stepped into the dining room.

"Hey honey," my mom said.

George was nowhere to be seen. I let out a huge sigh of relief and hoped my mom hadn't noticed. I plopped down in my usual seat and started eating.

"Where's George?" I asked.

"He had to work."

"Oh. Well, it's nice for it to be just the two of us. He's been here so much lately," I said.

"I know. I hope it hasn't bothered you," she said.

I'm not sure what she expected me to say. The answer was yes, but I couldn't very well tell her that, at least not without hurting her feelings.

"I do miss our one-on-one time," I said, hoping it would be the right thing to say.

She looked at me with sad eyes. I could tell she agreed, but she didn't say anything else. After that, the atmosphere dripped with awkwardness. I went up to my room to escape from it and got online to check my email. I hadn't checked it in weeks. I couldn't wait to see what Kelly had been up to. I expected to find numerous emails from her but was disappointed when I only had one.

Abby,
How is the school year almost over?? I can't believe it! Does it feel like it went by in the blink of an eye for you too?
I broke up with Isaac two weeks ago. It really sucks. I really missed our normal breakup ritual—ice cream, mani's, pedi's and movies. I couldn't bring myself to hang out with any of my other girl friends, and it feels like I'm mourning two relationships. The sad part is, I think I'm more upset that you weren't here than I was about ending things with Isaac. I miss you. Are you planning a trip here this summer? I really hope so! I hope things are better for you than they are for me. I'll talk to you soon.
Love,
Kelly

I checked when the email came in—a week ago. She was hurting, and I wanted to be there for her more than anything in the world. I loved our breakup routine. I could have used that ritual after my breakup with Pete. I don't know why I hadn't even thought about it at the time. It used to be second nature; now I wasn't sure what *normal* was any more.

I couldn't write her back just yet, my email needed to be carefully worded, and I just couldn't focus on it right now, not with the somber mood settling in the pit of my stomach. I lay back on my pillow and stared at the blank ceiling.

The next thing I knew, the light had brightened in my room, and the sun had descended into its afternoon place in the sky. Falling asleep in the middle of the day had become a habit. The obstacles I had been enduring must have been taking more of a toll on me than I had realized. I stretched my arms and legs and rolled out of bed. It took me a moment to get my bearings before I could form a clear thought.

I hadn't heard from Eli all day. I decided I wouldn't wait to hear from him any longer.

He picked up on the first ring. "Hey Abby." His voice seemed far away.

"Hey, is everything okay?" I asked.

It took a moment for him to respond, and that worried me.

"My mom didn't come home last night."

"What?"

"It's not like her. I don't get it." He sounded like he was panicking. I could hear a lot of shuffling as he spoke, and I imagined him pacing back and forth.

"I'm sure she's fine," I said, trying to reassure him while my mind raced. *What could this mean?*

"My dad isn't answering either," he said.

"Well, he's probably just busy."

"I have to go," he said, and the line went dead before I could say another word.

I set the phone down beside me on the couch. I should have known sooner that something was wrong. He would never have gone that long without talking to me if everything was fine. What could I do? My chest filled with anxiety.

I went into the kitchen to find my mom. She was talking to George. *Ugh! When did he get here?*

"Mom? Can you take me to Eli's?" I asked.

"Sure honey. I'll grab my keys. Want to come along, George?" she asked.

I rolled my eyes and walked out of the room. Grabbing my bag, I headed to the car to wait. Eventually, they emerged from the house together. George made large gestures as he spoke, and my mom giggled at something he said.

Grudgingly, I climbed into the back seat and tried to push away the annoyance I felt toward this man. He was like a moth to the flame; he didn't seem to know when he had overstayed his welcome, at least as far as I was concerned. I put my earbuds in so I didn't have to suffer through another conversation with him, grasping at whatever little detail he could find to make small talk about.

When we arrived, I stepped out of the car, shut the door, and waved at them. I watched my mom drive away, carelessly talking to George as she went about her day. I couldn't remember seeing my mom so carefree with anyone but my dad. It gave me a sinking sensation that George wasn't going away anytime soon. I sighed.

I knocked on Eli's door and was met with an empty echo that stretched on for what seemed like ages. The silence from within worried me. Maybe he had left, but where would he have gone? I shifted my weight nervously and knocked again, much louder this time, to make sure I had been heard. I waited a few more moments and turned to walk away. I had gotten to the driveway when a noise from within the garage caught my attention. I listened more closely, and I could faintly hear the clanking of what I could only imagine were tools. I leaned toward the garage door to listen more closely, pressing my ear to the metallic surface. I heard the same clinking, only louder.

"Eli?" I called out.

The clanging stopped abruptly and was replaced by shuffling. I jumped back when the garage door jolted and began to open. It lifted out of view, exposing Eli's car with its hood up. Eli stood near the garage door button in shorts and a tank top. His hair was tousled and his arms covered in grease. I had never seen him so disheveled and I was surprised to find that I was extremely attracted to him like this.

"Hey," he said.

"Are you okay?" I asked.

He didn't answer right away, but when he finally did he looked up at me with his gorgeous blue eyes full of dread. "I'm worried."

"I know," I said.

I stood there, not knowing what to do. I wished we could talk to Vince. He seemed to have that magic touch that made everything better. Finally, I built up my courage and walked over to where Eli stood, wrapping my arms around him. He didn't move at first, but ever so slowly he leaned in and hugged me back. I could feel the tension in the hardened muscles of his back. I stroked the groves between them, trying to relax him. There wasn't much more I could do. I didn't have the powers he did, so I just hoped my arms around him would comfort him.

The rumble of a motorcycle engine filled the once-quiet street. It pulled into the driveway, and came to a halt. The rider swung his leg over to dismount from the bike. He wore leather chaps, and his half helmet and skeleton face mask hid his identity. I watched with eager eyes, waiting for him to reveal himself. He stood before lifting his helmet off of his head, exposing his face.

Vince.

CHAPTER ELEVEN

The moment Vince walked into the garage, a whirlwind of action commenced. Vince searched the house for clues and he rattled off people to start calling to Eli. After only a few outgoing calls their phones began ringing non-stop. Operation Find Elizabeth was in full swing.

"Hello?" Eli answered his phone when it rang for what seemed like the hundredth time.

I excused myself. I couldn't hear who it was anyway, and listening to only Eli's side of the conversations had been driving me crazy. I went outside to Eli's backyard and paced around the patio, at a loss about what I could do to help. I gazed up at the brilliant blue sky above, a striking contrast to the bright sun.

I felt out of place amidst the chaos. Nobody needed to talk to me or ask me any questions. It seemed like I was just in the way, and the last thing I wanted to do was get in the way of finding Elizabeth. Nausea seized my stomach. I could think of no reason why she would still be gone unless something had happened to her, though I wouldn't admit that to Eli. I tried my best to stay positive and hopeful for him, trying to give him hope. It wasn't working though; the strained look on his face told me all I needed to know, and I stopped trying.

I sat on the porch swing and swung back and forth as my feet dangled in the air like those of a child not quite tall enough to reach the ground. I leaned my head back and closed my eyes, listening to the chains squeak with each pass. Back and forth, back and forth. It reassured me, bringing me back to the days when I flew on the tire swing my dad had made in the tree in front of my childhood home. The whine of the rope sliding to and fro on the branch created a soothing rhythm that I would always find calming. Back and forth. Back and forth.

"What are you doing out here?" A soft voice startled me, snapping me out of my childlike bliss.

My eyes shot open, and my head whipped around. Ren stood there with a sympathetic look on his face.

"Hey," I said.

"Hey yourself. What are you doing out here?" he asked again.

"Trying to relax. I feel like I'm in the way in there, and I have no idea what's going on. I'm going crazy trying to piece together the little bits of the conversations I hear. So I figured I would be better off out here where I don't stress anyone out."

He came around the side of the swing and sat down with me, giving a deep sigh. "I know how you feel; it's the same for me."

"I guess," I said, but I didn't think it really was the same for him. He had known the family for what probably seemed like an eternity. "I didn't even really know her. We only talked a few times."

"I don't think it matters how well you knew her. I know you want the same outcome the rest of us do."

"Of course I do. I just...I don't know..." I stumbled over my words.

"It's hard all around. Right now, all Eli needs from you is for you to be there for him, and Vince too."

"I know, I'm trying."

"I know you are," he said.

We sat there in silence for a while longer. I tried to think of things I could do to help. *What would my mom do?*

Suddenly an idea popped in my head. I jumped up and went inside so quickly that Ren was left in my dust, going straight to the kitchen and pulling ingredient after ingredient out of the refrigerator and cabinets. After washing my hands and rolling up my sleeves, I set to work. Cooking calmed me, but it also helped keep them fed while they tried to piece together Elizabeth's whereabouts.

Eli wandered in some time later. I couldn't be sure how much time had passed, but I wasn't going to stop cooking until I had whipped up everything I could from what I had available. They would be eating it all for days.

After watching me for a few minutes as I worked, he came up behind me and wrapped his arms around my waist. "What are you doing?" he asked.

"I'm cooking."

"Why?"

"It's the only thing I can do to be helpful. You have to eat." I shrugged.

"You don't have to do this." He turned me to face him.

"I know. I want to."

"Thanks," he said, trailing kisses down the side of my face.

Slowly, he released me. He walked over to the island and leaned over it, placing his head in his hands and letting out a huge sigh. I wanted to ask if he had gotten any closer to finding her, but I couldn't find the words, so instead I clamped my mouth shut and continued cooking. A few minutes later, I pulled out a nicely-browned, bubbly, oven-baked macaroni and cheese. It smelled amazing, and my stomach grumbled, but I didn't stop there. I grabbed the potato skins I had just finished topping with bacon and cheese and placed them in the vacant space in the oven. I worked my way around the kitchen with ease, finding everything I was looking for as if I had organized it myself. Elizabeth and I must have a lot more in common than I ever could have imagined. Regret filled me. *Why hadn't I spent more time trying to get to know the person that was there for Eli the most?*

Then Vince burst into the room, words flooding out so fast I couldn't keep up. I managed to catch bits and pieces—something about Elizabeth being seen with someone at some time, somewhere. The people and places he mentioned were lost on my ears. And with that he was out the door, with Ren trailing close behind.

I turned to Eli. He seemed to be concentrating very hard on a darkened spot on the granite countertop. A sudden dryness on the tip of my tongue brought my senses back to me, and I realized that I was, in fact, standing there with my mouth wide open. I clamped it shut and went back to the stove to busy myself again.

I tried to run through what Vince had said a few more times in my head, but it didn't make any more sense than it had as it was leaving his lips. The one thing I was fairly certain about was that they had a solid lead about her location, otherwise Vince and Ren wouldn't have run out the way they did. I hoped they were hot on the trail.

Should I ask Eli what he said? No, it would be best to just leave him alone. I tried my best to push away my anxious thoughts once again. The rush of excitement seemed to have brought it all back with a vengeance as I impatiently waited to hear from them once again. *Would there be another fight?* Suddenly my anxiety turned into worry.

I finished frying the popcorn chicken, pulled the baked potato skins out of the oven, and slid the first batch of cookies into their place.

Grabbing a plate, I loaded it full of chicken, macaroni, and potato skins and slid it in front of Eli.

"You need to eat," I said, trying to hand him a fork.

I realized at that moment that I had never cooked anything for him before and suddenly became nervous that he wouldn't like the food. As if that was what mattered right now. It was a stupid thought. So stupid. I turned away, reprimanding myself.

"It smells great, but I'm not sure I can eat. I have a horrible feeling," he said.

"What kind of feeling?"

"Like…like something is wrong…really wrong." He almost couldn't get the words out.

I held my breath as I listened to him stumble helplessly over the words. I turned away and tried to push back the fear I felt for him. I understood what he was trying to say, though it was unthinkable. Given his intuitive sense of my emotions, I could only imagine what he felt about the other people in his life. I was sure beyond a doubt that he knew his mother's fate, whatever that might be. I tried to think happy thoughts, conjuring up beaches and ice cream, but it didn't seem to help.

"You can stop trying to get rid of your emotions. It's not working," he said.

"I'm sorry."

"It's fine. I wouldn't expect anything else but what you are feeling. I just wish I could help you, but I can't muster the strength right now," he said.

I walked over to stand behind him and wrapped my arms around his waist.

"That is not something you need to be worried about right now," I whispered into his back.

I slid my hands up and massaged his shoulders. The rock-hard knots hurt my fingers when I tried to rub them out.

"Eat," I said, walking back to the stove to take out the cookies. They smelled amazing, and my mouth watered. I heard the fork hit the plate behind me a few times as I scooped the cookies off the pan. I took comfort in knowing that he was at least eating.

Once all the cookies were baked, the clean-up began. Eli had long since finished his plate of food and retreated back to the garage to tinker with his car, leaving me to clear the counter. It suddenly felt strange to be alone in his kitchen. I imagined Elizabeth standing right where I stood, doing dishes. She was probably the last person to stand here, cleaning up.

In a way it made me feel closer to her in some ways; yet I suddenly felt like I had overstepped some boundary. As if by moving things in her kitchen from the places she kept them had somehow removed her presence from the kitchen.

I shook off the feeling. She would be fine. I tried to tell myself that over and over again, but I found it difficult to think positively now that I knew Eli's sense of the situation. His feelings, good or bad, were always spot-on. I knew that the outcome wouldn't be good.

I cleaned every last dish in the sink, not allowing myself to slow until the task was complete. As much as I hated doing dishes, today it felt cleansing. Busy work that kept my mind away from bad thoughts hopefully spared Eli from my ever-changing moods.

After all the food was wrapped up and the kitchen was clean, I went into the living room to wait. I wondered how long Vince and Ren would be gone. Would they come back with answers? Would they come back with Elizabeth? I had to stop sitting around waiting every time danger came up. I needed to take more responsibility off of Eli, Ren, and Vince.

Even though I knew that Eli would never allow me to be put near a dangerous situation, I decided right then that whenever this was over, whatever the outcome, I would ask Ren to take me to the elders to discuss my role in the future. Eli wouldn't be happy when he found out, but that was a risk I was willing to take. They needed help and Eli told me more than once the police were not an option. From what I gathered, the Protector's were a very private group and they wanted to keep in that way.

These nightmares had to be some kind of gift. Maybe the elders could help me figure them out, and then I would be able to do more. If I could see into the future, there was no telling how I could aid them. Maybe it wasn't a bad thing after all.

The garage door opened slowly. I sat up straighter and saw Eli standing at the threshold, looking like he had seen a ghost, his face stark white and his arms hanging limply at his sides. The self-closing garage door hit him square in the back and bounced off his hard body multiple times until it banged to a stop. His body jolted forward with each blow. I jumped up and ran to him.

"What is it?" I asked, grabbing his arms and pulling him from the doorway.

"She's..." he sobbed. "S-she's…gone."

"Gone? What do you mean?" I asked.

A lone tear ran down his face, and my stomach filled with dread.

"She's dead." My heart broke for him.

With those two little words, my world exploded. Eli's muscular body slumped against the door frame and slid to the floor. Nothing I could say would make this better. Nothing. I knew that. There was not one thing I could do to ease his pain. I knelt down in front of him and wrapped my arms around him, hoping to at least comfort him with my touch. His body shook with silent sobs. We sat like that for what felt like an eternity. After a while I could no longer feel my feet beneath me. It didn't matter; I wouldn't move, not until Eli did.

He stood so suddenly that he knocked me over flat onto my butt. He didn't even seem to notice as he stepped around me, striding into the living room. I stayed there on the floor, watching him with my knees pulled to my chest, shrinking back into the shadows. He seemed to be pacing as if he didn't know what to do with himself. I slid up against the wall and let him be. *Give him space. He needs space.*

Once again the garage door opened and Ren walked in. I tried to scoot further out of the way, but he stepped around me too. His face looked red and puffy, as if he had been crying. I felt the familiar sting in of tears in my eyes. Vince walked in next.

Ren looked at me, sitting on the floor in the fetal position, with such sadness that it made my heart hurt.

Vince wouldn't even look at me. "Abby, it's time for you to leave," he said.

"Oh, um...okay. I'll call my mom."

I hadn't even considered that they wouldn't want me there, but I understood. I wasn't part of the family. Grieving could be a very private thing, and it was clear I was no longer wanted.

I rose and went outside to call her. She picked up on the second ring.

"Hi Mom. Can you come pick me up from Eli's?"

"Sure. I'll be there in a few minutes."

"Thanks."

I hung up and went back inside. All three men were still gathered in the living room. It appeared I had interrupted a tense discussion—they all silenced themselves the moment I stepped into the room again. Ren and Vince lifted their faces to look at me, waiting for me to say something.

"Um...my mom will be here in a few minutes. I just thought I would say goodbye. I made food and cookies. It's all in the fridge." I motioned toward the kitchen. "I'm so sorry. I know that doesn't make it better." I turned and walked out the front door. I halfway expected—and hoped—that Eli would come out to say goodbye, but he didn't. At every noise I found myself turning back towards the house to see if it was him. My mom pulled up to the curb, and I hopped in. I gave Eli's front door one last look: It didn't budge, and we drove away as a tear rolled down my cheek.

CHAPTER TWELVE

I lay in bed that night sobbing until I fell asleep. Eli's mom was gone. We weren't close, but the void I felt could not be encompassed with words. I hurt for him. Losing your mom was unthinkable. You don't think it will happen until you are far older than eighteen, and even then I didn't think you could really prepare yourself for your mother's absence. I would never wish that on anyone, and I realized how grateful I was to have my mom there for me. I hugged her a little tighter that night before I headed to bed, and I'm sure she understood why—she herself had lost her mom five years earlier.

I woke the next morning feeling like I had just stopped crying. My eyes were red and swollen, and my cheeks felt tight and stiff from the salt water streaming down them. It wasn't a dream. Not that it would have mattered much these days—my nightmares became reality.

I didn't want to get out of bed. Once I did, I would have to face reality. I would have to face Eli, without a clue as to what he needed from me or what I should say to him. After the way he acted when I left the day before, I wasn't even sure he wanted to see me.

A sudden realization hit me—I had to talk to Bailey. She had lost her mom. Maybe she could tell me what to do. I grabbed my phone, and my fingers slid across the screen.

Can you come over?

I tossed the phone on the bed and threw on the first outfit I saw; at the moment I didn't care if it was clean or dirty. I didn't even bother going down to breakfast. The thought of food nauseated me.

I opened my laptop and checked to see if Eli was online. He wasn't. I couldn't help but feel a little dejected, yet part of me understood. If I felt this horrible, what he felt must be immeasurably worse.

Then I had an idea. My fingers raced across the keyboard as I typed into the search engine:

What to do when your boyfriend's mom dies?

I felt silly as I pressed the search button. Turning to the internet for this seemed a little bit insane, but maybe, just maybe I would get lucky and find a helpful morsel in the sea of answers.

The little circle spun on the screen indicating that the search was underway. 868,000 results. *Yikes.* Maybe this search wasn't so uncommon. I stared at the screen, overwhelmed by what I saw—results from message boards, psychiatrists, advice columns, and beyond. I clicked into a few of them and after reading bits and pieces from each I realized that nothing would cover my uniquely immortal situation, nor did they touch on the fact that Elizabeth was murdered. I had a pretty good idea who was behind it too, but Vince seemed pretty determined not to share those details with me. In fact, last night he had seemed pretty determined not to share any details with me. The thought bothered me. Vince seemed to go from warm and fuzzy toward me to ice cold. The look he had given me had carried so much venom.

I heard a quiet knock on the door. I slammed my laptop screen shut as if I had been looking at things I shouldn't have been, embarrassed at the thought of my mom seeing my search. I wasn't sure that she would understand the reasons behind it, and I wasn't in the mood to discuss it.

"Come in," I called.

"Hey, what's up? You didn't text me back." Bailey's worried voice seemed to flood the room.

I didn't expect the abrupt sense of relief I felt when Bailey walked into view. I got up and threw my arms around her, and the uncontrollable flood of tears began all over again. I didn't try to hold back. She would understand; I knew she would. She stood there, giving me the time I needed without saying a word. Maybe she didn't know what to say; I'm not sure I would have if I were in her shoes. She stroked my hair, pulling it from my face as she lent me her shoulder.

"Eli's mom is dead."

"What?" she shrieked and pulled away from me to look me in the eye.

I sat on the edge of my bed and stared at my hands.

"What happened?" she asked, sitting down on the bed next to me.

"I don't know...she went missing, and after a lot of searching and phone calls, Vince and Ren found her, but it was too late." I paused, trying to decide whether I should say my thoughts aloud. Finally, I got the courage. "I think she was murdered."

It was such a bold statement, and I wasn't sure I should have made that kind of assumption when that word had never been spoken by Eli, Ren, or Vince. Yet, I couldn't imagine what else could have happened to her. I wish Vince had let me stay. Not knowing what had happened was killing me.

"Oh my gosh," she said under her breath.

My sniffle broke the silence and startled Bailey.

"What do I do?" I asked, almost pleading, searching her eyes for a sliver of hope.

When I didn't see it, my eyes fell on a spot on the wall as I waited for her to respond. The spot seemed to shift and change in front of my eyes as an excess of tears blurred my sight. I squeezed my eyes shut to eliminate the salty liquid, and it fell down my cheeks in warm streaks.

"I don't know," she said. "How's Eli?"

I shrugged. "Vince kicked me out as soon as they found out. Eli didn't even say goodbye."

He didn't say goodbye. A lone tear rolled down my face as I remembered how he had just sat there as I walked out of the house. He didn't even say goodbye. It was Ren's and Vince's voices I heard as I replayed it all in my head. Eli's eyes never lifted from the floor. *Why didn't he say goodbye?* I could dwell on that alone for days.

"Wow." She paused as if she was thinking. "I don't think there's anything you can do."

That was not the answer I was looking for.

"I was hoping you could tell me what you would have wanted someone to do for you," I said, hoping I could shake out at least a few ideas.

"I was so young. I don't even remember much of what happened when she died, or even how I felt."

"Oh," I said.

"I'm sorry, I don't think there is any specific thing you can do for him; everyone grieves differently. Maybe he just needs a little space and time," she said.

"Yeah, maybe."

I agreed with her verbally, but inside I didn't. Space would be the last thing I would need from him at a time like this, so how could he need space from me? We were supposed to be there for each other.

"He'll come around, really, just give him time," she said.

I mustered a half-smile.

"Do you work tomorrow?" Bailey asked.

"Yeah," I said.

"Darn. I was going to say we should go do something, help get your mind off of things."

"That would have been nice." It was my voice, but it felt and sounded far away.

I wished I could get his mind off of things.

Bailey stayed over for a few hours that afternoon, pampering me and not expecting me to return the favor. She painted my fingernails and gave me a pedicure. The small flowers she drew on my big toe seemed a little over-the-top for how I felt. They looked so cheery and happy that I didn't even want to look at them.

I ate dinner in my room that night. It felt like I hadn't left my room all day, but I wouldn't have changed that in any way. Except maybe to have had Eli with me.

I avoided calling him all day. It wasn't that I didn't want to, I did. I just worried that I might say the wrong thing. Or maybe he wouldn't even want to talk to me. I picked up my phone and flipped it around in my hand, inspecting its exterior and cleaning off all the lint and smudges. And when I couldn't procrastinate any longer, I called him. It rang and rang until finally his voicemail greeted me. I ended the call without leaving a message, feeling disheartened that he hadn't answered. I slid my fingers across the screen again. But then I deleted what I had typed and put my phone down. I thought about it for a moment more, then typed my message again.

Call me. I hope you're okay.

I hit send, and the text disappeared from the screen into thin air as it made its way to its final destination. I debated in my head whether I should have sent it or not, but either way it was too late now.

I got ready for bed and tried my best not to stare at my phone, willing it to beep. I checked online one last time to see if by chance he was on. He wasn't.

I fell asleep holding my phone so I wouldn't miss it if it vibrated. Eventually it fell from my grasp and startled me awake. It was already morning, but I felt as if I had just fallen asleep. I scooped it up to check for messages, but there were none.

I got up to get ready for school, hoping to see Eli when he picked me up, and ran downstairs and ate my breakfast at an alarming rate. I had to swallow hard to finish the last humungous bite I inhaled and almost choked on.

"Are you even breathing?" my mom asked, staring at me as if I had grown wings and was fluttering about the kitchen.

"Yes," I mumbled through a mouthful of food.

I tossed my plate in the sink, grabbed my bag, and dashed outside to wait. Watching in the direction his car should have come from, I rocked back and forth on my tiptoes and heels as I nervously awaited his arrival.

My mom pulled out of the garage to head to work. "Bye honey! Have a good day!" she called out the window.

"Bye," I said, only glancing in her direction briefly.

After my mom's car pulled out of sight, my eyes darted up and down the street, waiting to catch a glimpse of his car. Maybe he would come from a different direction today. But as I stood there, I felt less and less hopeful that I would see him. It was five minutes until the bell would ring at school. Even if he got there now, we would be late. Eli was never late. Never.

I started walking. *Where was he?*

I knew I would be very late now, but I kept to my usual pace because I didn't care. I would make it eventually. I didn't particularly care when. He wouldn't be there, so what was the point?

My neck ached from craning around to watch for Eli behind me. Though I didn't know why I bothered, since I knew deep down he wasn't coming.

It was almost second hour by the time I arrived at school. I weaved in and out of the cars in the parking lot as I approached the front of the building, searching for his car as I went, but I knew it wouldn't be there. Instead of going to sweep, detention for those who were late, I found a bench and waited. I watched the entrance, hoping he might show up. But I was just setting myself up for more disappointment.

I could hear the wind blowing through the leaves in the trees above me. It was peaceful, so I sat there and let nature calm me, closing my eyes and tilting my head back, letting the sun warm my face.

I didn't hear him approach, but I wasn't startled when I heard his voice. It was almost as if on some level I expected him. As if it was him I was waiting for.

"Abby." His voice was solemn.

I opened my eyes and saw Ren, his face red and swollen, like the last time I had seen him. My heart sank. I opened my mouth to speak, but nothing I could think to say sounded right in my head, so I shut it again. I sat there for a moment with a stupid, dumbfounded look on my face. Then I stood up and wrapped my arms around him. He accepted my embrace and enveloped me in his large arms. I could feel him shaking, his body ravaged by silent emotion. After a minute or so, he pulled away. He looked the same as before, his face swollen and eye ringed in red, any tears gone from his face as if they had never existed in the first place.

"Eli's not coming," he finally managed.

"I gathered that when he didn't show up to drive me to school." It came out sarcastic and angry. I felt awful the instant it was out of my mouth.

"Yeah, he's not doing so good," he said, not making eye contact.

"He won't talk to me," I said, as if Ren didn't already know, though I was sure he did.

"He took off last night. We don't even know where he is," he said, his eyes still on the ground.

It didn't surprise me. I had a feeling I knew just where he was, though I would never go there because I knew I was unwanted at the moment. I just wished he would let me be there for him. *Oh, Eli, why won't you let me in?*

"Have you talked to him?" I asked.

He didn't answer.

The bell rang, and a sea of students surrounded us.

"Ren?" I whispered, my voice almost carried away by the commotion.

His eyes met mine, and I could see the regret in them.

"You did, didn't you?"

He nodded.

"When?" I demanded.

"We have to go to class. Come on." He tried to grab my arm to guide me to class. I yanked back, suddenly angry. Eli was ignoring me, and only me. I walked away from him without listening to another word.

"Abby, wait!" he called, jogging to catch up.

He grabbed my arm and spun me around.

"Please talk to me."

"No!" I shouted. I didn't care who heard me anymore.

I pulled my arm away from his grasp and went to my second hour. I sat in my seat fuming. Why did everyone think I needed to be told what to do, and that I couldn't handle the truth? I was so tired of the secrets. And to top it off, Eli was ignoring me.

At lunch, Bailey tried to convince me everything was fine. I wasn't buying it. Everything was not fine.

"If I was having a hard time, I'd want him near me," I said.

"Abby, just give him time. Trust me."

I was trying. I truly was, but it didn't make any sense to me. None at all.

I left lunch early and went outside to call him for the third time that day. Once again, I got no answer. I couldn't say it surprised me. But it still hurt.

Why are you ignoring me?

I texted him, then threw my phone in my bag and refused to look at it until school got out. I knew better than to think he was going to respond.

I ignored everyone except Bailey the rest of the day. They must have thought I was a jerk, but I didn't care. What was there to care about if the one person that meant everything to you wouldn't even talk to you?

When the final bell rang, I prepared myself for the long walk home. I checked my phone as I walked out of the building and, as expected, found no messages. I called him three more times in a row. I was running out of patience. It had been two days since I had walked out of his house without so much as a goodbye. He had to know I wasn't going to give up on him. I loved him.

I set a record for speed walking on my trip home, of that I was sure. My anger fueled my stomp session. When I arrived, I threw open the front door and slammed it shut behind me. I was headed toward the stairs and up to my room when my mom's voice startled me. I had been so lost in my frustration that I hadn't even considered that she might be home.

"Abby?"

I rolled my eyes at the intrusion on the few minutes I had to myself before I went to work. I walked into the kitchen and knew from the look on my mom's face that it wouldn't be good.

"You weren't in first hour?" she asked, her eyebrows raised.

This was the last thing I needed. My boyfriend's mom was dead, he had gone on a hiatus, and she freaked out because I missed one lousy class. As far as I knew, he might not even be my boyfriend anymore, and that could very well be the worst thing that could happen to me.

"I didn't make it in time," I said through gritted teeth.

"What do you mean you didn't make it in time? You were ready when I left."

"Eli never showed up so I had to walk. It took me a while. What's the big deal?" My temper was beginning to boil over despite my attempts to cool it.

"He didn't show up?" she asked.

"Nope, his mom did just die, you know?" I spat. I waited for her to say more, but after a full minute of silence I gave up. "I have to get ready for work," I said, walking out of the kitchen without waiting for a response.

I headed out the door ten minutes later without saying goodbye. I didn't bother calling Eli this time, though it didn't stop me from dwelling on the fact that I was still in the dark. Vince, Ren, and Eli had no intention of letting me know what was going on, and I was mighty sick of being babied.

I walked in the door of the restaurant and pasted a fake smile on my face. It was time to put on a good act. I waited tables and smiled until the muscles in my cheeks burned. Nobody seemed to catch on to my performance. After a couple hours, I excused myself to the bathroom and locked the door. Leaning against the frame, I massaged my face until the pain went away, fighting back the sting of tears that threatened my lashes. After a few minutes, I decided I had better check on my tables. I took a deep breath and strode out of the empty bathroom.

Holding the fake personality wasn't easy, and by the time my shift was over, my cheeks ached. I was sure that tomorrow I would be sore from smiling. That couldn't be normal.

I grabbed my small pizza box and started my trek home, eating a slice as I walked. The multitasking was harder than I expected it to be. Toppings and cheese fell to the ground when I wasn't paying close attention, but I kept walking, not caring what kind of mess I left in my wake.

As I turned down my street, I noticed a car parked across the street from my house. My heart rate quickened as if I had just run the whole way home. I picked up my pace. *Could it be? Could it really be him?* As I got closer, I grew more certain. My stomach filled with butterflies. All I wanted to do was wrap my arms around him. To go back to the way things were before. I knew we couldn't really do that with his mom gone, but I could be there for him. He was going to let me.

I tried to calm myself as my stomach flopped with excitement. I breathed in and out, trying to keep myself from running straight to his car. I shuffled to my doorstep and set my things down before walking back down the driveway to meet him. But when I lifted my arms to hug him, he stopped short. It was like he had slapped me in the face, catching me completely off guard. I dropped my arms and crossed them over my chest protectively. If he didn't want to hug me, why was he here?

"Stop calling me, would you! I don't want to talk to you! Can't you see that?" he shouted.

"What?" I was stunned.

"Stop calling me," he said, calmer this time as he glanced around us. He looked like he was worried about causing a scene. "It's bad enough that I endure all your temperamental moods. I can't even think without you being there too, and then you have to go and call me incessantly. Just stop!"

"I'm sorry! You haven't said two words to me since..."

"Yeah, I think I know my mom is dead, thanks!" he yelled. "It's your fault you know! She would still be here if you hadn't stuck your nose where it didn't belong with Pete. You just had to go out with him and ignore all of my warnings. Just leave me alone, okay?" He stomped down my driveway and drove away, squealing his tires as he went.

I stood there, shocked and hurt. My head swam. *How could he do this to me?* He blamed me. Her death did have something to do with Pete. How could I disagree with him? It was my fault. If I had never come along, none of this would have ever happened. His mom would still be alive.

I went straight to my room and buried my face in my pillow to muffle my sobbing. I cried myself to sleep for the second time that week.

When morning dawned, I realized I had slept through my alarm. I rushed to get ready, throwing my hair into a ponytail, knowing that if I missed first hour again, my mom might flip her lid. Not that I cared at the moment, but I didn't need an enraged mom on my back adding to the list of problems I was dealing with. I practically ran the whole way to school and walked into class just as the bell rang. It took every ounce of focus to even hear the lecture. I watched the whole class write line after line, listening to the teacher, while I sat with my arms lying still, flat on my desk.

I felt disconnected from my body. I shook my head to clear my thoughts, and for a little while it seemed to work, so I repeated it several times as the day dragged on.

The end of school that day wasn't just welcomed: I embraced it with relief and open arms.

CHAPTER THIRTEEN

There was no telling how long Eli's ice-out was going to last, or if it would end at all. Maybe he would never want anything to do with me ever again. The thought made me sick to my stomach, but there wasn't much I could do about it. The last thing I was going to do was sit in a corner waiting for him to come around.

It had been days since Ren and I had our heated discussion. The first thing I did that morning at school was march right up to him and confront him. It wasn't like he hadn't tried to talk to me since our disagreement. I just hadn't responded, ignoring him as Eli and Vince ignored me. After days of trying, he had given up.

"I want to arrange a meeting with the elders," I said. I think my request surprised him, or maybe his eyebrows rose at the fact that I was talking to him at all.

He didn't say anything for a moment, as if he was weighing my words.

"I can't do that," he finally replied.

"Why?"

"They don't meet with non-Protectors who aren't gifted."

"Eli didn't tell you?" I asked, as if my secret was common knowledge, even though I knew full well that we were keeping it quiet. But Ren didn't know that.

"Tell me what?"

I hadn't planned to tell anyone about my dreams, but Eli had been understanding, so maybe Ren would be too. I wasn't as scared anymore either. Maybe I could prevent some terrible things from happening. Though at the moment I wished Eli had told Ren so I didn't have to explain it, especially at school.

I looked around us as we stood in the courtyard. The midday sun shone straight above our heads, warming my skin, but there weren't any other students in close proximity to us. A few small groups had congregated on the other side of the courtyard, but nobody paid us any attention.

I leaned in to him and whispered, "I *am* gifted."

"What?" His disbelief was written all over his face.

"I've been having dreams...well more like nightmares...and they come true."

He lifted his eyebrows.

"I've had two recurring dreams. Both ended up happening in real life. Eli was going to help me figure them out, but..." I trailed off, choking back a sob. "As you can see, he wants nothing to do with me." My voice quivered.

Ren didn't say a word. His hand gripped his mouth and slowly slid down his five o'clock shadow, before running through his hair as if he didn't know quite what to do. He stood, staring off into the distance for a few more moments. I wasn't sure if he was just letting me pull myself together or if he was thinking. Either way, I was grateful for the moment to get a grip on my emotions. I took a deep breath and willed myself to relax.

"So you'll set it up?" I asked when he still hadn't responded.

"I don't know..." he said. "This is something Eli should handle, not me."

"Yeah, well, I think he's kind of done with me, don't you?" My voice dripped with sarcasm.

I could see his pronounced jaw clench.

"Fine," he said before storming off.

He might have been mad, but I had gotten what I wanted, and I knew he would calm down eventually. Ultimately, I think he was more mad at Eli for not taking care of his responsibilities, but I probably would never know for sure.

I had more spring in my step than I'd had all week. For once, I was getting somewhere. Maybe I would begin to get some answers.

At the end of the day, I bounced my way out of school and into the parking lot. Ren pulled up next to me and beeped his horn twice. I opened the door, climbed in, and looked at him expectantly.

"Well?" I asked.

"They aren't happy about the whole situation, but given the circumstances they agreed to meet with us."

"When?" I asked.

"Tomorrow."

Tomorrow. What great news!
He stopped in front of my house. "I'll pick you up at nine. Okay?"
"Okay!"

I skipped to the front door, unable to contain my excitement. By the time I got to my room, the butterflies had set in. I was going into this meeting with the intention of getting answers about me, Eli, and my unique situation, and above all to find out what I could do to help Eli in the midst of his mom's passing.

Questions churned through my mind. *Why me? Is this my only 'gift'?* But it seemed the questions coming to me focused only on myself. The other things I wanted to know eluded me, and they were just as important. *What could I ask about them?* Maybe Ren would help me. Then again, maybe he wouldn't approve of me trying to help my Protector. I still couldn't be sure if the elders would take kindly to that, but that wasn't going to stop me from trying.

I finished my homework and went downstairs to cook dinner. This was the first time I had cooked in what felt like a month. The last time had been at Eli's house on that fateful day. I had a hard time not thinking of Elizabeth as I worked in the kitchen. I tried to clear my mind, but the questions were getting to be suffocating, so instead of holding them in I wrote them down.

-Is my gift genetic?
-If so, who else in my family has a gift?
-Does that family member know about this world of immortal beings?

My thoughts wandered to Eli. What would he think of all this? I wanted to pretend that I didn't care, but in truth I longed to find out more about my gift with him at my side. Sometimes he knew me better than I knew myself. It didn't matter at the moment though, because he wanted nothing to do with me. He had even taken a leave from the restaurant.

My mom would arrive home soon, and I hoped for some quality time with her to help distract me from the meeting.

-Can I control it?
-How do I know which dreams are real and
which are just dreams?
-Do I have any other gifts?

The timer dinged, and I set the table. I figured Mom must be running late, so I sat down and began eating without her. A few minutes later, she rushed through the door, apologizing.

"It's fine," I said.

She was full of conversation about her day, filling the room with chatter so it didn't feel so empty, something about hot new gossip about one of the other secretaries. Seeing her babble on about the things that made her day go faster and, in a way, made her happy warmed my heart. She seemed to be getting back to her normal self, the one I have always known, the person she was before she and my dad started having problems.

"Oh honey, you're so quiet. Here I am rambling on about work. How are things going with Eli?"

I shrugged.

"He still won't talk to you?" she asked.

I didn't want to answer that question, so I didn't.

"So, I was talking to Dad, and we were thinking the week after school gets out I could go to California for a couple of weeks. What do you think?" I asked instead.

"Wow, is the school year almost over already?"

"Three weeks left!"

"Yikes. Where did the time go?"

I laughed.

"Sure, that would be fine," she said between mouthfuls.

"Awesome, I can't wait! I have to email Kelly. She will be so excited!"

"I bet. You two are like twins separated at birth."

I shoved the last bite of food into my mouth as quickly as I could.

"I'm going to go email her now," I said through the food in my mouth, and dashed to put my dishes in the sink on the way to my room.

Kelly,
Guess what?!? I'm coming home! School gets out in
three weeks and I'll be coming a week later! You will be
out of school by then right? I hope so. I have lots of
beach days in mind for us. My tan is non-existent. The
sun here is just not the same, and the lakes are so far
away. Can't wait to hear from you!
                              -Abby

I sat there staring at the screen for a few minutes after I hit send,
hoping Eli would sign on and talk to me. Eventually, I gave up.

-What can I do to help Eli?
-Are the elders doing anything to stop the
people that did this to Elizabeth?

I lay in bed that night trying my best to clear my mind. Falling
asleep didn't come easy. Happy and horrifying thoughts clambered for my
attention. I hoped that by the time my dreams beckoned me the happy ones
would have the upper hand.

*   *   *   *

The next morning I climbed into the car with Ren, accompanied by
a bellyful of nerves and armed with a full-page list of questions stowed in
my pocket. My hands fumbled on my lap like there wasn't a comfortable
place for them to rest.
"Nervous?" Ren asked.
"Is it that obvious?"
He glanced down at my lap, and I slid my hands beneath my legs.
He chuckled.

"Are the elders..." I couldn't quite think of the right question. My words hung in the air while Ren waited for me to finish the sentence. I hoped my words would come easier once I was sitting across from them, but judging by my anxiety I wasn't counting on it. "...easy to talk to?" I finished. Those weren't the words I was hoping for, but they were the best I could think of at the moment.

"Uh," he said, pausing to think for a moment. "I guess. I think it depends on the topic. You'll be fine though. Don't worry."

I took a deep breath. If I wanted them to take me seriously, I needed to be sure of myself, not a bumbling mess. That might take some good acting skills and a whole lot of willpower, but I was going to do this. I would nail this meeting.

Ren drove for twenty minutes before coming to a stop in front of a dirty, run-down warehouse that seemed like a weird place for immortal beings. I guess I pictured something a little classier. A hotel penthouse. A mansion. Something. But not this.

"This is where we're meeting them?" I asked, unable to keep the disdain from my voice.

He laughed, "Yeah."

I looked at the building again. I couldn't understand what they would be doing in such a place.

"Ready?" he asked.

I took a deep breath. "Yeah, I guess so."

We climbed out of the car and entered the building through a door with rusted hinges that looked like they might fall apart at any second. It creaked loudly as it swung open. I took one last deep breath and entered. I hadn't even stepped all the way through the door when I was hit with a flood of negative energy so strong that I stopped in my tracks. My chest felt tight. I gripped the door frame to steady myself.

"Are you okay?" Ren asked.

"I don't know," I said.

What could be causing such a strong feeling? I couldn't explain what I felt. I tried to take a deep breath to steady myself, but my lungs just wouldn't expand enough. Ren put his hand on the small of my back and guided me into the room. The bright light from the sun faded as the door slammed shut with a bang, and I was pleasantly surprised to see the sumptuous room that awaited me. It was as if I had walked through a time machine and was transported back to the Victorian era, when elegance was at its peak. Elegant white pillars stood in each corner of the room, and exquisite draperies hung over pristine windows. I caught a glimpse of the scenery beyond them—rolling hills with beautiful mountains in the background. I looked behind me, and the door we had just entered through appeared to be made of cherry wood, the rusted hinges gone as if they never existed. Ren seemed to understand my confusion.

"It's some kind of trick. I couldn't tell you how they do it. Amazing isn't it?" he whispered in my ear.

I nodded as my eyes roamed around the room, taking in all that it offered. The deep reds that filled the chamber were complemented by an exquisite gold chandelier hanging from the center of the room.

A door burst open from the far end of the room. But the person who emerged from behind it startled me more. Eli traipsed into the room, and I froze. The negativity doubled, and I panted for air. I had never expected to see him here. My tongue felt dry, and I realized my mouth was half-open as I stood there and stared at him. He came toward me. His ice cold eyes trained on me.

Three steps away.

Two.

Until he stood directly in front of me, so close I could feel his hot breath on my face.

"You have no business here." The disdain and anger in his voice made me falter, and I took a step backwards, bumping into Ren's solid frame. The venom in his voice terrified me. "You should know better," Eli spat in Ren's direction.

Ren didn't falter. My back was pressed solidly against him.

"What are you doing here?" I asked.

"What am *I* doing here?" He chuckled. "You ask that as if I would never be here." He looked around. "This is my workplace, and like it's any of your business, I came to request a leave. Right now my priorities don't include protecting you from yourself!" He said it so coldly I shivered.

He sidestepped me and stormed out the door, taking the negative energy with him. I could never have imagined him treating me that way, and it hurt worse than anything I had ever felt. I couldn't understand how he had turned so against me. I had never meant for anything bad to happen, but he was treating me like I had murdered Elizabeth myself.

"I'm sorry. I didn't know he would be here," Ren said. "He hasn't exactly been himself lately."

Seeing Eli shook me more than I would have expected. I wasn't sure how I could meet with the elders now, but I didn't have a choice. I had asked for this, and it would be rude to leave now.

"Come on," Ren said.

I shoved my trembling hands into my pockets and absently walked in the direction Ren led me. We reached the same door Eli had come from, and I hesitated before passing through. I closed my eyes, took a cleansing breath to push all my bad energy away, and stepped through it.

The next room was decorated like the first, except in off-whites. Again, a gold chandelier hung from the center of the room. From the moment I stepped inside, six eyes were trained on me, watching my every move. Two men and one woman sat comfortably on the two couches located below the chandelier I had been admiring. They didn't look much older than my mom.

"Hello Abigail," said the man seated the furthest from me.

"Hi," I said, but it caught in my throat and came out as a loud, awkward croak.

"Please have a seat," the woman said, motioning to the chair across from her.

I trudged over to the seat she suggested, and Ren followed me and stood behind it.

"Ren, it was so nice of you to accompany her," the woman said in an almost condescending tone.

He just smiled in return.

"My name is Edward. This is Theodora and James," the first man said, motioning to the other two elders. "It's good to finally meet you. I hear you were quite interested in meeting us. What can we do for you?"

I nodded, and tried to recall some of the questions that I had scribbled on the list in my pocket. I didn't dare take it out in front of them. Finally, one came to me. "Why do I keep having nightmares that come true?"

This time James spoke. "Because you have the gift of seeing the future, of course."

He said it so matter-of-factly, as if it was commonplace. Maybe it was for him, but it wasn't for me. His bluntness was unwelcome, and I wasn't sure I would like him.

"Okay, why me?"

"You were born with it," Edward said. He paused and looked at me. I was sure that my face screamed confused. He looked down at the floor, as if considering what to say next. "There isn't any other way to phrase it. There may be someone in your bloodline with gifts. Sometimes it's genetic. Either way, as you near the age of eighteen, the gift will grow stronger, increasing in regularity. The other gifts you were given will emerge by then as well."

"There are more?" I asked.

"Most definitely." Edward smiled at me.

I was glad to be sitting because I felt as if I might faint. More gifts. My head spun. The thought overwhelmed and excited me. Then I got an idea. My connection with Eli. Was that one of my gifts too?

"Eli and I have, I guess you would say, an unusual connection. Is that a gift too?" I asked.

"She's being modest. They have a bond unlike anything I've ever seen," Ren said, but then stopped as if he felt he was speaking out of turn.

"It could be, but sometimes those connections happen with your soulmate as well. They aren't always associated with any type of gift," Theodora said.

My soulmate. The thought didn't surprise me. Our bond transcended was unlike anything I had ever felt before, but it didn't matter anymore. I never thought I would see the day that he told me to stay away from him. My world had come crashing down around me then, and now I was trying to figure out how to climb out of the rubble. The last thing I wanted to hear was that we could be soulmates. We were fated to be together, and now it was up to Eli to come back to me.

"Do you know who murdered Elizabeth?" The question came out before I had thought about the repercussions of such a bold inquiry.

I felt Ren stand up straighter behind me, gripping the back of the chair. When nobody spoke right away, I began to worry I had overstepped, but finally Edward broke the silence.

"That is something we are working on." Tension lined his face. "We have two leads; one is guilty. We do know that much. I assure you that we will get to the bottom of it."

"I want to help," I said.

James burst into laughter until he caught sight of the glare Edward was giving him.

"I don't think that is a good idea," Edward said.

"Please."

Ren's hands fell from the chair. I turned to look at him from the corner of my eye, and his fingers were in his hair. I turned back to Edward and tried to ignore the look on Ren's face. Edward seemed to be thinking. I could almost see the wheels turning in his head.

"You can't be considering letting her help?" James asked.

I had been right about James. I hadn't even been in the room with him for twenty minutes, and I already wanted to punch him in the face.

"I think I can find something for you to help with," Edward said, a slight grin on his face.

"Really? I'll do anything you need. What can I do?"

"Go home," he said. "I'll call you when I need your help."

"Okay. Thank you so much!" I got up and shuffled to the door, forgetting the rest of the questions I'd had.

Once Ren and I were back in the car, he broke his stony silence.

"You can't be serious! Is this the real reason you wanted me to arrange this meeting?" he demanded.

"Only partly," I said, bracing myself for his outburst.

"I may not be your assigned Protector, but that doesn't mean I don't care what happens to you. I can't let you get wrapped up in this!"

"Well, it's a good thing it's not your decision to make," I said.

"Don't you care what Eli would say?"

"Why would I? He hates me. The least I can do after what he's done for me is make things right, even if it doesn't change anything between us."

"And you think this will make it right?"

"Maybe," I said.

"Abby, none of this is your fault, regardless of what Eli has told you."

"Maybe not, but that's the way he sees it," I said.

I didn't admit I believed it too; then again, he didn't need to know that, and I knew how he would respond.

Edward

The minute Abby left the room, I knew what was coming. Allowing her to tag along on the investigation was a bold choice, even I knew that, but I needed to keep close tabs on this one.

"I cannot believe you," Theodora said. "Are you serious?"

"I am," I said sternly.

"Why?" James asked.

"If I let her help, I'll have a front row seat when she perfects that amazing gift of hers."

"Her dream foresight? It isn't that great of a gift," Theodora said. "Surely we have many of our own with that talent, if you wish to see it perfected."

"Yes, but they are all one of us. She isn't. It's not as ordinary as I led her to believe. She's the first I've ever met."

CHAPTER FOURTEEN

The call from Edward came two days later, after waiting with my phone in hand at every moment of the day since I had left Ren.

"We have a job for you," he said.

"Great."

"Let's meet and go over the details," he said.

We made plans to meet at a coffee house next door to my work at nine when I got off my shift that evening. The excitement I felt was amplified by a buzz of indecision in my nerves.

I thought of Ren after I had hung up. I hadn't spoken to him since he dropped me off at home Saturday afternoon. I knew he was angry, but in the end he knew he could do nothing to change my mind. I hoped I wouldn't lose him over this too, but it was something I had to do, no matter what.

I didn't tell Bailey about my meeting with the elders. I knew she would be against it just like Ren was. I didn't want to have that talk with her, and she was sure to do everything she could to stop me. So instead, I told her I had asked for more hours at work now that Eli wasn't around, so I wouldn't have much time to hang out in the evenings. She seemed to accept it without question.

I was still on the receiving end of Eli's silent treatment, so when I walked into work, his presence startled me. *Could this be a sign that he was back?*

"You're here," I said, sounding dumbfounded as I put my things down in my cubby in the backroom.

"Yeah," he said, and walked away without another word.

I knew that it didn't change anything between us, but it sure felt like progress in the right direction.

As the night went on, I realized how wrong I was. The tension in the air sucked the breath out of my lungs. He refused to even look at me, and in passing, he tried his hardest to not even let his arm brush against mine. A few times he failed, and our arms touched for a half-second. I heard his breath catch. The electricity of his skin on mine overwhelmed me. The split second that it lasted wasn't enough; I wanted more. Oh, how I wished things were different. I needed him back.

For once, I decided to forgo my pizza that night. Between Eli and my meeting with Edward, food was the last thing I needed. I clocked out and threw open the front door, rejoicing in the fresh air outside before rushing a few doors down to the coffee house, anxious to get there.

When I walked in, I didn't see Edward at first. After buying my coffee, I looked around once more, searching all of the faces my eyes met until I found him in the middle of a small group. I could feel my adrenaline spike as I approached him, giving me the nervous shakes. Thank goodness my coffee had a lid, otherwise it would have been splashed all the way down my legs by the time I reached Edward's table.

There were more people with him than I had expected, and they all stared at me when I walked up to the table. My heart caught in my throat, but I pushed it aside. That shy person wasn't going to be allowed to come out anymore, I decided. It was time for a new me—assertive and bold, the person I always lacked the courage to be. I took a deep breath as I strode the last few steps to the table, and smiled.

"Abby, it's so nice to see you again," Edward said, standing to greet me. "These are the people who will help us achieve our goal."

I turned my attention to the four other people who sat around us. All were boys, or to be more correct, men.

"Hi Abby. I'm Casey. This is Luke, Ferdinand, and Brad," said the tallest of the men, motioning toward each person as he introduced them.

"Nice to meet you all." I nodded to each of them.

"Consider them your team from here on out. You will be working together to get to the bottom of this," Edward said.

"Who are our suspects?" I asked.

Someone chuckled at my question. It was Luke. This time I was not that shy girl, and it was time I showed it.

"Is something funny?" I asked him.

He shut up. "Oh. No." His face flushed.

I turned my attention back to Edward, and he handed me a folder. Inside I found two pages with a photo paper-clipped to each one. The last name on both caught my attention immediately: Denali. They were both related to Pete. My heart sank. My suspicions were confirmed.

"It wasn't your fault," Edward said, as if he sensed my emotion.

I wondered at his intuition. However he had figured it out, I was grateful for his reassurance. It meant a lot coming from someone in his position.

I read the profiles a little more closely. Neil Denali, Pete's dad, and Ian Denali, Pete's uncle, looked to be about the same age, and I could easily see the resemblance. It saddened me to think that some ancient feud that culminated in me meeting Pete had cost Elizabeth her life. She had never even been involved in the first place—or had she?

"What started this feud in the first place?" I asked.

Nobody answered at first, but after a moment, Casey broke the silence.

"Eli's dad, Vince, found out about some indiscretions on the part of Reginald—Neil and Ian's father. Murder. Some other things, not unlike what you experienced with Pete. Vince reported Reginald to the elders. As you can imagine, the elders didn't take this lightly and agreed to strip Reginald of all his gifts, including his immortality."

"He died the next day," Ferdinand said, his voice barely above a whisper. "It was tragic, and not something anyone could have predicted, hit by a car, but Ian and Neil blamed Vince. It was rumored that they've had a vendetta against him ever since."

"Oh." Eli had never told me the story behind it all. I couldn't help but wonder why he hadn't opened up about it. Vince had done nothing wrong. In fact, he had done exactly what I had come to expect from him: he had righted the wrong.

"Okay, let's move on," Edward said, without confirming or denying the story.

My team seemed to have had time to prepare their plan, but they tried their best to get me up to speed, and I felt like I was catching on quickly. Looking around at my team, watching them talk, I felt a sense of pride that I would be working with them. I liked the way they carried themselves, and their plans were efficient and well-thought-out. I knew would learn a lot from them.

We exchanged phone numbers and made plans to get started the next day. Luke and Brad would pick me up from school. Once again, not having a car or a license presented a problem, though they didn't seem to mind acting as my chauffeurs.

We said our goodbyes, and I strolled outside, heading for the parking lot exit, but when my team saw I was walking, all four jumped at the chance to drive me home. It must have been the inner Protectors in them trying to keep me safe. In the end, it was Casey who was headed in my direction.

At first it was excruciatingly quiet in the confines of his car, but that changed quickly.

"What is Eli like?" he asked, breaking the silence. His voice sounded shaky and rushed, as if he was nervous to ask.

I didn't understand why he would ask such a strange question. It was Eli after all, he was perfect whether he was mad at me or not, but I couldn't understand why someone like Casey would even care. I was sure that Casey had the same qualities Eli had as a Protector, and while I knew Casey didn't have the same gifts as Eli, he probably had some that were equally useful.

"He's pretty amazing," I said. "But why?"

"Eli's kind of a celebrity in our world. Didn't you know?"

"I guess I hadn't thought about it."

It made sense. Eli always had an air about him that bespoke superiority, but I had never thought anything of it because he was so modest. I wished I wasn't thinking about it now. The whole Pete debacle probably made headlines, if there was such a thing, in the Protector world. My throat felt tight. Was every move I made now under a microscope? I wanted to forget Casey had ever given me that thought.

"Why?" I asked.

Eli had never given me any reason to believe he was out of the ordinary when it came to his 'kind.' I shouldn't be so surprised—there were a lot of things he hadn't disclosed to me, and the list kept on growing. I wondered if I knew who he was at all. But maybe even he didn't know how popular he was. But in the end, I realized that of course he had to know. How could he not?

"Vince, of course. He's one of the most powerful Protectors."

Now that didn't surprise me either. His presence spoke power.

"Oh," I said, leaving the car to fall quiet again.

"I'm glad you're on our team," he said.

And suddenly I became very aware that I was alone with him. My hands grew clammy in my lap.

"Uh, thanks."

At my house, I got out and waved as I walked to my door. I headed straight to my room. My exhaustion kicked in, and I climbed the stairs at a snail's pace. Just another thirty seconds until I could fall into bed.

"Abby?" my mom called from the living room.

I stopped dead in my tracks and looked at the floor, hoping she wouldn't want me to come talk. My bed was screaming my name.

"Yeah?" I called back.

"Come here."

I sighed. Grudgingly, I trudged back down the staircase, my feet aching with each step.

"What?" I asked, trying to keep the frustration out of my voice.

"Where have you been? It's eleven o'clock. You were supposed to be off at nine," she said.

I hadn't expected the third degree from her. She hadn't seemed to care about what I did for months. Why now?

"I worked late," I lied. I turned to leave, figuring she would leave it at that.

"No you didn't," she said. "I called the restaurant. Eli said you left at nine." Her voice was angry but steady.

Thanks Eli.

I was sure he was more than happy to rat me out. I rolled my eyes and whipped back around. "Fine. I went out and got coffee with some friends."

"Who dropped you off?" she asked.

"Really?"

"Abby," she said.

"My friend Casey."

"From now on, if you're not coming straight home from work, you need to check in to let me know."

"Okay," I said with an attitude.

I didn't know what her problem was, but I worried she might check up on me more often now, and with my new adventure beginning tomorrow that would not bode well.

*　　*　　*　　*

The darkness around us concealed our presence as we sat in the car, watching and waiting. I hated stakeouts, waiting for something to happen but all the while knowing you could be sitting there for nothing. For hours.

Casey and I had been sent to watch Ian's house, and the three others were watching Neil. I was glad we weren't watching Neil, Pete's dad. I shuddered at the thought of sitting for hours in front of the house Pete most likely grew up in. *Bleck!* Even though Ian was Pete's uncle it felt different, somehow, more distant.

A woman emerged. It was impossible to make out her face, but even in the darkness I could see her long blonde hair. I sat up straighter, my heart racing. I leaned forward, closing the gap between me and the windshield to try to get a better look.

The woman glanced around, almost as if she thought someone was watching her. I leaned back into the shadows of the car so she wouldn't see me as she looked our way. Then she got into her car and drove away. Casey didn't budge.

I looked at him expectantly, wondering why he was just sitting there.

"Shouldn't we follow her?" I asked.

"No."

"Why not?"

"Our orders are to watch Ian," he said.

Ugh! I wanted to do something. I was going crazy sitting there doing nothing. I hoped the whole mission wouldn't be a series of stakeouts.

Unfortunately the next night was the same. We spent hours waiting for something to happen, and it didn't look like anyone was even home. I was beginning to wonder if we had the wrong address. Nobody had come or gone from the darkened house since the lady the night before.

It didn't seem like we were going to get any information this way. Maybe I just didn't understand what we were waiting for. I thought we should be knocking on doors and shaking people down, pushing them out of their hiding places, making them do things they normally wouldn't. Then again, maybe another team did that. Edward wasn't exactly giving us all the information. We had just enough to get our job done.

I was thankful that I had work the next night and wouldn't be stuck in the car with a numb butt. Another team would fill in for us, and I was grateful for the break. No matter how much I wanted to help find

Elizabeth's killer, this didn't seem like the right way. Or like we were doing anything at all. I craved action.

Casey dropped me off in my driveway two hours later. It was 11 p.m., and Mom was waiting up as she had done the last few nights since I hadn't come home on time. Perched in the chair by the window with a book in hand, she sat like an owl waiting for the moon to rise.

"Hi Mom," I said, rolling my eyes after I turned my back. "Good night."

We hadn't spoken more than simple greetings since the night she accused me when I came home late. I had nothing to say to her. My dad on the other hand was encouraging me to be lenient on her. "She's just trying to be a good mom," he had said, but I wasn't buying it. I had done nothing wrong. My curfew had always been 11. I was home on time, yet she had acted like I was hours late.

I was exhausted, but my homework wouldn't do itself, so I worked on it until I fell asleep in my chair. I finished it the next morning instead of going downstairs to eat breakfast with my mom. It was the perfect excuse to avoid her. I heard the door close as she left for the day and breathed a sigh of relief before heading downstairs to grab food and head off to school.

I didn't mind walking to school every morning any more. It was nice to have some time to myself to think and be alone. In the afternoons, Casey had been picking me up from school, and I was glad I didn't have to worry about the heat.

On Thursday afternoon, Casey drove me straight to work, and Eli arrived at the same time we did. I sat in Casey's car watching him watch me. His eyes stayed trained on me as he walked. I could see anger wash over each feature of his face when he recognized me in the car next to Casey. He turned away and walked into the restaurant. He looked furious, and if it were possible I was sure I would have seen steam coming out of his ears.

"Here goes nothing," I said as I climbed out of the car.

"See you at nine," Casey called out the window just before he drove away.

I had never hated my job more than I did that night. Eli's dirty looks and cold shoulder left me edgy. So edgy in fact that I jumped when my boss told me it was time for me to leave.

Relief washed over me when I clocked out. I grabbed my pizza and headed for the door, and then toward Casey's car at the end of the sidewalk. *Thank you for being on time.* I made a beeline for his car, anxious to sit down for the first time since my shift started.

"Are you stupid?" Eli's voice bellowed from behind me.

"What?" I said as I swung around to face him.

"Are...you...stupid?" he demanded, enunciating each word.

I glared at him. The last thing I was going to do was stand there and listen to him yell at me again. I spun back around and stomped away without another look in his direction.

He caught my arm and pulled me back to face him.

"Stay out of this," he spat in my face with more force than I had ever heard from him.

I could hear Casey's door open and gravel move under his shoes.

"Abby?" I heard him call out.

"Stay out of what?" I asked. I batted my eyes like a schoolgirl. I couldn't help it when a devilish smile crept across my face. If he acted like this, the least I could do was play along.

I could see Eli eyeing Casey behind me.

"I'm okay, Casey." I called. For once I was sure I had this under control. I could hear his feet shuffle, as if he was unsure what to do.

"Don't play games with me," Eli said through gritted teeth.

"I don't have a clue what you're talking about," I said as I yanked my arm from his grasp. I could feel the sting of his nails on my flesh. I opened the door to Casey's car and climbed in before he could say another word. Casey got in and pulled away from the curb.

I let out a deep sigh as I sat back against the seat and closed my eyes.

"You okay?" he asked. "That looked...ah...intense."

I let my head roll to the side and looked at him. "Yeah...I'm fine."

I sat there, staring at the ceiling of Casey's car, and tried to figure out when it had been decided that Casey would be my personal chauffer. It frustrated me. Always living at the mercy of others. Always feeling like a burden.

"Let's go do something," I said, full of energy. I didn't want to go home. I wanted to break free of the everyday routine. Let my hair down.

Casey laughed at me. "Like what?"

"Mini-golf!" I said.

"Mini-golf?" His full-hearted belly laugh filled the car.

"What?" I asked.

"You sound like a little kid!"

"Thanks," I said. "Seriously, let's go play mini-golf."

"All right," he agreed.

I texted the warden to let her know where we were going, and when I looked up again Casey was already turning into the parking lot of a mini-golf course. A large castle sat at the entrance. We wandered inside, paid, and picked up our clubs and balls.

"I haven't played mini-golf in years," I said, waiting for Casey to go first. His ball sunk into the hole on his first swing. My jaw dropped. "I think you're going to beat me."

"Nah, you'll do fine," he said.

As I stood there next to him, I realized for the first time that he towered above me by a good eighteen inches. He was huge, not just in height but in build as well. Muscles bulged from his sleeves, and his shirts never seemed to fit loosely.

My nerves kicked in as I lined up my ball. How embarrassing would it be to really mess up my shot after his hole-in-one. Casey's eyes were on me—I knew it without even looking at him. I hit the ball a little too hard. It hopped off the green and rolled into the pond. *Great!*

I shot him a look that challenged his faith that I would do well.

"Well, maybe you do need a little practice," he said, smirking.

He went to the pond and retrieved my ball. Then he set it down, lining it up with the hole again. "Come here."

I walked over to the ball and got ready to try again. Casey came up behind me as I focused on the ball. He lightly rested his hands on mine, guiding them the direction they needed to go. My breathing slowed as I all but froze in his grip. I could feel his breath on the top of my head, and it sent chills down my back. Goosebumps rose on my arms. I tried to bring my focus back to the ball. Relaxing, I let his muscular arms guide my swing, and the ball sank into the hole with as much ease as his had.

"Yes!" I said, jumping up and down and throwing my arms around his neck. I hugged him before I realized what I was doing. "Thanks!"

"Of course," he said as he put his arms around me to return my affection.

I gracelessly released him, stumbling backwards. I felt strange for latching on to him the way I had, even in celebration.

He helped me with each hole until the sixth, when he said that he thought I had it from there. My arms felt bare as I swung without him there to guide me. The ball sailed just an inch away from the hole. I smiled, knowing I had gotten better.

"So how old are you?" I asked out of the blue as he lined up his next shot.

"How old do you think I am?" he asked.

"I don't know. I would say eighteen, but I know better than that."

"Do you now?" He grinned.

I nodded, smirking at him.

"I'm twenty," he said after he had taken his next turn.

That isn't that much older than me. I don't know why, but I had assumed he was so much older. Maybe it was because he had been given such an important task by the elders. Then again, so had I, maybe I had things all wrong.

"What day is today?" I asked.

"May 8th," he said with a confused expression.

"Oh my gosh."

"What?" he asked

"My birthday is in three days. I almost forgot."

My mind raced. *Who does that? Who forgets their own birthday?* I would be seventeen in three days. And I almost forgot my own birthday.

"Awesome! We'll have to go celebrate."

"Yeah..." I said.

Since I had become friends with Eli, I had imagined spending my birthday with him, maybe going to the lake or to our park; but clearly that wasn't going to happen, and that hurt. For the first time ever, I dreaded my birthday.

"Are you off work?" he asked.

"Uh..." It took me a moment to recall. "Yeah I'm off."

"Cool."

We finished our round of golf, and my score came in just behind his. It seemed pretty good to me, considering how the night had started.

"See, you didn't do so bad," Casey said.

"Yeah, but I had help," I said, nudging him.

When I got home and checked my phone, I had a missed call from Bailey. It was too late to call her now. I tossed my phone on my nightstand. Yet another person to answer to.

CHAPTER FIFTEEN

Sunday morning came with a surprise intrusion from my team, bright and early at 7 a.m.

"Happy birthday!" they all shouted, waking me from deep unconsciousness.

They showered me in confetti, and when I opened my eyes again I could see each of them holding balloons, except for Casey. He held a stack of rainbow sprinkle-covered pancakes with a single blue candle glowing on top, in the center of a huge dollop of whipped cream. Syrup drizzled down the sides.

"Make a wish," he said as he came forward, holding the plate out.

The awkward look on his face confused me. I could see his arms trembling as he held out the cake. *What was he so nervous about?*

I closed my eyes and made a wish. The candle whooshed out when I barely breathed on it. Everyone cheered, as they always did when someone blew out their candles, as if I had just completed some significant feat. If you asked me, blowing out a candle was not clap-worthy, and I felt even sillier being the center of attention.

"Thanks guys," I said, smiling.

"Eat," Luke said.

Casey plopped the plate in my lap, and all four boys belly flopped in different spots on my bed and over my legs to watch me eat. Once my bed stopped shaking and my laughter subsided, I didn't hesitate to dig in. The pancakes smelled heavenly.

When I was halfway finished, my mom popped her head in and smiled at the scene.

"I just thought I would come in and say happy birthday to my baby girl," she said.

"Thanks Mom."

"I'm going to run to the store. Do you need anything?" she asked.

"I think I'm good," I said, giggling at the funny faces my new best friends were making.

"Okay, see you in a few." She began to shut the door but opened it again. "Oh, and don't forget to think about where we're going to celebrate tonight." Then she was gone.

"Want some?" I asked Casey as I heaped a large pile of whipped cream on my next bite.

"Nope, it's all yours."

He certainly didn't expect what I had planned. In a swift motion, I took the forkful and splattered the extra whipped cream onto his face. We all burst out laughing at the same time. Suddenly, all four guys' hands came toward my plate. Each of them loaded up a finger full of whipped cream, despite my attempts to stop them. Their devilish smirks told me I was next. I squirmed away from them to no avail, and a moment later, whipped cream was smeared from one side of my face to the other. No skin was spared. We laughed until it hurt.

I would never have imagined the turn my life had taken, but I couldn't have been happier at that very moment, with or without Eli. I had become part of a group of Protectors that accepted me as their own, and to me that was a huge honor. One I would not take lightly.

"Well, I'd better go shower," I said, motioning toward my whipped-cream-decorated face.

"We'll wait downstairs. We have plans for you today," Brad said.

They filed out of my room one by one, and I sat there for a minute, letting myself enjoy the small moment of happiness.

Fifteen minutes later, I marched down the stairs free of whipped cream. I found them raiding the cabinets in the kitchen as if they had been there a hundred times before. It felt good to see them all on my home turf, instead of on stakeouts and in whispered meetings held at night. I loved seeing them relaxed.

"So now what?" I asked.

All of them looked at Casey, the only one without a mouthful of chips or pretzels. He seemed uncomfortable being put on the spot. His eyes flickered to each of the other guys, as if he hoped someone else would speak.

"Uh. How does bowling sound?" he asked.

"Sounds like I'm going to lose!" I laughed.

Casey eyed me skeptically. "You didn't lose as badly as you thought you would in mini-golf."

At that moment I felt suspended in time, as if we were the only two people in the room. I could almost feel his arms on mine, as if he were once again assisting me with my golf swing. I felt my cheeks warm. And then I shook myself out of the daze. The other guys looked at each other in confusion.

"You guys went mini-golfing?" Luke asked.

Casey rubbed the back of his neck. "Ah...yeah," he said.

"All right. Let's go," I said, bringing the discussion of our time alone to an end.

The smell of leather and spray-in shoe cleaner filled my nose as we entered the bowling alley. The sound of pins hitting the wood floor echoed through the building. My shoes stuck to the ground in some places, where beer or soda had been spilled. Brad paid for us all, and we headed off to pick up our shoes and balls. I hadn't thought about money until we got to the counter. Protectors didn't usually work. I would bet Eli had been an exception. On the other hand, Eli had told me that the Protectors never ran out of the funds they needed. The elders made sure of that.

I wasn't completely wrong when I said I would lose. I came in second-to-last—barely—in front of Luke by a single point. Casey kept his distance from me the entire time, never helping me correct my game or offering any advice on how to improve. I couldn't help but feel a bit disappointed, but at the same time I didn't want the others to see that part of our relationship. In our own way, we had crossed some kind of boundary; we were closer than the rest of the team. Like best friends.

Ferdinand was the first to razz Luke for coming in last, and Brad was the first to point out that I hadn't done as badly as I had thought I would.

"Yeah, but I wouldn't say coming in second-to-last is something to brag about." I stuck my tongue out at him.

We piled into the car and headed back to my house. As we rounded the corner onto my street, I saw Ren's car parked in front of my house. Nerves set in, and my stomach got a little queasy. *What would he say about me hanging out with Brad, Ferdinand, Luke, and Casey?* I knew that he opposed my involvement in the first place, and he had been avoiding me ever since the meeting with the elders. I couldn't imagine what he wanted.

Brad maneuvered into the driveway, careful to park on the opposite side from where my mom parked. I stepped out of the car and walked around the back, hoping to beat the rest of the guys out.

"Who's that?" Casey whispered from behind me, before Ren emerged from his car.

"Ren," I said.

My nerves tortured me. *Had he forgiven me for deceiving him?* I got to the end of the driveway just as Ren stepped out of his car, and the guys emerged behind me seconds later. All of them seemed on alert, including Ren. Maybe they could sense my anxiety.

"Hey," I said. "What are you doing here?"

"I came to bring you a birthday present," he said, holding out his hand. In it he held a small box wrapped in blue paper with a pink bow. "I didn't expect to find you with guests." He paused for a moment. "Can we talk? Alone?"

I hesitated before turning to Casey and tossing him my keys. "You guys can head inside. I'll be there in a minute."

Casey closed the gap between us and placed his hand on the small of my back. "Let me know if you need me," he said close to my ear, giving Ren a challenging look and walking inside.

His hand felt strange on my back. It left a ghost outline of his fingers long after he had gone inside.

I felt like I could breathe easier now that half of the tension had left.

"What are you doing?" Ren asked.

"I'm not going to talk about them."

"You shouldn't be involved in this. They're immortal. You aren't. You're going to get yourself killed!" He gritted his teeth together, and his voice was beginning to rise higher.

"I'm fine. I know what I'm doing."

"Do you?" he asked.

"Yes."

"You know that you're going after a murderer?" he asked.

"Of course," I said. "Why do you think I decided to do this in the first place?"

"How exactly are you going to protect yourself when you find the murderer? Have you thought about that?"

"I'll be fine!" I shouted, a little louder than I had intended.

My front door swung open, and Casey stood in the doorway, Ferdinand right behind him. I gave them a wave to go back inside. Casey didn't budge. He stayed planted in the opening, watching with his arms crossed.

"You need protection," Ren said, pulling my attention back.

"I don't need protection! Besides, my Protector gave up on me. Remember? And what does it matter to you, anyway?"

Minutes went by, and Ren didn't speak. We stood there awkwardly.

"My team will keep me safe. That's what they're there for." I gestured toward Casey standing in the doorway.

"Your team, huh?" he mocked. "Is that all they are?"

"What are you talking about?" I asked, confused.

"I see the way Casey looks at you." He tossed the present to me. "Eli doesn't need to lose you too," he said, more quietly now.

"Eli already lost me."

"Maybe, but one day he's going to come to his senses and realize you're the best thing that ever happened to him."

"What am I supposed to do? Wait around for that to happen?"

"I don't know, but are you willing to throw away that chance for a fling with Casey?" He got into his car and shut the door before I could form a response. He rolled down the passenger window. "Happy birthday," he called, and drove out of sight without another word.

Casey? I knew that there had been a few weird moments, and that we were really close, closer than the rest of the team, but I had never considered him anything other than a friend. But, as I looked up toward my house and saw his face peeking through the curtains, I wondered how I had been so blind. I should have seen it for what it was. He had feelings for me.

I looked down at the box in my hands. It wasn't very big. I hadn't even thought Ren knew when my birthday was, let alone that he would show up with a present. I couldn't imagine what he would have gotten me.

Carefully, I slipped the lid off the box. Inside lay a silver, ancient-looking locket, neatly tucked in tissue paper. My fingers slid over the design on the face. An owl. My heart tore a little. Ren had brought me such a beautiful gift, and yet he was so angry with me. I lifted the locket into my hand and held it up to the light. Just as I was about to put it back in the box, a small folded piece of paper caught my eye. I opened the note. The paper trembled in my shaking hands. It read:

The tawny owl so beautiful, and majestic, mates for life.
Just like you and Eli.
-Ren

A single tear streaked down my face. Briskly, I wiped it away, shifted the lid of the box back into place and turned to go inside.

That night my mom and I went out to dinner at our favorite Mexican food restaurant. Our conversation was minimal and strained, but then the whole night changed. My dad strutted into the restaurant and caught my eye. I jumped out of my seat and ran up to hug him.

"Dad! What are you doing here?"

"You didn't think I would miss my little girl's seventeenth birthday, did you?" He held me tight.

The three of us ate dinner together like old times. We ordered sopapillas for dessert, and when the waiter brought them to the table, the whole wait staff paraded behind him. They sang happy birthday to me off-key, making us all laugh.

It had been one of the best birthdays I'd ever had. I felt silly now for dreading it. I had great friends and family.

My dad and I talked until I fell asleep that night. The next day I skipped school to spend as much time as I could with him. We went out to lunch and browsed the mall together. He even promised to come out sometime that summer and help me find a new car. I was grateful that he didn't ask about Eli—my mom must have caught him up on that touchy subject, otherwise I knew he would have been wondering.

My dad's flight departed at 6 p.m., and I wished with all my heart that he had more time here. I headed out to walk to work at the same time he and my mom took the car to the airport. I watched the car sadly as it whisked my dad further and further away from me.

Casey was leaning against his car on the next street, as if I had told him when and where to wait for me.

"Hey," I said.

"So, anything exciting happen for the rest of your birthday?" he asked with a hint of boastfulness, and I had a feeling he already knew.

"My dad came and surprised me all the way from California," I said.

His large smile confirmed my suspicion.

"You knew, didn't you?"

"Yeah," he said, grinning. "But I only found out yesterday morning when we came to surprise you for breakfast. Your mom told me."

Eli was working the same shift as me again. I cringed when I saw him. I used to look forward to it, but now I couldn't wait for my shift to end, and it had me seriously considering finding a new job, even though I loved working at the restaurant. It wasn't fun anymore, and I didn't know how long I would be willing to wait if things didn't improve soon.

As much as he made me miserable now at work, I missed him. The sweet, caring Eli. Not this new evil clone. I missed the boy who always had my back and knew what I needed before I did. I needed that Eli back.

On my break, I sat there remembering how great being with him used to feel, recalling that bond I had with nobody else. I missed our connection. My eyes welled up with tears once again. I felt like I had cried for him a thousand times before. A single tear slipped from my eyelash and rolled down my cheek. I lifted my head to wipe the tear away as quickly as it had come, and searched the room, hoping that nobody had seen. In the corner of the restaurant, not far from the booth I sat in, Eli stood frozen, staring right at me. Our eyes locked, for a moment we held our gaze, but then he looked away again. It was the first time since I had left his house on that fateful day that his face wasn't disgusted when our eyes met. It felt like something passed between us in that moment, something meaningful, but I brushed away the hopeful thought. Probably just my imagination.

That night after work Casey and I went back to our stake-out spot, but this time something different hung in the air. I felt on edge. My nerves didn't help, either. Ever since Ren had gotten angry with me the day before, I hadn't shaken the feeling that he was right. Casey and I had been getting close. Really close. Our night mini-golfing was almost like a date, especially with all the assistance he had given me; but he had to know we were only good friends.

A movement on the side of the house had me sitting up straighter.

"Did you see that?" I whispered, as if whatever or whoever was sneaking around would hear me.

"Yeah," he said. He picked up his phone and began dialing a series of numbers.

Was this what we had been waiting for? I listened to him tell the person on the other end of the line—Ferdinand, maybe?—that we had spotted movement. Besides the mystery woman, we hadn't seen anything since we had started this mission.

"They're coming," he said once he got off the phone.

My eyes darted back and forth for any sign of motion. For the first time, a light flicked on inside the house, and within a minute the whole house glowed in the dark like a scorpion under a black light. My body coursed with adrenaline. Tonight was the night.

Ian hadn't been seen since Elizabeth's death, and his house had remained dormant as if abandoned. Neil, on the other hand, had maintained his presence consistently. Brad, Luke, and Ferdinand had been kept busy following his movements all around town, but he appeared clean. We had come to the unanimous conclusion that Ian was hiding for good reason: He was guilty. Now it appeared Ian was ready to re-enter the world. Time to make our move.

"You should change," Casey said.

"Change?" I asked.

"There's a black shirt in the back. It's mine, hope you don't mind." His voice sounded a little nervous.

He was already clad from head to toe in black. I glanced down at my work uniform, which consisted of a bright white shirt and black pants. I would stand out like a sore thumb in it. I climbed into the back seat to change. I slid my white shirt over my head and carefully folded it, setting it on the seat next to me. My eyes lifted to the rearview mirror, where they met Casey's. I froze. I felt bare sitting there in only my bra. His eyes looked down and away from mine. Even Eli had never seen me that undressed. Hastily, I grabbed the black shirt and threw it over my head, smoothing it down over my stomach. It smelled good, like Casey. Slowly, I climbed back into the front seat.

"Are they here yet?" I asked.

I looked around the neighborhood and tried to find anyone that hadn't been there before.

Casey's arm came across the car and pointed down the street at a car I recognized immediately.

His phone lit up, and after glancing at the screen he turned it in my direction for me to read.

Talked to Edward, we have orders to move in and apprehend. Now.

My nerves hit me all at once. *Would I be able to hold my own?* My time investigating with Eli had never gone well. I always seemed to mess things up. My breathing grew erratic, and I gripped the seat beneath me.

"Hey, are you okay?" Casey's arm was suddenly on mine.

"I don't...know...if I can do this..." I sputtered.

He turned my body toward him. "Look into my eyes," he said.

My chest heaved up and down unpredictably with each uneven breath. I lifted my eyes to his.

"Now take deep breaths with me. In." My eyes held his. "Out," he said.

My breath, unsteady and labored, passed out of my lungs.

I closed my eyes and listened to Casey's instructions. "In and out."

Eventually my breathing settled, and I opened my eyes again. Casey's hands still gripped my arms, holding me.

"Thanks," I said.

"Are you okay?" he asked again.

"Yeah, but I should stay here."

"What?" he asked.

"I don't want to mess anything up. We've been waiting so long to get to him."

"You aren't going to mess anything up. We need you out there. We're a team," he said.

I took another deep breath, and realized he was right. When I took on this mission, I decided to be brave and independent.

"You're right," I said. "Let's do this."

"That's our Abby."

We slid out of the car and slipped into the shadows of the night. Casey motioned for me to trail behind, so I followed his lead. I could faintly make out three dark shapes creeping up to the house opposite from us. They lined up at the corner. I could vaguely make out who was who in the shadows based on their darkened shapes. Ferdinand motioned for us to move up the other side of the house, toward the backyard. He was going to the front door, and the other two would wait out front; at least, that was the way I understood his hand signals.

Finding the right footing in the pitch-black night proved more difficult than I had anticipated. Twice I stumbled and fell forward into Casey. After the second time, he guided me in front of him and didn't let go of my hand, holding me steady. The side of the house seemed to go on for longer than I would have expected, or maybe it felt like it because my hand was in Casey's. I wondered if he felt the same way. My palms began to sweat just thinking about it, and my grip on his hand began to slip.

When we finally reached the gate leading into the backyard, Casey leaned around me to peer over it before reaching out to the latch. We walked ever so cautiously into the yard.

I peered around the back corner of the house, trying to hide myself from anyone who might see me. The patio light illuminated most of the yard, leaving just enough shadow for us to hide in. There didn't appear to be anyone outside, so I moved forward at an even slower pace, keeping my body as tight against the wall as I could.

Casey's hand was slick in mine, and I wondered if I wasn't the only one with a sweaty palm.

We came to a window, and I turned to Casey, motioning that I would crouch below it. Slowly, he nodded and released my hand. I kneeled down and began to crawl past the window.

In the blink of an eye light flooded every angle of the back yard. Not a single shadow remained. Three men rushed out the back door. All carried large guns. My breath hitched in my throat, and my first instinct was to run. Instead, I stood tall, as if my body alone would be intimidating. Without warning Casey grabbed me, threw me behind him, positioning his large body in front of mine, shielding me from them.

"Don't move," the first man shouted.

The gun was now pointed at Casey. Frustration boiled up inside me. This was not how things were supposed to go. This was not the plan. We had watched this house for almost a week. And we weren't the only ones—a team had been on duty around the clock. And no one had seen a soul until today. How could there be so many people inside? It made no sense.

"Move," the man ordered. He signaled with his gun for us to walk toward the house.

I followed Casey onto the porch. Without warning, Casey lunged forward, tackling the guy closest to me. They wrestled on the ground for control of the gun, which was yanked this way and that. I stood there, dumbfounded and afraid to move.

Then the gun went off. The shot resonated around us, making my ears ring while everything else fell silent. Casey fell on his back clutching his side. *Oh my god.* There was so much blood. I dropped to my knees beside him. A wave of nausea overtook me.

"Casey!" I screamed.

I didn't know what to do. Casey looked up at me with pain and sorrow in his eyes.

"You're going to be okay," I told him. "You are."

The man who had shot him kicked my leg, "Up!"

I didn't want to leave Casey, but my body moved as if robotic. I felt detached from the movement. I was propelled forward in the direction I was ordered. When I turned back, just before we entered the house, the rest of the men had surrounded Casey. I stopped briefly, grasping for a little more time with him. He needed me.

Someone jabbed a gun into my back, causing me to stumble and almost fall. "Move!"

I turned around to glare at him before I stepped through the door. Inside, I saw only one man, sitting in the center of the room, looking comfortable and smug. He turned to face us, and there was no mistaking his identity. Ian.

"Protectors running with mortals now, eh?" he said in a disgusted voice. "The elders must be getting desperate." He laughed at his jab. "Is there any particular reason that you and your friends have chosen to invade my home tonight?"

"You know why we're here," I blurted out before I thought better of it.

"Do I?" Ian asked, amused at my apparent embarrassment.

"We're here about Elizabeth," I said.

At this, Ian's face twisted into disgust. "And why would you be here?"

"Because you killed her."

I don't recall what happened next, but when I woke I tried my hardest to remember. When I opened my eyes, darkness surrounded me, and I waited to adjust to the harsh inky void to no avail. My head pounded, and it felt as though my hair was sticky and wet.

I didn't want to move and alert anyone who might be there that I was stirring. However I had gotten here, I was positive that it hadn't been good. Slowly, I tried to slide my hand from my back to the front of my body. Pain sliced into my wrists, which were both restrained behind my back. Gingerly, I tried to move my legs, and failed again; my ankles fought against the ropes that bound them. I started to panic. *Where am I?*

I felt a coarse, cold surface beneath my fingertips. Concrete.

"Casey?" I whispered, hoping I wouldn't be rewarded with a beating—or worse.

"I'm here," he responded.

I wasn't alone.

"I'm so happy to hear your voice. I was really worried about you," he said. I heard shuffling and then something brushed my leg.

"Worried about me? What about you? You were shot. Are you okay?" I asked, remembering the events that led us there. The blood. So much blood.

"I'm fine," he said.

I wasn't sure I believed him, but there wasn't much I could do to help him.

"Where are we?" I asked.

A door flew open before Casey could answer. "Look who's awake," a guard snarled. He hoisted me up by my bound hands and dragged me through the door, my feet scraping the floor.

"Wait, don't take her! Take me," Casey yelled after us.

The door slammed shut behind us, silencing Casey's protests. The man struggled to get me into the room and then tossed me onto the couch. I barely stopped myself from tumbling face first off of it. I shot the man a look that could kill and tried to reposition myself.

"I thought maybe you might be ready to talk, now that you've had some time to think." Ian's voice came from just feet away.

My head shot up and my eyes found him, perched comfortably in the same chair as before looking smug.

"So, do you care to tell me why it is that the elders are letting you run missions with Protectors?"

"Why would I tell you anything?" I spat.

"Maybe you value your life."

I sensed his confidence in his dignified position, dangling my life in the balance. What he didn't count on was my bull-headed stubbornness.

"I guess I don't." My voice held fury that I didn't know I had in me.

"Wrong answer." He gestured to his guard with his finger and, for a split second, I felt blinding pain in the back of my head, and then there was nothing.

When I awoke again, the lights were finally on, and I could see Casey lying on his back beside me, about two feet away. His head was rolled to the side, facing away from me. I struggled to turn my body closer to him. Blood covered nearly his entire shirt. *Was he breathing?*

"Casey?"

No answer.

"Casey," I said.

Nothing.

I felt myself panic. *What did they do to him?* It felt like something sat on my chest, blocking my airway. My heart pulsed blood rapidly through my arms and legs. I could feel the swell of my veins with each unique throb.

I looked around. A garage. Big enough for three cars, yet it was empty. The thought boggled my mind. *How had they all gotten here without cars?*

Casey groaned, bringing my full attention back to him. His head rolled toward me, and his eyes met mine. They were overloaded with water, and the pain in them broke my heart.

"Are you okay?" I asked.

"I'm fine," his hoarse voice mumbled. He sucked in a deep breath, like he was biting back pain as he scooted his body into a different position.

This time I could hear more sadness than pain in his voice. "I'm sorry," he said.

"For what?"

"I should have protected you. I failed."

"Casey, it's not your job to protect me. I knew what I was getting myself into. I can protect myself. And if I can't, well then I guess that's the way it was supposed to be."

"I should have prepared you better. Taught you some self-defense skills. Something."

"Don't think about that now. You're...hurt." The words wouldn't come out easily. My vision faded, becoming spotty in places, and I felt myself slipping away again. I tried to form words, but as much as I willed myself to speak, when my mouth opened nothing came out.

My last coherent thought was that my head was killing me.

Walking, I was walking slowly. Almost creeping along. The sweltering heat made even a deep breath difficult. So much humidity. My hair was damp and clung to my head grotesquely. I wasn't in the desert, that much I knew, though my surroundings were unfamiliar: Row after row of trees, high above my head, casting shadows on the ground from the midday sun. The leaves blazed green all around me. An orchard?

I wasn't alone. Eli was there. But he wouldn't respond to me. I felt like I was screaming at him. He never looked in my direction. Frustration coiled just below my tolerance threshold, threatening to strike. I kept walking. Soon Eli would be in front, and I would be following. He didn't tell me so, but I knew. How did I know?

Ren strolled out from the trees that had obscured him moments before, startling me. I jumped. He nodded to me but said nothing and strode out in front of me to walk next to Eli. Shiny metal up ahead caught my attention. Railroad tracks. Eli and Ren approached them with caution. My senses roared to life. Apprehension took hold, and I stopped moving. I didn't like this, not one bit. A person without a face emerged and lunged at Eli. Another faceless someone materialized out of what seemed like thin air. Had he just appeared? His fist connected with Ren's cheekbone without warning. Ren slumped to the ground. No.

My chest heaved as my lungs tried to compensate for my angst. *I'm in the dark. Where am I?* I tried to orient myself, thrashing. The hard ground underneath me bit into my hip and shoulder.

"Abby?" Casey's voice startled me, and it all came back in one overwhelming rush.

It took a long time for my breathing to even out.

"Are you okay?" he asked after my terror began to pass.

"I'm fine," I said, but I knew that wasn't true. I felt like I was coming unglued at the seams. A new dream. Nightmare. A new vision. It was going to come true. I knew it with every fiber of my being. Edward had confirmed my gift, and I known it would only be a matter of time before another dream reared its ugly head. But why did it have to come now of all times?

"We have to get out of here," I sobbed.

I was frantic. So much for staying calm and collected. This dream had rattled me far more than either of the others. This time I didn't speculate whether it would come true or not. There was no question. My friends would be ambushed as I stood there, watching, frozen. *What were we doing there?*

Casey seemed to sense my panic.

"Abby, take deep breaths. Breathe in and out, in, out, in..."

I did as he instructed and felt my blood pressure lowering. A shuffling sound came from his direction. I heard him suck in a loud, deep breath. Finally, the movements stopped, and he grasped my hand. He let out the breath in one loud huff, and I wondered how painful the wound must be for him. It felt good to know that I wasn't alone. Having his hand right there gave me hope.

"Can you untie me?" I asked.

"No," he said. "The rope is too thin for me to grip. It needs to be cut."

We lay there silently for a long time, hand in bound hand. I think we had given up. There was no way out. We were at the mercy of Ian.

CHAPTER SIXTEEN

When you have hours to think while being held hostage, your idle thoughts are not predictable. Every little thing you ever felt guilty about presents itself in a nice, pretty package of regret. Every. Single. Thing.

I sighed.

"What are you thinking about?" Casey asked.

"Trust me, you don't want to know."

"Try me."

I debated whether I should tell him. *What could it hurt, it's not like it mattered.* "All right. When I was ten, I stole a candy bar from the gas station when my mom wasn't looking."

It was silly. I knew that. But I felt loads better after finally telling someone. I had never told anyone, not even Kelly.

He laughed. "Really? You're tied up in the dark with me in this garage at the mercy of a psychopath, and you're thinking of something frivolous that you did seven years ago?"

"Yeah. It's silly, I know. I felt so guilty I couldn't even eat it and ended up throwing it away a week later."

Pop! Pop! Pop! Three loud shots rang through the air. Casey's body jolted with each explosion. We huddled closer together, as if trying to dodge someone coming for us. But nothing came.

"What was that?" I whispered once the commotion subsided.

My pulse drummed in my ears.

"I don't know." His voice was a breathless whisper, as if he had been holding it in. "I think it might have been gunfire."

"That's what I was afraid of."

Moments passed, letting the suspense and fear really set in and leaving us on edge and jumpy. My heart rate never slowed.

Then the door burst open, letting bright light stream into the garage and across my face. For a moment, the harsh light blinded me. Once I blinked the shock away, my eyes focused. Eli rushed to my side. *Eli?* The relieved look written all over his face surprised me. *What is he doing here?*

"Abby! Are you okay?" he asked. He fumbled clumsily with the ropes that bound my hands together. Finally my hands slipped free of the their tight embrace, giving me instant relief. Eli wasted no time pulling me upright into his arms, my legs still bound.

He put my head between his hands. "I thought I would be too late. I'm so sorry. I'm so, so sorry." His words trailed off into my lips as he kissed me with more passion than ever before. Electricity pulsed between us as if nothing had ever parted us. Heat rushed to every part of my body. In that moment I needed his touch as much as I needed air. When he pulled away, I was panting.

Casey cleared his throat, and I realized that he still lay on the floor, restrained, not even a foot away with a gunshot wound in his abdomen. I cringed.

Eli helped me down to a sitting position and pulled out a knife he must have forgotten he had moments ago when he burst into the room and struggled to liberate my legs. Before long, both Casey and I had been freed.

Casey tried to stand upright, but he couldn't do it on his own. I helped him to his feet as the rest of our team entered the garage from inside the house. They all looked saddened, their faces grim and tense.

"Oh my god," Brad said, jogging over to Casey to help hold him up. By then Casey had managed to stand on his own, but I could tell by the look on his face that he was biting back the pain.

"What happened in there?" I asked, pointing toward the house.

Eli's expression darkened. "I don't want to talk about it."

"Eli?" I pushed.

"The less you know, the better." His tone was strict and serious. I knew not to argue with him. No matter what I said, he wouldn't budge.

I looked at Casey, and he looked just as frustrated as I. This had been our mission, and now it was over with what I could only imagine was a catastrophic ending.

"Let me look at you," Eli said to me.

He held each of my arms and looked into my eyes for a moment before checking for injuries. Sadness and worry I had never seen before dominated his eyes.

He started by thoroughly looking over my head. His fingers gingerly slid through my hair, moving it out of the way until he found the source of all the blood.

"Right there," he said, holding a good chunk of my hair on top of my head.

He grabbed a water bottle and poured it down my head to rinse away the excess blood. I sucked in a deep breath as the icy water drizzled down my arm, and I leaned over, trying to avoid getting any of it on Casey's shirt. The cold slightly numbed the pain.

"It's not a bad cut. I'm going to use the super glue in the first aid kit to glue it shut, okay?" Eli said.

I nodded.

He didn't waste any time. I winced at the sudden sting of the glue and the pressure from his fingers pushing the cut closed. Casey slipped his hand in mine to help me cope. I was grateful for the comfort he offered and wished I could do something for him. I took a deep breath, remembering what Casey had told me—in and out. Eli's fingers lifted from my head at last.

"Done," he announced.

"Thanks," I said.

I watched Eli's smile turn to a frown as he noticed Casey holding my hand, but I refused to let go. He turned back to the first aid kit to close it up.

"What can I do to help?" Casey asked Eli.

"I'll take it from here," Eli said, without so much as a glance in his direction. He walked between Casey and I as if it was the only path, pushing Casey's hand away from mine and bumping into Casey's shoulder, knocking him sideways. Casey winced and righted himself with Brad's help. He looked at me as if his anger might boil over and hobbled out of the garage without another word. Ferdinand and Luke followed behind, nodding dolefully to me as they went.

"You don't have to be so rude!" I said to Eli.

"Look at the mess he got you into, and I'm supposed to play nice?" Eli closed the gap between us until his face was mere inches from mine. "What would have happened if I hadn't gotten here when I did?" He shuddered. "He should have known better."

I gave Eli a menacing look and ran after Casey and the others. I caught Casey as Brad was helping him into the passenger seat of his car. Ferdinand and Luke were nowhere to be found.

"Wait," I called as I jogged the rest of the way to his car. "I'm sorry about him. He's a bit..."

"Of a jerk?" Casey said.

"Protective of me." I finished biting my lip. *When he wants to be.*

"Yeah," he sighed. "I can't say that I blame him. He's right, you know. I should have done better. We shouldn't have gotten into that position."

Brad went around the other side of the car and got in, pretending to ignore our conversation, giving us privacy in the only way he could.

"It's not your fault. We were a team. You aren't my Protector. I'm fine, anyway. Really."

He didn't agree. Yet he didn't disagree either. He didn't say anything at all.

"Are you okay?" I asked.

"I'm fine," he said. "I've got to go."

It was a lie. Nothing about him said he was fine. The blood-soaked shirt was screaming out at me.

"I'll call you tomorrow, okay?"

"Sure," he said, and they drove away.

I stood there, feet planted on the ground, going over the night. My head ached. The stickiness I had felt earlier on my scalp was now a dried, crusty redness in my hair.

Ren and Vince cruised up to the house, stopping in the driveway. I shrunk back into the shadows, hoping they wouldn't see me. I couldn't guess what they would say to me, but I knew it wouldn't be good. I wasn't ready for it. For now, I needed to be alone. I sat down across the street and waited, hoping Eli would emerge soon. I pulled my knees to my chest and curled myself into a tight ball.

Despite Eli's unwillingness to divulge the truth, I knew what waited inside that house. The thought made me sick. I leaned my head on my knees, looking down at the ground to help the nausea pass. I took deep breaths through my nose, which seemed to help a little. Eventually the nausea loosened its grip on my abdomen, and I was able to breathe easier, knowing I wouldn't hurl right there in the street.

When I had volunteered to help with this mission, my goal had been to find out who was responsible for Elizabeth's death and make them pay for it. Killing them never crossed my mind. Not once. I wondered if that was what Edward had in mind for the killer all along, but I doubted it.

Would Eli be in trouble for what he had done? I didn't want to think about it. We were back together, or at least I thought we were, and that was something I had never expected to be able to say again. I had given up hope, despite Ren's reassurances.

Footsteps on the asphalt pierced the soundless night. They were coming closer. The crunch of gravel under shoes came to a halt directly in front of me. I refused look up to see who it was, even though I knew there were eyes boring into my back. I could almost feel them, but I didn't look up.

"Are you okay?" It was Ren's voice.

I wouldn't look at him. The last time we had spoken it hadn't gone so well. Actually, that was an understatement; the last time we talked he had yelled at me for my decision to get involved. Now look where we were.

"I'm fine," I said.

"Abby, you don't have to be so distant. We are friends, aren't we?" he asked.

"Are we? It's been hard to tell lately. Every time I see you, you tell me I'm doing something I shouldn't be and then avoid me for days."

He seemed to ponder this for a moment. After a while I rolled my head to the side and looked at him. His mouth had tightened into a thin line as he thought. His eyes flickered to mine.

"You're right. I have been a crappy friend. I'm sorry. I should have been there for you more." He sat down next to me and nudged me with his shoulder. "Forgive me?"

I nudged him back. "I guess."

He slid his arm around me and gave me a big side hug. I leaned my head on his shoulder.

"I'm glad you're okay," he said.

I nodded, unsure of what to say. I may have forgiven him for not being there for me, but I was still bitter that he couldn't accept that I was capable. And maybe I was bitter because he had been a little bit right.

"How did Casey react?"

His question caught me off guard. "To what?" I asked, confused.

"To Eli coming back. I'm sure his arrival was quite...heated." He looked at me expectantly.

I knew then what he meant without any further explanation. It had occurred to me seconds after our momentary lapse in judgment as we embraced our reunion that our PDA might have bothered Casey. And we had succumbed to it before untying him, making him bear witness to it all without an option of escape. I should have thought of it in the moment before passion had taken hold. Casey and I were friends. We had gotten close. Really close. But part of me knew he wanted to be more than that.

"I don't know," I said. "Eli wasn't very nice to him."

"I imagine not," Ren said. "You know I may not have agreed with your choice to get mixed up in all this, but good did come from it."

He was right, in a way. I knew that. We had found Elizabeth's killer, and Eli had come back to me, but I still had a horrible feeling in my gut. Murder didn't feel like justice. It felt more morbid. *What made Eli's actions any better than what Ian had done?*

I knew better than to rejoice. Death was in the air, and I knew retaliation was on the horizon. We were not in a good place as far as I was concerned. This battle was far from over. If I had learned anything from our encounters with Pete, it was that he had a lot of friends willing to help him out. Eli had killed his uncle. History was repeating itself, except a lot more sinisterly. The thought of people we didn't know coming at us terrified me. It was a lot easier knowing who your enemies were.

Eli emerged from the house, and Ren stood up. "I'm going to go help Vince, but for what it's worth I'm glad Eli's come to his senses and realized what you mean to him. He needs you, especially now." He smiled before he turned to leave. The warmth of his smile comforted me.

Especially now? What did that mean? I didn't have a chance to ask him before he walked away.

As Eli approached, I tried to think of what I wanted to say to him. After all, he was the one who had dropped me like the plague. What was going to stop him from doing it again? *How could I really trust him now? How could I truly let my guard down with him?* I wanted to move past this and go back to where we were before any of it happened, but I didn't know if I could do that.

He stopped in front of me and held out his hand. Hesitantly, I took it. He pulled me to my feet and into his arm, kissing me.

"I've missed you so much," he whispered, his lips brushing against mine as he spoke.

"I've missed you too. Don't leave me again," I pleaded in a whisper.

All my reservations were forgotten the moment his skin touched mine. The dynamic buzz of his touch was exhilarating. Somehow, the world felt right again and all my worries slipped away as if they had never existed at all.

"Let's get you home. It's late."

"Oh my, what time is it?" I asked. I was sure I had missed my curfew. My mom was probably fuming by now.

"Midnight. Don't worry, Ren called your mom, she thinks you're at a movie."

"Okay." I relaxed, knowing we had time, and the warden wouldn't be seething when I got back. "Would you mind if we walked?" I asked.

"I think that's a great idea," he said, smiling.

We ambled along the dim street, enjoying the cool night air. The moon played peek-a-boo behind a scattering of meager clouds, and a gentle breeze rustled through the bushes that lined the street.

We remained silent for the first few streets, as if we didn't know how to talk to each other anymore. It was more than awkward. I longed for the carefree time I spent with him before we had ever become more than friends—the easygoing conversations that weren't complicated.

I slipped my hand out of his. "Eli?"

"Yeah?" His steps didn't falter.

"How do I know I can trust that you won't leave me again?" I asked. My vulnerability shone through the mask I had worn over the last few weeks since he had rejected me.

He stopped, his face tense. He closed his eyes and looked at the ground. Eventually, he spoke, his voice barely above a whisper.

"I'm sorry I ignored you, and..." His voice trembled. "I'm sorry I was so..." He didn't open his eyes while he searched for the right words. I gave him the time he needed. "...mean to you. I can never forgive myself for the way I treated you."

When his eyes opened they were filled with sorrow, and I felt myself wishing I could take away his pain.

"It's okay..."

He stopped me from continuing. "No it's not. My grief took over. I shouldn't have let it."

I took his hand again, kissed his cheek, and resumed walking, letting our voices fall silent again.

"I'm going to California in two weeks," I blurted out a short time later.

"Really? That's awesome," he said. Then he was quiet for a few minutes. After a while he said, "Am I invited?" His voice was hesitant and nervous.

I had hoped he would want to come with me to visit my dad ever since we had become a couple, and even more so since he hit it off with my dad.

"I wouldn't have it any other way," I said.

He stopped in his tracks and grabbed me, wrapping me in a big bear hug and swinging me around in a circle. When we stopped spinning, he set me down, letting my body slide down his. When my feet landed on the ground, he kissed me. Lovingly. Tenderly. His hand cradled my chin. "I'm so looking forward to moving on from this mess."

Then, just as quickly, he grabbed my hand and we were walking again.

"Me too," I said. "Wait a minute, you're graduating."

He chuckled. "Yep."

During our separation I hadn't had time to think about what the end of the school year meant. Eli was eighteen. In mere days he would finish school. He would don his cap and gown and graduate next week, and his mom wouldn't be there to see it. She wouldn't be able to tell him how proud she was. It brought a swell of tears to my eyes, and I tried to stifle the sniffles. All of that had been taken away from him, for what?

I tried to think of something else to push the tears away, and instead said the first thing that popped into my head. "I'm going to be lonely without you at school for the next two years."

He laughed. "I'm sure you'll be fine."

I jutted my lip out, pouting. "No I won't."

He stopped and looked me in the eyes with skepticism. When I laughed, he poked my shoulder with his hand.

He walked me to my door and was hesitant to leave. I could tell in the way he held me for longer than he ever had before as we stood on the doorstep. As much as I loved being in his arms, I was anxious to get inside to wash the blood out of my hair. I felt gross and dirty. And, I had to admit, wearing a shirt that smelled of Casey while I was in Eli's arms felt wrong somehow. *Could Eli smell his cologne on me?* He had to notice, at the very least, that the shirt was too big for me.

"I should go in, call me later?" I asked.

"Of course," he said.

After Eli left, I went inside and hoped my mom wasn't paying close attention to me as I raced up to my bathroom. She was in the kitchen, and I could hear the water running. An occasional pan clunked in the sink.

"Hey Mom," I called as I took the stairs two at a time.

"Hi honey," she mumbled.

I could hear a man's voice whispering, and I knew George was there, holding her attention. For once I was grateful for his presence. It distracted my mom from any intense scrutiny of my behavior. I let out the breath I had been holding when I closed the bathroom door. Tossing my purse in the corner, I took a deep breath and turned to face myself in the mirror.

The whiteness of my face startled me.

"Oh my," I whispered to myself, my voice so low even I hardly heard it.

My fingers brushed a darkened mark on my forehead. I frowned. Eli had never mentioned that. The darkened blue skin turned yellow when I pressed on it. That would be difficult to hide.

I got in the shower and washed my hair, taking extra care around the cut to ensure I didn't break the glue free. The water on the shower floor turned pink as it pooled around the drain before swirling around and down.

Eventually the water ran clear, and I shut off the spray. I felt like me again, that is, except for the splitting ache that had taken up the majority of the space in my head. Brushing my hair was the next challenge, and after a couple minutes of gentle combing, I gave up. Tangled, I decided, was my new style until my head healed.

It wasn't until I had climbed into bed that I realized Eli had never answered my question. *Could I trust him?*

Getting comfortable in my bed was a short-lived struggle. In no time, I fell fast asleep, though staying asleep proved a lot more difficult. My nightmare beckoned me into its disastrous clutch.

My feet came down in front of me, one right after the other. Our pace was so slow that I watched the powdery dust rise and settle with each step. Heat rose on my back, causing me to sweat. My lungs felt heavy, as if I was underwater, and I tried to gather a deep breath. I slid the back of my hand across my forehead to stop the beads of perspiration from rolling down my face.

I rolled onto my side gasping for air and winced when my cut brushed the pillowcase. I opened my eyes, but nothing had changed in the darkness of my room. I yawned, and my eyes lulled closed again.

Trees high above my head surrounded me in neat rows. Bursts of sunlight drifted through spaces between the leaves, casting strange shadows on the ground. Eli trekked ahead of me, almost close enough that I could touch him. He would not respond. Confusion and desperation jostled with my patience for control. Ren appeared out of what seemed like thin air. He lifted his head toward me in an attempt at a greeting and fell into stride next to Eli. The trees ended abruptly, and I stopped short of their edge. Someone stepped into view. Who? I couldn't tell.

I startled awake as my arm fell off the bed. I could feel the anxiety in my chest welling up from the dream's relentless pursuit. I sighed and took a deep, calming breath. I rolled onto my back and settled in to fall back to sleep.

I squinted my eyes as if the sun was causing a glare, but that wasn't the problem. The mystery person broke into a run and lunged at Eli. Suddenly another person came out of hiding, his face obscured. His fist connected with Ren's cheekbone without warning. Ren's listless body fell to the ground in a heap. I took a step back. The grinding of gravel under my feet alerted the strong-arm of my presence. My heart thumped in my chest. His foot came forward, and before I realized what was happening, he stood in front of me. His fist came forward...

My hands were clenched into fists as I sprang out of my bed, ready to strike. Sun peeked through my window. I stumbled to the window, wringing my hands until my knuckles blanched.

I lifted a single blind flap to peer out at the blue sky. I stood there for a long time, trying to make sense of the dream and wishing it was wrong. I sighed, wondering if life would ever get less complicated.

Wrapping myself in my robe, I went downstairs. Over breakfast, I thought about Eli's return to me. *What will Vince think of me now?* It hurt to even consider that he might not accept me after all that had happened. But I couldn't dismiss the thought. After the coldness I felt from him the day they found Elizabeth, I wasn't sure our relationship would ever be the same.

*   *   *   *

Falling back into the same routine at school seemed so normal, except that Bailey wasn't there. When I texted her to ask where she was, she informed me that she had a dentist appointment, then lunch with her dad, and wouldn't be there the whole day. I breathed a sigh of relief that Pete hadn't shown up and involved her again, but at the same time I felt bummed that I wouldn't have her there to chat with.

Eli pulled up to the curb at the end of the day, and I ventured into the parking lot toward his car. I smiled at him before I hopped in.

"Have a good day back?" I asked.

"Eh, it was all right," he said.

"All right?" I asked.

"Yeah, you weren't with me for most of the day. Now if you had been, the day would have been amazing."

I blushed at his answer, and I tried to hide it by looking out the window. Eventually, I snuck a peek at his handsome face. It hadn't changed a bit in the time he had been on his little 'sabbatical.' I could stare at him for hours. The slightest stubble was beginning to surface, darkening his chin. I wanted to reach out and stroke it, to feel the prickle of his five o'clock shadow on my skin.

Eli's jaw clenched. I looked away from him and saw why. Casey stood in my driveway, shifting from one foot to the other.

"What is he doing here?" Eli asked.

"Casey?" I asked. I was relieved to see him. He had taken off the minute we had gotten free, and I hadn't heard from him since. I had hoped Brad would take good care of him after he had been shot, and seeing him in my driveway was a good sign. Eli, on the other hand, was not happy. "I don't know," I said. "I didn't know he was coming."

I didn't like the way this situation was headed. I could tell Eli wanted Casey to have nothing to do with me. Unfortunately for him, that wasn't how things were going to happen. He was just going to have to accept that Casey and I were friends.

I opened the door before the car even stopped rolling.

Casey didn't look himself. His face was pale, his dark, sunken eyes the only contrast to his skin. He was standing upright, a significant improvement over last night, but I was sure that even immortals took time to get back their strength and heal from something as serious as what he had gone through the night before.

"Hey, what are you doing here? You should be resting," I chided.

"I was worried about you. I came to see how you were doing."

"I'm fine," I said. "How are you?"

"I've been better," he said with his head down.

Eli's footfalls behind me stopped me from reaching out to touch Casey's arm. Then I got mad at myself. *Why should I change my actions because of his irrational jealousy? But then again, was it irrational?* Of course it was, and I pushed the thought away.

I gathered my courage and stepped forward, reaching out to grasp Casey's forearm. "Is there anything I can do?"

His eyes darted to Eli and then back to me. "Uhm..." he began, but then he changed his mind. "No, I'm fine," he said. He squared his shoulders. "I should go."

I could only guess how awful the glare from Eli was. I wanted to elbow him in the stomach to make him stop, but I refrained.

"Okay," I said, understanding why he shut down.

Before he could walk away, I shrouded his body in my arms. His hands remained at his sides at first, but he slowly lifted them and gave me a half-hearted hug back. I held him there for a moment before whispering, "Call me later."

He pulled out of my embrace more quickly than I expected. "I'll see you later Abby," he called over his shoulder as he sauntered away.

I whipped around to see Eli giving Casey's back a death glare. I smacked his chest, and it drew his attention back to me faster than a spooked deer disappears from sight. His face softened the moment his eyes landed on me.

"You're cute when you're mad," he said.

I rolled my eyes and turned to walk into the house, but he snatched my hand, twirling me back around into his arms and against his chest.

"Don't be mad," he said.

He kissed my forehead. Then my cheek. One by one, he planted a trail of kisses leading from my cheek to my lips. I couldn't help the smirk that spread across my lips. At first I didn't respond to his kiss, but then, reluctantly, I kissed him back and felt my frustration and anger melt away. He was good. He was really good. Something about Eli's touch encouraged me to throw caution to the wind.

He led me into the house with his hand on my lower back. "You aren't off the hook," I said. It may have come out as a joke, but deep down I knew I was serious.

My mom was doing dishes in the kitchen when we walked in. The surprised look on her face when we entered, talking and laughing, was priceless.

"Well hello there stranger," she exclaimed.

Eli sobered, his awkwardness apparent. He cleared his throat. "Hi."

CHAPTER SEVENTEEN

"He's back!" I squealed into the phone.

"Who?" Bailey asked, confused.

"Eli!"

"Really?" Her voice seemed a little more than surprised, and if I didn't know any better, I would have thought I detected a little doubt.

"Yep," I said.

"That's great! How did that happen?"

Uh oh. In my excitement, I hadn't thought this far ahead. Lies always did end up catching up with you like a shadow that always looms behind.

"Ah..." I said. "Come over." I didn't want to confess more secrets and lies to her over the phone. It was risky to assume that she would even listen when she sat in front of me. I wouldn't chance her hanging up before I could explain.

"All right," she said, her voice happy. "I'll be there in a bit."

I hung up before saying goodbye. My nerves were getting the better of me, and I thought through what I would say.

Cookies. Everything was better with cookies, or better yet, cookie dough. I ran downstairs as a sudden jolt of excitement shot through me, giving me butterflies in my stomach. The jittery excitement made me hopeful that in the end she wouldn't actually be mad, but instead be happy for me.

I was mixing in the chocolate chips when the doorbell rang. I stuck my cookie dough-covered finger in my mouth and ran to the door.

"Hey," I said happily when I opened the door.

She giggled. "Someone's in a good mood, eh?"

I didn't answer. Instead, I grinned and pulled her into the kitchen. I grabbed a spoon, scooped a pile of cookie dough onto it, and handed it to her. I waited until a good sugar buzz set in before I laid on the heavy stuff.

"Yum," she said as she ate small bits of dough off of the spoon. "So what's up?"

"A lot has happened." I tried to think of where to begin. "I guess I should start by saying that I haven't been completely honest with you. I know we promised no more secrets, but I didn't think you'd understand." I waited a moment, and then added, "And I thought you would be mad at me if I told you my plan. Ren was."

"I'm not going to like this, am I?"

I shrugged and gave her a sympathetic look.

"All right, get it over with," she said.

"Okay, after Eli's mom died, Eli shut me out."

Bailey nodded.

"That much you know." I was talking in circles, and I knew it. "What you don't know is that I asked Ren to take me to talk to the elders." I made sure to leave out my nightmares. The fewer people that knew about them, the better. "I asked to help find Elizabeth's killer." I waited before I continued, expecting some sort of outburst that never came. "In Ren's defense, he didn't know my real reason for wanting to see them. I told him that I wanted to find out what I could do to help Eli; in a way, it wasn't a lie. Finding Elizabeth's killer would help. Ren was so furious with me afterwards that he didn't speak to me for a week.

"But the elders accepted my offer to help and put me on a team right away, so I wasn't always telling the truth when I told you I was working." I glanced at her with a look of hope. Hope that she would understand. Hope that she would be forgiving. Hope that she wouldn't immediately write me off. She waited patiently for me to finish, and I couldn't have been more grateful. "Things didn't go so well last night. My partner, Casey, and I were ambushed as we closed in on a house. Casey got shot in the stomach. I was hit over the head with god-knows-what." Absently, I reached up to touch the throbbing wound.

"The next thing I knew, I was tied up in the dark. Casey was there, also tied up." I felt myself drifting back to the previous night, and my voice became almost monotone as I replayed the events in my head.

"We lay there for a long time, or at least it felt that way. I was in and out of consciousness. Eventually, Eli found and rescued us. I still don't know what changed his mind about me, or how he knew where we were. But he's back," I said.

She remained silent for a moment. "Wow," she said. "I'm not sure what to say. I'm speechless."

"I know," I whispered.

"So, is Casey a boy?" she asked.

The question took me by surprise. "Ah...yeah."

"Ooh," she said. "How did that go?"

"What do you mean?"

"Eli meeting a guy you've been spending all that time alone with. It's almost like boyfriend meeting ex-boyfriend or something. I don't imagine Eli being the friendly type when it comes to sharing you." I thought she had finished, but then she added, "And then he had to rescue you...and him. Yikes."

"Casey's not my boyfriend. But yeah, Eli was rude to him. Really rude. He was awful to him again today when Casey came by to check on me."

"I would imagine so. How do you feel about that?" she asked.

"It makes me downright livid!" I growled, feeling my anger coming back at the reminder. "He has no right! Casey did nothing wrong. At least he was there for me when Eli refused to be. You should have been there on my birthday. Casey planned this whole amazing day." I looked out the kitchen window as I spoke. "Uh, well, I think he planned it. Our whole team was there..." I stopped talking when I turned and saw the look on Bailey's face. "What?" I demanded.

"Is there something going on between you and Casey?" she asked.

"What? Why do people keep asking that? We're just friends," I said, exasperated.

"Well," she said, "maybe because of the way you talk about him. Not to mention the whimsical look on your face."

"No," I said. "There is *nothing* between us, for the final time."

"Touchy. Okay, okay," Bailey said, putting her hands up. "I'll leave it alone, but I do think you should think about it a little more." The smirk on her face told me that she didn't believe a word I said.

Somewhere in my core, I knew I was lying. I knew Casey felt more than friendship for me, though had never discussed it.

*　　*　　*　　*

Later that night, my mom and I ate dinner together. I knew the conversation was coming, but I still hadn't put much thought into what I would tell her had changed Eli's mind. To be honest, I didn't know the truth just yet, and maybe I never would.

"So, Eli's back, huh?" she asked without beating around the bush.

"Well, that didn't take long," I said, amused.

"I've been dying to know what was up since I saw him with you earlier today."

I laughed. "We talked at work, that's why I was late last night. We went out after work."

"I thought it was Ren who called to tell me about the movie."

"It was." I knew I had stuck my foot in my mouth. "He came too."

"So why didn't you call?"

Crap! And this was how lies snuck up on you. "Ah, well, we decided to go to the movie while we were still at work, so Eli asked Ren to call you before we got off to make sure it was okay."

"I see," she said. "I thought you and Casey kind of had something going."

Really? I was going to get it from her too?

"No," I said, hoping she would just drop it as the others hadn't.

"Really?"

I sighed. "Yes, really."

"Well, in any case, I just want you to be happy with whomever you decide to date."

"Thanks Mom," I said.

When I sat down in my room after dinner, my head spun. I seemed to have narrowly escaped my web of lies, though I wasn't positive I really had. My mom's questions had been spot-on, and I was amazed she hadn't pressed any further. My thoughts drifted to Casey. Warm thoughts of our time together filled my mind, until I thought of Eli and became grounded once more. Eli and I were meant to be together. I liked Casey, and I refused to let Eli get in the way of our friendship. But that's all we were. Friends.

I picked up my phone and called Casey right then. He answered on the second ring, and his voice sounded a bit out of breath.

"Hey, do you want to do something?" I asked, skipping the small talk. I needed to get out of the house. It was only 7:30, and I was restless.

"Uh..." I could hear him shuffling around. "Right now?" he asked.

"Yeah," I said. He took a moment to answer. I wondered what could be keeping him from saying yes. "That is, if you aren't busy," I said, hoping I wasn't pushing him into hanging out with me.

"No, I'm not busy," he said. "Are you sure it's okay?"

"Of course it is. Why wouldn't it be?" I asked.

"Umm...well...I just don't think Eli likes me..." He trailed off. "I thought he might have a problem with it."

"No," I said.

"All right, if you're sure."

"Great. Any ideas?"

Again he fell quiet for a minute.

"I'm working out right now. Would you like to join me? That is, if you don't mind me being sweaty. Maybe I could teach you some self-defense maneuvers."

The thought intrigued me. Self-defense. I should have learned that a long time ago. Maybe the next time someone decided to mess with me I could actually do something about it.

"That sounds great."

"You sure you're up to it, with your head?" he asked.

"I'm fine," I assured him.

It only bothered me a little, at least when I had painkillers in my system.

"Would you mind picking me up?" I asked.

"Not a problem. Be there in fifteen minutes."

I hung up, changed, and pulled my hair back into a messy ponytail before going downstairs to tell my mom what I was doing. When his car pulled up to the curb, I was waiting outside for him in tight-fitting yoga pants, a sports bra, and a tank.

Casey's eyes were wide when I got into the car.

"Hey," I said.

"Uh...hey," he said, like he was trying to pull himself together.

What's his problem?

"Ready?" I asked.

"Yep."

It took only fifteen minutes to get to his apartment. I had never been there before, so I had no clue what to expect, but when Casey's car pulled into a large parking structure nestled beside a brightly-lit, fancy building, I was surprised. The garage connected to the apartment building; in the summer I could only imagine how much cooler your car would be while parked there away from the harsh rays of the sun.

The elevator chimed its arrival on the seventh floor. Casey's apartment was one of only four units on this floor, and my jaw dropped when we walked in his front door. The space was striking, boasting a modern glory. His living room featured a wall of windows, with a gorgeous view of most of Phoenix, including Tempe town lake at its core.

His furniture was all black leather, and the decor sleek and modern. I imagined curling up on his couch, enjoying the warmth from the tiled fireplace as we looked out at the glorious view. The marble floors showed off a white shag area rug at the very center of it all. I wanted to kick off my shoes and dig my toes into it. I turned to see Casey watching me shyly as I took it all in. I smiled.

"Casey, this place is amazing," I said in awe.

"Thanks." He blushed.

"Do you live alone?" I asked.

"Yeah."

How did I not know that? "It's so big," I said. I guess that was what came with being his age, and a Protector. Pretty soon, I supposed I would be on my own, too. I wondered what my life would look like then. Surely I wouldn't be able to afford a place this nice, but one could dream, right?

"Ready?" he asked, bringing me back to reality.

"Yes."

He led me to the next room, which showcased a whole wall of windows and was large enough to fit my bedroom inside it, twice. Exercise equipment covered the plush white carpet. It looked like a complete gym that people paid memberships for, with two of every machine. Hand weights, ranging from five to eighty pounds, lined one wall. The heaviest ones looked enormous. His hot physique showed he used the room, though until then I had never considered the hours that went into making him look so athletic. I walked over to the biggest weight, fingering the large numbers printed on it.

"Wow, you have a lot of equipment," I said, trying to get my mind off his toned, broad shoulders.

He laughed. "Yeah, it's sort of my hobby."

"So where do we start?" I asked, feeling a bit overwhelmed and embarrassed. "I can't say I've ever worked out before. You'll have to walk me through everything."

"That's okay," he said. "Let's start by seeing how much you can lift, and get you warmed up. Then we can move on to self-defense."

He handed me one of the ten-pound dumbbells and had me begin with a few small exercises, ten repetitions each time. Halfway through, he switched me to a fifteen-pound weight that made it seem like I had been lifting nothing before. My arms shook with each repetition. I could feel my head begin to hurt, and I knew it was almost time for more pain medicine. By the time he told me to put them down, I was panting, and my arms felt like they might fall off.

"Thirsty?" he asked.

I nodded.

"Why don't you go grab us a couple water bottles. They're in the fridge." He nodded in the direction of the kitchen. "I'll move some stuff around so we have room to work."

I wandered back into the kitchen. The fridge was enormous, with all kinds of buttons on it. For half of them, I couldn't figure out what they would do. For a brief moment, I stood mesmerized, until I felt silly.

When I opened the fridge, bright white light streamed into the room. The organization I faced surprised me. Everything had its place, and it sparkled. I grabbed two bottles, trying to not spend too much time holding the door open. I walked over to the counter that overlooked the living room as I took the first drink of ice-cold water. It slid down my throat and cooled me from the inside out. I looked through the windows for a brief moment of serenity, seeing the beautiful city below, the houses and businesses standing out like sparkling night lights against the dark.

I felt a hand on my back, and I jumped, spilling water down the front of my shirt.

"Hey, are you okay?" Casey asked.

"Oh. Yeah. I was just looking at this view," I said, gazing back at the twinkling lights.

His face twisted, as if he wasn't sure he could believe me.

"Really, I'm fine." I smiled.

"Your shirt is soaked. I'll get you one of mine."

He left the room before I could protest. So I followed him. I found myself standing in his bedroom. "Really, I'm fine. It's actually cooling me down." He emerged from the closet with a shirt in his hand.

"Are you sure?" he asked.

"Yep."

I turned on my heel and left his room, feeling a bit in the spotlight. Seconds later, he stood behind me. He caught my hand in his, turning me around. "Are you sure you're okay?" His face seemed concerned, but there was no way I could tell him what my problem was; I wasn't even sure what was wrong with me.

"F-fine. Really," I said.

His musky sweat and the last remnants of his cologne filled my nose. It smelled so good. I let myself enjoy it for too long as I stood frozen in his grip.

"All right," he said. "But if you need to talk, you know I'm here for you."

He tossed me a black shirt. I tossed it back. "It's fine, thanks."

He threw it on the floor of the weight room. "It's there if you decide you need it."

I realized I was still holding his water bottle when a bead of dew dripped down my arm. "Here," I said, thrusting it toward him.

As casually as I could, I walked back into the workout room, out of Casey's grasp. Away from his curious eyes. Away from his scent. I had to get control of myself. *What is wrong with me?*

The center of the room had been cleared. A couple of mats were placed in the middle, giving us somewhere to land safely if we fell. I slipped my shoes off and walked onto the mat to test its squishy texture under my feet. Casey grabbed me from behind and held me in place. It took me off guard, but it only took me a moment to realize my training had started. I struggled at first, recognizing his strength, and how incapable I was. After several attempts, I felt like I was more stuck in his grasp than when I had started.

"Okay, I give. How do I get out?"

He chuckled. I could feel his Adam's apple moving up and down on the back of my head. Suddenly I was very aware of the pressure the rise and fall of his chest created on my back.

"Stomp on my foot, then immediately bring your elbow back into my stomach and spin, all in one fluid motion."

He demonstrated it on thin air and resumed his position, attaching himself to me. I ran through the instructions in my head, imagining what I would look like doing them. I stepped on his foot, elbowed him in the stomach, and spun...well, I tried to spin. I failed, miserably.

"I know you've got more in you than that," he scolded.

"I don't want to hurt you," I said.

"I'll be fine."

"Are you sure?" I asked.

"Yes."

"All right." *Here goes nothing.* I stomped as hard as I could on his foot, followed by a sharp jab to his stomach. I didn't wait a second after my elbow left him to spin out of his grasp. I stumbled to catch my balance, hurting my throbbing head, and threw my hands in the air the second I stabilized. "I did it!"

I turned to see Casey holding a lopsided grin on his face, but he was hunched over, holding his stomach. In which he had been shot the day before.

"I'm sorry," I said, rushing over to him. "Maybe we shouldn't do this? It can't be good for you."

"No, I'm fine. Just give me a sec," he said. His voice sounded winded and hoarse.

"You were just shot," I said. "This isn't a good idea."

I stood there, nervously biting my thumbnail, watching him recover from the pain I had inflicted. Seeing him in pain twisted my insides in knots. Finally he stood tall again and appeared unphased once more.

"Ready for another?" he asked.

"I don't know," I said, unsure I wanted to continue. "Maybe we should do something else."

"I'm fine," he said. "You're okay, right?"

I nodded, but looked at him apprehensively.

"Oh, come on," he said.

He lunged at me and grabbed both of my wrists.

"Now what?" he asked, smiling.

I tried to pull my hands out of his grasp and only tightened his hold. The grin he wore while I pulled made me more determined to do it on my own, without his instructions, just to prove I wasn't incompetent.

After no amount of pulling or twisting seemed to help, I was losing hope.

"Give up?" he asked.

I gave one last tug and still didn't succeed.

"Okay, wise guy. What do I do?"

"Wise guy, huh?"

"Just tell me what to do," I said with put-on impatience.

He laughed. I could tell he enjoyed teasing me a little too much.

"Raise your hands above your head, then bring them in and down in a circular motion as hard and fast as you can. But be sure to take advantage of the space between my fingers and thumb."

This time I didn't hold back at all, and my hands broke free the very first time.

"Wow, that was really easy," I said, rubbing the burn on my wrists.

"Easy as pie," he said.

"You know, I've never understood that saying, 'easy as pie.' Have you ever made a pie?" I asked.

He shook his head with a smirk on his face.

"Pie is not easy to make," I said.

He laughed. "Oh, well piece of cake then."

I smiled. "Better."

"Okay," he said. "One more. Turn around."

I hesitated, looking at him suspiciously. *How was he going to trap me this time?* He held up his finger and twirled it around in a circle, indicating that I needed to face away from him. Slowly, I turned around, only taking my eyes off him when I could no longer see him without craning my neck.

My heart started beating faster as I anticipated his next move. It was so quiet I could hear the rush of blood in my ears. It was taking him longer than I expected, and the suspense was killing me. Just as I was about to look at him, he grabbed my shoulders. The jolt surprised me, and I jumped.

"Sorry," I muttered.

This one should be easy to get out of. A grip on my shoulders couldn't possibly be worrisome. I dropped to a crouch, and his grip on me got stronger; he got ahold of my arms. I stood again, and his hands moved right back to my shoulders. "Try again," he said.

This time, I thought for a moment before I acted. I dropped one shoulder and twisted my body, and one of his hands slipped off my shoulder. I could almost taste victory. But before I could twist out of his grasp, he grabbed my arm under the shoulder he still had his hand on, and he pulled me close. My face was pressed tightly against his chest. I heard his heartbeat pick up its pace as he held me there for a moment. Before I could say anything, he thrust me forward to face away from him once again, and he put his hands back on my shoulders.

"Put your arms straight up in the air and spin," he said.

All these instructions sounded ridiculous, but so far they had worked, so I did what he advised, and once again I broke free of his tight grasp. Putting my hands up and spinning was the last thing I would have thought to do if this situation were real; maybe that was the reason they worked so well in the first place. No attackers would anticipate these methods of escape.

"I think that covers the basics," he said, his voice a bit winded. "Do you want to move on to the harder stuff?"

"I'm exhausted!" I grabbed hold of one of the bigger machines that had been moved out of the way. "I'll help you move everything back."

"No. I'll get it later." He put his hand on mine to stop me. "Just leave it."

I stood up, putting my hands up in surrender. "All right, I'll leave it."

He chuckled.

My phone's ringtone echoed through the silent apartment. I bounded from the workout room to the entryway where I had stowed my purse, answering without looking to see who it was, knowing that Casey was behind me.

"Hey," Eli's voice sounded weary.

"Hey," I said back, walking over to the giant window.

"What are you doing?" he asked.

Knowing his dislike of Casey, I felt apprehensive about telling him the truth, but I would not let him dictate my friends. I would not falter.

"Hanging out with Casey," I said.

"Oh." He sounded a bit surprised.

"We just finished working out," I said, feeling compelled to keep talking. I knew he could feel my strange moods shift in the blink of an eye, and I wondered what it made him think. I was sure that it didn't help.

"Well, I guess I'll let you go then. I'd hate to interrupt." He was gone before I could argue.

Great!

"Eli?" Casey asked.

I nodded. I thought I saw a disappointed look on his face, but he turned his back to me, and the next thing I knew a large screen lowered itself from the ceiling. It seemed Casey and his apartment were full of surprises, and I was enjoying discovering them. Hopping over the back of the couch, he landed right on it and beckoned me to join him with a goofy, lopsided smile and a couple loud slaps on the seat next to him.

All awkwardness was gone in the blink of an eye.

"You're a dork."

I sat on the couch next to him, and he playfully threw his arm around me. "The biggest," he said, beaming.

I zoned out as we sat there. The TV rambled in the background. How nice must it be to have this whole place to himself. I was envious.

My thoughts drifted to Eli; maybe knowing he disapproved made this all so much more enjoyable, and in a sense I was glad he resented it. Doing something so spiteful made me feel good after everything he had put me through, and it helped that Casey was loads of fun. I smiled. This was for me, and I deserved it.

CHAPTER EIGHTEEN

I woke up the next morning, and without even moving I could tell that my whole body ached. Gradually, I lifted my arms above my head to stretch out my stiff muscles. As I rolled my wrists around in half-circles, I found a new pain I hadn't expected. My wrists were spotted with bruises. I sighed. *Of course.* I caressed each one as I counted them. Nine. Nine bruises total.

I threw back the covers and got dressed. Heading straight to my jewelry box once I finished, I threw on a couple thick bangles that matched the color of my shirt. They almost covered the bruises. The rest I would have to try to hide myself.

I ran downstairs and met Eli at the door, completely skipping breakfast. I took a deep breath. A week and a half left of school. That's it. I could do it.

"So Casey taught me some ways to get away from an attacker last night," I said, broaching the subject casually on our way to school.

"Cool," he said.

"What did you do last night?" I asked.

"Nothing."

I sighed. I guess I would have to get used to the tension that my friendship with Casey caused. As far as I could see, there was no way around it. I hoped it would get easier with time, but I wasn't going to hold my breath.

Eli's hand lay idle on his lap. I reached over and looped my fingers through his. I hoped the spark of our touch would bring him out of his funk. When he didn't say anything more, I resolved to give him space and sat quietly.

We walked to class, and I kept my fingers crossed that by the end of the day his spirits would lift.

"Earth to Abby!"

I looked at the person behind the arm waving wildly in front of my face.

"Where are you today!" Bailey exclaimed.

"S-sorry," I stammered. "Just have a lot on my mind, I guess."

I finally took the first bite of my lunch to break the spell her inquisitive eyes had on me.

"I said," she enunciated, "what happened to your wrists?"

My eyes darted to my wrists. My bracelets no longer concealed the deep black and blue marks, and the spots popped out like beacons under the fluorescent lights. Eli's hand shot over, and he gently fingered one of the larger blemishes.

"Did he do this?" Eli asked.

My heart thumped harder in rhythmic fashion. My mouth went dry. I stared at Eli with a look of shock on my face, unable to utter a word.

"He did, didn't he?" he demanded.

I could feel his anger coursing through me, as strong as if it were my own.

"He didn't do it intentionally," I said, defending him. "I didn't even know they were there until this morning," I added, hoping that would calm him and alleviate his worry.

He pulled his hand away, stood, and stormed out of the room. I shot Bailey a helpless look and jogged out behind him to catch up. I wanted to smack her for asking.

"Wait," I called after him into the empty hallway.

"Wait for what, Abby?" He whirled around to face me, nostrils flaring.

"Just wait. You're overreacting. He was teaching me self-defense. He showed me how to get out of different holds if someone attacked me."

"That doesn't need to end in bruises."

"I must bruise easy or something," I said.

"No, he was too rough. That's all there is to it. And why was he putting his hands on you at all?"

"He was teaching me!" I shouted, startling even myself. I looked around to make sure we were still alone before finishing. "It took me a few tries to get out of the holds, it was probably my fault."

"It was not *your* fault! Are you serious right now?" he growled through gritted teeth. "Where does he live?"

"I'm not going to tell you that." I stood there, stewing.

"Fine, but I want to speak with him," he said.

"Okay," I said. "Can we go back to lunch now?"

He hesitated briefly, and then grabbed my hand before I knew what was happening, pulling me into a bear hug. We both needed the embrace, and I could feel the tension between us gradually slip away. When I slid my hands down to his waist as I pulled away, his muscles didn't seem as tight as they had been.

We walked back into the cafeteria, running into Ren and a few of the other guys who were headed out. They pulled Eli along with them. Their laughter was contagious, and I giggled as I watched the tension on Eli's face transform into a carefree expression. Then he was out the door, and I was left alone with Bailey. The inquisitive look on her face told me I had a lot of explaining to do.

"Why'd you have to ask about the bruises in front of Eli?" I was exasperated, but still joking.

"Sorry! How was I supposed to know? Nobody ever tells me anything!"

"They're from Casey."

As soon as I said 'Casey,' Bailey's eyes practically bugged out of her head.

"I know, that's why I was hiding them. He's so jealous."

"Abby, that looks so bad. They couldn't be in a worse place," she said.

"I know! I was hoping he wouldn't see them," I said. Looking at them now, I realized how stupid that had been. How could he not have noticed them?

"How'd you get them?" she asked.

"He was teaching me how to get away if someone were to grab me."

"Well, he certainly grabbed you."

I shot her a dirty look. "Not helping."

"I know, sorry. So what did Eli say?" she asked.

"Of course he was furious. He didn't even want me hanging out with Casey in the first place. Now he wants to talk to him. That'll go really well."

"Yeah, I'm glad I'm not in your shoes."

I smacked her arm. "It's all your fault!"

"Come on," she said, getting up and pulling me from the room. "Let's get to class."

*   *   *   *

When I heard the knock at the door that afternoon, my feet felt leaden. Casey had agreed to talk to Eli, though I had omitted the reason. I really hoped things would go smoothly, and that there wouldn't be some kind of testosterone explosion. Thankfully, Ren made sure he was present after what he had witnessed from Eli at lunch. He would be a calming presence if nothing else.

I got to the door and took a deep breath before letting it swing open to admit Casey. I gave him an apprehensive grin and motioned for him to go ahead of me. There was no turning back now. Ren and Eli were both standing, facing us from the opposite side of the couch. Ren stood closest to Casey. I held my breath, waiting for the first word to be spoken. My eyes darted back and forth between the three guys.

"I don't appreciate my girlfriend coming home with bruises from you," Eli snapped.

Casey turned to me with a surprised look on his face, and I threw my arms behind my back to hide the blemishes.

"I gave you bruises?" His quiet voice barely broke the silence in the room.

I regretted now not telling him why Eli wanted to see him. I had left him unprepared, and I could see now that he was devastated that he had hurt me.

"I didn't even know until this morning." I shrugged. "I guess I bruise easily." I hoped that would make him feel better.

His eyes locked on my shoulders where my arms were hidden behind my back. He took a step forward, but then stopped and didn't come any closer. He looked back at Eli, his back tall and strong. "I never meant to hurt her. I was just showing her some self-defense."

I silently commended him for his respectful response. He was older than Eli, and his maturity showed.

"I appreciate the intention, but I'm kindly asking you to refrain from putting your hands on her from now on," Eli said.

"Okay," Casey said. He turned back to me, "I'm so sorry, Abby. I hope you know I would never intentionally hurt you."

I nodded. "I know." I closed the distance between us and hugged him. I noticed Eli's jaw clench, and he looked away. When I pulled back,

Casey's hand grasped my forearm to inspect my wrists. He dropped my arm at the sight of the marks, and his eyes fell to the floor.

"They don't even hurt," I said, trying to make him feel better.

The silence in the room stretched on longer than it should have before Ren finally spoke. "Hey, why don't we all go grab dinner together."

I could see Eli's head whip back in Ren's direction, though I didn't catch his expression. I could guess that he didn't like Ren's suggestion.

I mouthed 'thank you' to Ren when nobody was looking at me. He grinned and nodded in response.

I didn't wait for Casey or Eli to object. "That's a great idea. I'll go change." I headed out of the room. "Be right back," I called over my shoulder.

This might have been one of the best ideas Ren had ever had, or one of the worst. I guessed we would find out, but I hoped it wasn't the latter.

An hour later we sat at a table in a new Chinese restaurant, chopsticks in hand. Before the food came to the table, we kept almost completely silent. I looked around awkwardly to avoid eye contact, wishing I hadn't been so ready to do this. But then, when the food arrived, something changed. Casey was the first to speak.

"I can never seem to work my chopsticks the right way. I always end up with half my food in my lap." He laughed at himself.

"Me either," I chimed in, giggling.

"I usually ask for a children's set," Eli admitted.

He was trying. I had to give him credit for that at least.

The conversation seemed to flow freely after that. Even Eli was laughing and seemed a lot less tense than when we arrived.

We stood in the parking lot talking for a while before heading our separate ways. It wasn't until we were saying goodbye that I realized Eli hadn't spoken for a long time. I hugged Casey and urged him to call me later. I wanted to make sure he understood I wasn't mad at him. I waved at Ren before I got into Eli's car. He revved the engine to life and sped out of the parking lot, squealing the tires as we went.

"Was it really that bad?" I asked.

"I don't understand why you want to be friends with him so badly," he said.

"Why not?"

"I don't like him, and if it even has to be said, he put bruises on you. If you must be friends with him, please don't make me be a part of it."

"Okay," I said, and left it at that.

I realized then that we were not headed to my house.

"Where are we going?" I asked.

"A surprise," was all he would divulge.

We wound around a curvy road as we headed up a hill into the desert. When we reached the top, Eli got out and pulled me to the edge. The view took my breath away. The whole city sat nestled below us, and I gazed out for what seemed like a hundred miles. I felt like I could see everything. The wind whistled around us as it pushed its way up and around the mountain. He turned me around, and I sucked in my breath in awe. The sun on the horizon was just beginning to kiss the earth. We found a place to sit, away from the others who were out taking advantage of the Arizona beauty. He pulled me onto his lap as we watched the colors in the sky change and transform as darkness took hold behind us. Just as the last sliver of light retreated for the night, Eli's hand slipped into my hair, gently cradling my head. He stared into my eyes. The glow emanating from the disappearing sun's rays lent his eyes a striking glimmer. Finally, he kissed me so tenderly and passionately that my knees might have buckled beneath me had I been standing. When he pulled away, I was breathless, and I laid my head on his chest, watching the stars begin to light up the darkening sky. These moments were the ones I had longed for in the midst of the chaotic life we lived. This was what made it all worth it.

"I love you," he whispered into my hair before placing a gentle kiss on the top of my head.

I smiled. "I love you too."

CHAPTER NINETEEN

The final day of school came in glory, welcomed by the whole student body. The entire school was in an uproar of excitement as teachers tried to rein in students' boisterous celebration. Yearbooks were passed around in each class, and mine was the fullest it had ever been, filled with signatures and special notes both from close friends and those who weren't close to me at all. I saved a special place in the back for Eli to sign later.

Most of the graduates rode a roller coaster of emotion: One minute they grinned from ear to ear, the next they were crying with no end in sight. Eli, however, was not one of them; his mood stayed consistently happy, though I sensed some nerves had settled in.

He left me at my house after school to get ready for graduation. My mom got home early to attend with me. "You look beautiful," she said when she popped her head in to say hello. "I'll be ready in a few minutes and then we can go."

When we ascended the stairs into the stadium, hardly anyone else had turned up yet. We sat in the front row. Our view would be great, but I couldn't tell if Eli had arrived yet. A large cap-and-gown clad group had congregated behind the graduates' chairs, waiting for their grand entrance to be announced.

I shot off a quick text message to him and hoped he would get it before he walked in the ceremony. *Good luck. We're in the front row. I love you.*

The crowds were really filling in now. I was elbow-to-elbow with my mom and a stranger who didn't seem to understand personal space and smelled like an armpit. Each time someone said something amusing he rolled with laughter, throwing his elbows wildly out to his side and right into my arm. My elbow throbbed so much after countless blows that I finally shoved him back with all my might.

"Hey," he wailed, shooting me a glare.

I returned it. "Watch your own elbows if you don't like it!"

He was about to say more, but the announcer began by inviting the graduates to advance onto the football field to take their seats for the speeches. I spotted Eli among the crowd and waved, but to my dismay he didn't see me, so I lowered my hand back into my lap.

Whoever decided to make graduations such long affairs must not have had anywhere else to be. There was speech after speech that came from people that nobody in the crowd really knew, except of course the valedictorian. If it were up to me, that would be the only full speech that took place, followed by a couple words of encouragement from the principal, and then the presentation of diplomas would begin. Trying to stay awake on the bleacher seats for two hours proved more tedious than I would have liked. But when it came time for Eli to walk, I stood and cheered as loud as I could. This time he spotted me. His bright blue eyes sparkled under the harsh stadium lights. He lifted the diploma high above his head in victory. I smiled at the cheerful expression on his face.

Then it dawned on me: He had graduated. Now what? We had never talked about what would happen next. *Would he go to college? Would the elders have other plans for him?* I would be in high school, still stuck, left immobile by my age and lack of diploma.

All the caps flew into the air, jerking me away from my dismal thoughts. The crowd in the stands stood all at once and started rushing the field to congratulate the new graduates.

"Mom," I shouted so she could hear me over the commotion. "You can head back. Eli will take me home."

"Okay honey, stay out late, celebrate!"

"Thanks Mom!"

In moments, she disappeared into the sea of people, and I was left alone, trying to find Eli. I picked my way through the groups of families and friends congregating together, snapping pictures. Their laughter and excitement made me smile. I passed a few of my friends and congratulated them as I went by.

"What's that big grin for?" His voice came from my right.

My smile spread across my face. "Hey! Congratulations!"

Eli swooped me into his arms. "Thanks," he said against my ear. He released me swiftly. "Can you take a picture of us?" he asked someone over his shoulder, and it only took a moment for him to step beside me, revealing the photographer.

Vince.

He stood there with Eli's phone in hand. My heart plummeted to my stomach. My eyes darted to Eli, and then to the ground. *Did he realize how awkward this was for me?*

Eli slid me to his side. "Smile." He seemed completely uninhibited, oblivious to the tense atmosphere surrounding Vince and me. I forced a smile to my face. The flash blinded us twice, and I let my smile fall with my eyes. I had nothing to say, and I regretted telling my mom to leave.

"I...ah...told my mom she could go...I figured we could do something...to, you know, celebrate...but if you already have plans I can call her back..." I trailed off, leaving my invitation hanging in the air. I was sure Vince's eyes were on me, scrutinizing my every move.

"I'd love to do something!" Eli said.

"Okay."

My hands fidgeted as I waited for Eli to say or do something, but he didn't. Instead, he seemed to be looking around as if he were waiting for something or someone.

"All right son, I'm going to head home. Enjoy your night. I'm so proud of you, and I know your mother would have loved to be here to see this moment, but I know that she is watching from above." Vince gave Eli a tight hug and held it for just a moment, then released him. "Bye." He turned and walked away.

"Thanks Dad, bye," Eli called after him.

"So, what do you want to do?" I asked him the second Vince left my line of sight.

"When do you have to be home?"

"Doesn't matter." I smiled at him. "My mom said to 'stay out late'." I used my fingers to quote her exact words.

"Come on," he said, dragging me off the field. He was almost jogging to the car, as if every second mattered. I giggled at his sudden burst of energy and excitement. A few fellow graduates congratulated him as we sped by. He waved his hand behind him in thanks. I shot each of them sympathetic looks and kept on moving.

He opened my door for me before slipping into the car too. He sped out of the parking lot at the first chance we got, driving faster than normal. I stole a glance at him, and the happiness displayed on his face made me giddy.

Pulling into a drive-thru, he ordered us a bucket of fried chicken, and then we were off again. The smell enticed me even though I had already eaten. *Though that was hours ago*, I tried to reason.

"Where are we going?" I asked for the second time since leaving the graduation.

"I told you," he said. "It's a surprise." He smiled coyly as he shot me a sideways glance.

We were headed up the freeway now, in a direction I had only been a couple of times. We drove for a long time. Longer than I expected. Though to be honest, I knew there were no expectations, especially now that we were in the middle of nowhere.

The freeway seemed to end, though I don't think it actually did. It appeared to turn into a highway, though it sure didn't look like one. It was pretty dark out here with only an occasional street light to illuminate the road around us. We passed through a small town, but within minutes it was back to nothing on either side again. When we approached a turn that led into a neighborhood that sat in the middle of nothing, I really became confused.

I shot Eli a puzzled look, and he smiled, knowing he was tricking me well. I crossed my arms and turned away from him to look out the window, pretending to pout.

Then, as if an invisible line restricted any further development, the buildings ended, giving way to desert. At least that's what it looked like in the dark. Maybe there were other things out there, but I positively could not see anything. The pavement and street lights stopped at the end of the development, leaving us in the pitch-black night lit only by the headlights of Eli's car and the moon. It was eerie and brought me back to the night I was taken by Randy. I wrapped my arms around myself as my mind went through a quick replay of the events of that evening. I couldn't help but dwell on Vince. He had saved me then. I had put all my trust in him, knowing he wouldn't let me down after that. Then he made a complete turnaround after Elizabeth's death. I felt disheartened that things between us had evaporated into thin air in a split second. I wondered if our friendship would ever be mended, and if tonight's cold shoulder gave any indication, I knew not to have any expectations.

"You okay?" Eli asked. He eyed me with suspicion.

"Huh? Uh...Yeah I'm fine," I said, trying my best to bury the dark thoughts as deep as possible, to be forgotten, if not for good then at least for now.

"You sure?" he asked.

I knew he could feel my apprehension and remorse, but I didn't want to talk about it. The last thing I wanted was to ruin the night with old news.

"Honestly, I'm fine."

He hesitantly turned his full attention back to the dirt road ahead, and I retreated back to gazing out the window, trying to make out shapes in the distance to distract myself. He made a couple turns and finally pulled off to the side, stopped, and shut off the engine. The headlights switched off, plunging us into darkness. He sat there for a moment and let the silence sink into the car.

Then he reached over and latched his hand onto mine, lacing our fingers together. He hit the button to lower the convertible's top, and it slid away without disturbing the quiet, revealing a breathtaking sky above. Stars shone bright everywhere my eyes fell, twinkling above us like beacons in the night. The half moon glimmered bright white in contrast to the blackened sky.

"It's beautiful."

"Not as beautiful as you," Eli said, his eyes on me instead of the sky.

He leaned over and kissed me. We had never shared such an awkward kiss before. The center console got in the way, digging into our sides as we tried to deepen the kiss. I tried unsuccessfully to bite back my giggle. I could feel Eli's body begin to tremble as well. I opened my eyes and looked into his smiling face.

"Well, that wasn't the most graceful, was it?" he said, poking fun at himself.

"No." I giggled.

He grabbed the bucket of chicken from the back seat and popped it open. The succulent smell filled the air around us, and my mouth watered.

"Oh my gosh, that smells amazing."

Eli held the bucket out to me, letting me have first pick. I grabbed a drumstick and sunk my teeth into it, not caring that Eli was watching me pig out. After a moment, I reached for a napkin and made sure I was at least being neat in his spotless car.

"Hungry?" he asked, his expression amused, as he watched me finish off the last of the drumstick in less than two minutes.

"I didn't realize it, but yeah I guess I was."

I snatched another piece of chicken, this time a breast. Not a word was spoken as we polished off the food. I was halfway finished with my second piece by the time Eli finished his first. I felt like a pig. When an air bubble gurgled to the top of my stomach, it popped out of my mouth without warning in the form of a loud belch. I couldn't hold in my outburst of laughter when I caught sight of Eli's shocked face.

"Who are you and what have you done to my girlfriend?" he said in a teasing voice.

I playfully pushed his shoulder away.

"Thirsty?" he asked.

I nodded, regretting my haste in eating now that I didn't have anything to drink. Eli stepped out of the car and popped the trunk. He was hidden from view only briefly, but it was still long enough to make me nervous, feeling like I sat alone in the desert. My eyes skimmed the brush surrounding us. Everything seemed to move until I looked at it. The jostle of the trunk slamming snapped my attention back to Eli.

"Miss me?" he joked as he hopped back into his seat, but I could tell there was an edge to it that seemed as if he might really be questioning. With our complicated situation, it didn't surprise me that he was a little apprehensive here and there.

I smiled. "Always."

His lopsided grin was sexy in so many ways. So enticing.

He handed me one of the ice-cold sodas he was carrying. So sneaky—he had planned this night, and I was never the wiser. He devoured two more pieces of chicken while we sat talking about his graduation.

"So, what are your plans now that you're done with school?" I asked.

"Oh," he said, surprised by the question. "I'm not sure yet."

"No?" I asked.

"Well, I applied to a few universities," he said, looking at me before he finished. "I got into all of them."

"Really?" I said, astounded. "That's amazing!"

"Yeah, I guess. I just don't know that I want to go to college."

"What? Why?" I asked.

"I mean, what's the point? I'm a Protector. That is my career. It's kind of pointless to try to go to school since I could end up re-assigned anywhere, any time."

The truth in his statement was like a jab to the jugular. It hurt. I couldn't even speak, but he was right. He didn't have a choice when a new assignment came up. Sometimes he might not have much notice before he would have to leave town.

"I'm sorry. I guess this is why I never brought this up before," he said.

"No. It's okay. We need to talk about this kind of stuff. It's just sometimes I forget about it, and it's kind of nice not to feel that your impending absence is imminent. Even if it's not immediate," I finally was able to say.

"I know."

"Let's not talk about it any more right now."

"Agreed. Come on," he said, getting out of the car.

He pulled a blanket from the backseat and spread it on the trunk. I got out and walked around to the spot he stood waiting. He hugged me close. I breathed in his manly scent and let it fill my nose. His aroma made me weak in the knees. The next thing I knew he lifted me into the air as if I weighed nothing and set me back down on the trunk. Then he hopped up next to me and put his arm around me. I leaned into him, finding comfort in his body.

"This is really pretty," I said. "How did you find this place?"

"My dad use to take me dirt biking on trails that wind through the hills that way," he said, pointing out exactly where, though it was so dark I couldn't even make out the hills.

A rustling in the bushes startled me backwards, and I almost fell into the backseat. He caught me just before my butt tilted over the ledge. "What was that?" I whispered, afraid to move out of his embrace.

"I don't know."

The bush began to rustle again, so much so that we could see it moving back and forth. Eli hopped down to investigate, leaving me alone on the car. I watched him tiptoe over to the bush. Slowly, he pulled his phone out of his pocket, and the beam from his flashlight lit up the area around him. He stole a quick peek in my direction. I couldn't be certain whether he was assuring himself that I was okay or that he was. He thrust himself forward, landing on the other side of the bush. Suddenly, a coyote bolted from it, running toward the car, but at the last minute it dodged to the right and scampered off into the scrub.

My hand shot to my chest, which burned from holding my breath. Then we both started laughing at ourselves. That little coyote had given us both the heebie-jeebies. Eli jogged back to the car and threw his arms around me, resting his head on my chest. I could feel his heart racing on my leg. We sat there, shaking with laughter. That is, until I realized his head was on my chest, nestled right in the center. I felt abruptly self-conscious. His head shot up, knocking into my face.

"Ow."

"Sorry," he muttered.

I rubbed my chin and looked back up at the stars, letting my mind drift back to what Vince had said about Eli's mom. I hoped she was looking down on him. He was an amazing person, and I was proud that he was able to graduate even after losing his main support system, his mom.

Eli reached over and hooked his hand in mine but didn't come back to sit on the trunk. Instead he leaned on it between my legs, resting one arm on my leg. I leaned forward and rested my chin on top of his head, inhaling the musky smell of his hair. With my free hand, I rubbed his shoulder.

When I looked back at the sky, I saw a shooting star streak across it. I silently made a wish. *I wish that Eli would not get called away from me, ever.* It might have been a selfish wish, but he was the best thing in my life, and without him I didn't know what I would do. I would never tell him my wish; I wanted it to be his choice whether he went away or not. If I held him back I would always regret it, and so would he.

I let my body relax against his, wrapping my arms around his neck. I turned my head upwards as I exhaled.

A dark cloud took hold of my mind once again as I recalled something I had forgotten. Something that I didn't want to think about. It grounded me faster than the shooting star had shot across the sky.

"Oh," I said, "that reminds me. There's something you need to know."

Eli pulled away from me to look me in the eye. His expression bordered on worry. "What?"

I took a deep breath. "I had another dream."

One week later...

Eli's car hugged the curves like a dream as we drove up the mountains that separated us from California. The heat forbade us from the ultimate freedom, riding with the top down. The drive just wasn't the same without the wind in your hair, and with the top obscuring a good portion of the sights. But the heat's evidence was laid out in front of us when we looked at the road ahead and saw an evaporation mirage on the pavement. Our music blared out of his speakers, and we sloppily sang along to every song. His hand lay casually on my thigh.

I couldn't wait to get to California. My dad anxiously awaited our arrival. He had been happy to hear Eli and I were back together and even happier to know he would be accompanying me to California.

Driving out had been Eli's idea. I couldn't fault him; road trips with him were becoming one of my favorite things.

Kelly would be waiting at my old house with my dad when we arrived. Seeing her was another highlight on the list of great things happening on this trip. I couldn't wait for her to meet Eli. I knew she would just love him.

We stopped in Indio for lunch. After we ate, we took a walk to stretch out our legs before getting back on the road. It felt great to be back in my home state, enjoying the cool breeze mixed with the hot summer sun.

After two more hours, we arrived at my house. Kelly was sitting on the swing in the front yard, waiting. I couldn't help but wonder how long she had been sitting there. Her brown hair swung back and forth with her. It had been cut shorter than I remembered, but her eyes were as blue as ever. Eli's car came to a slow stop, and I was out of it the moment the wheels ceased rolling. I threw myself forward, stumbling onto the curb.

"Kelly!" I shrieked.

"*Ah*!" she yelled.

We crashed into each other with a thud, knocking both of us to the ground. The eruption of giggles came so naturally. I felt like I hadn't laughed like that since moving to Arizona.

"Ahem." Eli cleared his throat as he stood on the driveway watching us. His amused expression just made me laugh harder.

Eventually our mirth subsided, and I jumped up, pulling Kelly up with me.

"Kelly, this is Eli, my boyfriend. Eli, this is Kelly," I said.

"It's nice to finally meet you," Eli said.

"You too," Kelly responded. She leaned over and whispered in my ear. "Oh. My. Gosh. He's so *hot*!"

I laughed. "I know, right?" Eli's eyebrows lifted. I smirked at him. "Where's my dad?"

She pointed toward the house, and off I went. I bounded up the steps and into my childhood home in a matter of seconds, without waiting for Eli to catch up.

"Dad?"

He came from the kitchen with a huge grin on his face. "Abbs!" I threw my arms around him, and he squeezed me tight. "I'm so glad you're here, sweetie. I've missed you so much."

"I've missed you too."

I looked around the room, and it was like nothing had changed. The same pictures hung on the walls, including the ones that featured my mom. It surprised me, yet at the same time I didn't know what I had expected. He wasn't like Mom. For him, moving on didn't involve erasing all reminders of the past. It felt like I had never left. It felt like home.

"Knock, knock," Eli called into the house as he peeked through the front door.

"Come in," my dad said. "I'm so glad you could make it up with Abby."

"I am too. I'm looking forward to seeing where Abby grew up." The flirty grin he shot my way sent a burst of excitement through me. I couldn't wait to show him all 'my' places.

"Come on," I said, grabbing Eli's arm and pulling him up the stairs. I turned back halfway up and motioned with my hand for Kelly to follow too. A smile filled her face, and she bounded up the stairs after us.

"This is my room," I said, rounding the corner and flipping on the light switch.

Nothing had changed. It looked as if I had never left almost a year ago. I couldn't believe it had been that long. My gray and yellow bedspread still messily sprawled across my bed, just the way I had left it. A picture of Kelly and me sat on the nightstand, our faces covered in green, exfoliating face masks. I went straight to the window, which was partly covered by my bright yellow curtains. Before I reached it, I stubbed my baby toe on the lounge chair that sat just before it. My knee shot up almost into my face as I grabbed my foot in pain.

"Ow!" I squealed. I started to lose my balance, falling backwards, my arms flailing. Eli closed the gap between us and unexpectedly caught me. My body gracelessly slammed into his strong chest.

"Whoa, you okay?" his husky voice murmured into my hair.

I felt so silly. I had almost fallen flat on my butt. I laughed at myself to try to hide my embarrassment. "I'm fine." I turned to flash Kelly an embarrassed smile, but the look on her face caught me off guard. Her mouth hung open. The instant her eyes met mine, she promptly clamped it shut again and changed the subject.

"So, how did you two meet?"

Eli and I exchanged a look. Neither of us spoke at first. For a normal couple that would have been an easy and even a fun question, but for us it was far from it. Our relationship started out complicated. Who was I kidding? It had never stopped being complicated.

"Uh..." I stumbled.

"We met on the first day of school," Eli said.

Then I considered that maybe it wasn't that hard of a question after all. It wasn't like I had to tell her all of the crazy events that had brought us together. Eli's level-headed temperament could see around all of the complication to the core of our relationship, without Pete's interference. It gave me a new perspective. I grinned at his save.

Love flooded my body. My hair even lifted off my shoulders from a light breeze. Eli had a guilty smirk on his face. I wondered if Kelly noticed.

"Yep, he caught my attention right from the start," I said. And it wasn't a lie. His piercing glare had grabbed me and kept my interest from the beginning.

She smiled, blissfully unaware. "You guys are really cute together."

My dad poked his head in the door. "Hey honey, I have to run to the store real quick. I'll be back in an hour or so. I was thinking we could all go out for dinner when I get back."

"Sounds great," I said.

Two hours later we arrived at my favorite restaurant and arcade, and I was thrilled to find all my old friends there, waiting. Kelly had arranged the whole thing, a welcome home party for me. Eli made quite the impression on all of them. He fit right in.

I ran to take a potty break and all of the girls tagged along. I felt like I had my own entourage. They all dished about how cute Eli was, and how great he seemed. What they didn't know was that there was so much more to him than what met the eye that made him even more desirable than they could ever dream. Just before we left that night, we headed to the ticket redemption booth to cash in for our hard-earned prizes. Each of the guys had won well over a thousand tickets, yet I had come up with a measly hundred. I picked out some candy and gave the rest to Kelly, then waited outside with my dad, escaping the loud chaos in the prize area.

"It's so good to have you here," my dad said. "I've missed hanging out like this. You're completely in your element when you're surrounded by your friends. Plus, it makes me feel young!"

I thought back to all the times my dad had tagged along with me. I had never realized he enjoyed it. I had always figured it was his way of keeping his watchful eye on me.

"It feels like I never left," I said.

Despite the crazy past year, I felt like all my friends and I had picked up where we had left off, as if no time had passed. Kelly even seemed happy being single, which was something I had never thought I would see coming from the boy-crazy Kelly I remembered. She had matured a lot since I had moved away.

Eli came out carrying a huge stuffed panda. He grinned from ear to ear. "I thought maybe you were lacking a giant stuffed panda."

"Oh my gosh! That thing is huge!" Laughing, I ran to his side and put one arm around his back and the other on the panda. I couldn't even reach all the way around it. I stood up on tiptoe and kissed him, hiding our smooch behind the stuffed toy. It might as well have been a wall, it was so enormous.

As the rest of the group emerged, we said our goodbyes and went our separate ways.

"Eli and I'll be home later. I'll call if it's going to be later than eleven, okay?" I said as I hugged my dad.

"Sure honey," he said. I couldn't help but notice a hint of sadness in his eyes as he walked away.

Eli put the top down, and we secured my new friend tightly in the back seat. I even buckled him in before we drove away. I gave Eli directions, and we took the opportunity to drive up the coast at night, barely able to see the waves crashing on the shore, but the salty, cool air coming off the ocean felt perfect blowing through my hair. I directed Eli to pull off the highway at the point where the edge of the earth ended and dropped off into the water. The cliffs had always been one of my favorite places to go at night. We pulled a blanket out of the trunk and spread it over us as we lay there stargazing and listening to the melody of the waves below. It didn't get much better than this right here. I made myself cozy on Eli, resting my head on his shoulder.

"I wish we could do this every night," I whispered.

"Me too," he said.

I closed my eyes, and I could picture the way the water would look as it sprayed across the rocks below. Then the ocean would suck it all back out, exposing colorful starfish and crustaceans that clung to the coarse rocks and coral.

"Your friends are great," Eli said when the silence stretched a little too long.

"You really think so?" I asked.

"Absolutely. I kind of wish some of them were back in Arizona."

I smiled. "Me too."

I must have fallen asleep because the next thing I knew, Eli was carrying me up the stairs into my dad's house. I drifted back to sleep moments after he laid me down in my bed, covered me with my blanket and softly kissed my forehead, but not before I heard him whisper, "Goodnight angel. I love you."

That night I slept fitfully, when I slept at all. My nightmare ravaged its way through my dreams, traipsing its way all over my happiness the next morning. I stomped down the stairs with my hair disheveled and out of place. Eli and my dad already sat at the table eating. A plate of pancakes lay in my place waiting for me. I plopped down in my chair with a thud and dug in without acknowledging Eli or my dad. Their uncertain gazes kept looking from me to each other, and their conversation dwindled.

Finally, after I finished half my food, Eli decided to test the waters. "Rough night?"

I glared at him. I knew full well that he knew exactly how I felt. My foul mood had taken over. I hoped a full belly and a shower would be the trick to get out of this funk, but when both were done, I still didn't feel any better. I grumbled to myself as I headed downstairs.

When Eli saw me coming he was at my side in seconds. "Let's go to the beach."

It brought a smile to my face for the first time that morning. "Okay."

We headed to the door when I stopped in my tracks, realizing I would be leaving my dad behind. I was here to see him; I shouldn't ditch him to go to the beach. Eli rammed right into me, pushing me a full step forward. But he knew right away what was wrong. He wrapped his arms around me and said, "He went out for a few hours. He said he would be back late this afternoon."

Despite Eli's good intentions, my irritation didn't fade. I stared out the window, ignoring his repeated looks of concern.

"You had the nightmare again, didn't you?" he asked when he shut off the car in the parking lot at the beach. His question hung in the air.

"Yeah."

He seized my hand in his. "I don't want you to worry."

"How can I not?"

"I won't let anything happen to you," he said.

"Eli, you know it's not about that. You have no idea how hard this is, not knowing when or where these dangers are going to strike, throwing us into chaos again." I sighed. "I just don't know how much more I can take."

I got out of the car without saying another word. I was done talking about it. Right now I just wanted to forget. Forget I was gifted.

Forget that my life was complicated by death and destruction. Forget that this wasn't home anymore.

Goosebumps rose on my legs when the wind hit them. Even in summer it was sometimes chilly on the beach in the morning. I wrapped my arms around myself, rubbing the bumps away. The sand called my name. I slid off my flip-flops as I ventured into the sand, letting my toes sink in. I could feel Eli coming up behind me, and I didn't waste another moment, taking off running down to the shore. The cold water drifted over my feet and up to my ankles, reinvigorating the goosebumps all over again. Eli laid out our towels before he came down to the water. He stood there, watching me frolic like a child. It felt so good to be back on the beach. I shot him a devious grin before I dashed toward him, water scooped up in both hands. When I flung it at him, he tried to dodge it, laughing as a few drops landed on him.

"Hey, you better watch it! I might have to throw you in, clothes and all!"

"You wouldn't dare," I challenged, lobbing another handful of water at him, missing him entirely.

He lunged forward, grabbing me at the waist and throwing me over his shoulder as he leapt across the knee-height water. I shrieked as he threatened to dip my head in. The tips of my hair dripped in front of my face.

"Okay, okay! I surrender!"

He stopped at once, heaving me to his front again, letting my body slide gradually down his until my feet dangled just over the water, and we were face to face. Nose to nose. Our moment of fun turned more intimate, more heated. I could feel his hot breath on my face, and I closed the gap and kissed him. His fingers dug into my back, pulling me closer. I wrapped my legs around his waist. Some kids up the beach squealed 'eww,' bringing us back to reality. I smiled against his lips, and we erupted in giggles.

"I don't think they like our kissing," I whispered.

I felt the rumble in his chest as he chuckled. I lowered my legs and felt the cold water slide up my thigh as he let me drop lightly to the ground.

He took my hand and led me back to the towels.

"You seem happier," he said.

"Yeah, the beach is my happy place."

A sailboat off in the distance caught my eye. Its majesty as it drifted across the water, powered by the wind, made it all the more appealing to watch. The sails filled with air, billowing to one side.

"Are you getting hungry?" Eli asked.

I thought for a moment, as if he had asked a really hard question. "Yeah, I guess I am."

Eli snorted at my indecisiveness. "How about I go get us some food, and you can stay here and soak up some sun."

"Sounds great," I said.

He kissed me on the forehead and walked away toward the shops that bordered the sand. I watched him until I couldn't tell which dot he was anymore.

Sitting on the beach with my toes dug into the sand, smelling the surf, was heaven. I had missed the tranquility. I closed my eyes and listened to the waves crash on the shore. I leaned on my hands, tilted my head back, and let the sun warm my skin. The breeze allowed my body to stay comfortable despite the high summer temperature. I felt at peace here, alone. It had been a long time since Eli had gone to get us food. My stomach grumbled in reminder.

Suddenly, goosebumps sprang up on my arms and legs, and not because I was cold. They trailed down my spine. My eyes darted open. I felt as if someone was watching me. When my eyes landed on a shadow lurking under the pier, my heart rate picked up. I squinted my eyes against the glare of the sun. *Who is that?*

The shadow was moving. Closer and closer it came. I felt myself moving backwards, though I couldn't explain how I was doing it. Eventually, the shadow reached the edge of the darkness.

I was on my feet now. Ready to run. My erratic breathing bounced between forgetting to breathe at all and almost panting as I tried to regain the forgotten breath. The figure stopped, as if waiting for something. Everything inside me screamed to run, but my feet stayed rooted to the sand. I might as well have stood in quicksand.

The figure's right foot came forward first, stepping out into the light. His leg was engulfed in sunlight, and then in one fluid motion he stood in the open, his face sparking instant recognition.

Casey.

I broke into a run and met him at the very edge of the pier, half-shadowed, half in the golden sun.

"What are you doing here?" I was more than shocked to see him standing there.

"I had to see you," he said.

He reached out and grabbed my hand in his. His clammy fingers fidgeted restlessly around mine.

"Why?" I asked, looking up from our entangled hands.

"Because." He stopped and looked at me like he was trying to find the right words. "Because...Eli isn't who you think he is."

"What?"

Confusion filtered through my mind, and I stared at him, bewildered. I turned to see if Eli was coming back yet, but he was nowhere in sight.

"He's changed. He isn't the person he once was. You have to see that. Please be careful." His eyes pleaded with me.

"I have no idea what you're talking about. Eli is the same as he always has been," I said.

"It's an act. Please believe me. I don't want you to get hurt."

Hurt? Why would I get hurt?

"Listen, I don't know what you think you know about Eli, but you're wrong. Eli has done nothing but protect me. I think it's time for you to leave."

I turned to walk away, but what he said next stopped me cold in my tracks.

"Didn't you ever wonder how he found you? How he knew right where you were?"

I whirled around, trying to stifle my anger. He had no idea what he was talking about. He didn't even know Eli.

I marched up to him and raised my finger, wagging it as I spoke. "You need to leave. Right now!"

He walked back into the shadows without another word. I watched him disappear before I went back to the towel I had been sunbathing on. My anger boiled hot in my veins. I lifted my hand in the air and swatted sand away from me.

"Whoa, are you okay? What happened?" Eli asked when he set the food down on the towel and enveloped me in his arms.

"I'm fine," I mumbled, trying to push it all away. I wouldn't ever tell him what Casey had dared say about him. There was absolutely no truth in it. *Or was there?*

"Did something happen?" he asked. Confusion etched his face.

I took a deep breath and plastered a smile on my face. "Everything is fine." I pulled him close and kissed him. My body hummed with desire as his strong hands wrapped around me. Playfully, I bit his bottom lip. My anger fueled my need. I needed to be close to him. I lifted his shirt off and wrapped my arms around his bare flesh. He sucked in a breath as I slid my nails softly across his back. He pulled back and looked into my eyes, deeply searching them for something—I couldn't tell what. Then his lips were back on mine. He leaned into me harder. When I couldn't hold myself up any longer, we tumbled over into the sand, bursting into laughter.

There was nothing sinister about Eli. Casey was wrong.

Eli handed me a brown paper bag with a sandwich in it, then grabbed his and took a huge bite. I giggled as mayo dabbed the corners of his mouth. I stared at the white smears, waiting for him to clean them off himself.

"What? Do I have something on my face?" he asked around a mouthful of food.

I couldn't help but laugh as he tried to get it with his tongue.

"Here." I reached over and wiped it away with my finger. He grabbed my hand just before I brushed it off on a napkin. He slid my finger into his mouth, gently sucking until he plucked it out again. "All clean," he said, his voice quiet and sensual.

My stomach leapt as his voice touched me in ways it had never done before.

The afternoon got away from us as we sat relaxing on the beach. By the time we made it back to my dad's, it was time for dinner. As we got out and headed inside, Eli grabbed my arm and pulled me aside. "I'm going to go run an errand and leave you and your dad to catch up at dinner."

"An errand?" I asked.

"Yeah, I won't be long. See you in a couple hours," he said. He pecked me on the cheek and was gone the next second.

His departure struck me as funny. Whether it was what Casey had said or something else I would never know, but one thing I knew for certain—I wanted to know where he had gone. I had to know. I tried to come up with reasons he might not tell me where he was going, but nothing feasible came to mind. Maybe he did just want to give my dad and I some time to catch up like he had said, but something in the way he had left seemed strange. I couldn't put my finger on it.

I marched into the house, resolving to forget about it for now.

"Dad?" I called.

"In here." His voice drifted through the house and met me at the door.

I followed it to the kitchen and found him stirring a thick white sauce that bubbled on the stove.

"Can I help you with anything?" I asked.

"Could you heat up the green beans?"

I washed my hands and jumped in. It felt good to fall back into our usual kitchen routine. We worked around each other effortlessly as if it was second nature; I guess it probably was.

When we sat down to eat, my dad suddenly seemed to notice something was missing. He looked around before asking, "Where's Eli?"

"He had some errands to run." I shrugged.

We sat down at the dining room table and ate the delicious fettuccine alfredo and green beans—my dad's specialty.

"I need to get this recipe before I leave. I have missed this. Yum!"

"It's a secret," he teased.

Between bites we caught up on things that we didn't talk about during our quick phone calls, like how my mom was doing and what kind of car I wanted. Then we decided to go out for ice cream.

"You don't think Eli will mind do you?" he asked just before we pulled away from the house.

"Not at all," I said, wondering where the heck he was. I had expected him back already.

When we arrived back at home, Eli's car sat out in front of the darkened house. I softly knocked on the door to the guest room, but there was no answer. I guessed he had gone to bed, and I decided to go to sleep myself.

Upon stepping into my room, the first thing I noticed was a beautiful bouquet of flowers on my dresser, along with a small white envelope resting in front of it. I tore into the envelope.

Abby,
I am sorry about tonight. I will
make it up to you tomorrow. Sleep tight
beautiful. I love you.
-Eli

My heart melted at his thoughtfulness when I smelled the glorious perfume of the flowers. I fell asleep that night staring at the bright blossoms. My dreams beckoned, transporting me to a field of dandelions. Eli held my hand as we ran barefoot, the cool damp earth beneath us. The brilliant blue sky was clear for as far as I could see. In the distance, glorious mountains filled with lush greenery dominated the horizon; and then my eyes caught a black cloud that loomed far ahead, so small it was hardly discernible. I squinted my eyes, but that didn't help me see it any better. Eli suddenly disappeared, leaving me alone as the threatening cloud inched closer.

I sat bolt upright in bed. Without a doubt, I knew that miniscule dark cloud was a sign of something more sinister closing in on me, and it wasn't going to be pretty.

Casey

This grungy hotel smells of bleach and stale cigarette smoke. That will teach me not to pick the first hotel in sight. I should have sprung for something nicer so I wouldn't wallow in such a stench.

I slammed my hands in frustration on the bathroom counter. Edward had me and the team tailing Eli and Abby everywhere. I saw every kiss they shared on the beach, and it made me sick to my stomach. When Eli left her alone on the beach, she looked so relaxed and beautiful. I had to move closer. I hadn't expected her to spook the way she did. She looked right at me, and I couldn't stop myself from stepping forward. She had looked so worried until she saw me. And then she ran toward me. Only then did I realize the deep water I swam in. Not once before had I considered how creepy I must have looked to her. Like some kind of stalker. *What was I thinking?*

My phone buzzed on the counter. I had long since lost count of the number of times Edward had called. I knew what he wanted, so I ignored him. The buzzing stopped, leaving the room to fall silent again.

I couldn't watch her vacation with him another minute. It hurt. I had to get away from them. Edward was sure to be livid at me for leaving my team. He had never been so persistent in calling me before, though I had never defied orders.

I had wandered around on foot for hours afterward, replaying every detail, torturing myself with my own stupidity until I found this dump. I tried to rest, but my head and body refused to cooperate, gaining me a sleepless night. I'd had too many of those lately. Under the fluorescent lights, my darkened, sleep-deprived eyes looked gaunt. I flipped off the light, plunging myself into darkness. Then I backed against the wall and crouched down, running my hands through my hair. My stress headache refused to go away. Stubble from my five o'clock shadow rubbed harshly against my forearms.

My phone illuminated the bathroom like a nightlight when it buzzed to life again. I was growing tired of the incessant buzzing that like clockwork sounded every few minutes since dawn. Sighing, I snatched it off the counter and shoved it to my ear just before it went to voicemail.

"What?" I said.

"Where are you?" Edward's voice filled my ear.

"At a hotel."

"What did you tell her?" he demanded.

"What do you think I told her? I tried to warn her."

"I need to know exactly what you said to her. You could have compromised the entire mission."

I sighed. "I told her he wasn't the same, that he was acting."

Edward fell silent.

"It doesn't matter. She didn't believe me anyway."

"You're sure?" he asked.

"Yeah. She was furious. Told me to leave. Why can't we just tell her?"

I knew in her eyes I had become *that* guy. The one who tried to come between a couple without regard for their feelings. I looked like a jealous idiot. She had undisputable history with Eli. I couldn't blame her for not believing me. I would be lucky if she even spoke to me again.

"It's classified."

"That's bullshit, and you know it," I said, raising my voice. "You want something from this."

"I assure you, I have no idea what you're talking about," Edward said.

"It's about her dream foresight, isn't it? Because she's mortal? Is that why you care? What do you hope to gain from this?"

"Knowledge."

"What kind of knowledge is worth putting her in danger? We're Protectors, not scientists!"

"Well, she's not really in danger if you and your team do your job, is she? Now, I suggest you stop questioning me and start following orders. You're letting your feelings for her cloud your judgment."

"How-"

"You'd have to be blind not to see the way you look at her. If you aren't going to help your team, come home. I'll be in touch."

There was a click on the line, and I knew he was gone. I tossed the phone across the room, and it slid against the bathtub with a thud. *Damn him!* My team had suspected my feelings too. It shouldn't come as a surprise that an elder would notice, especially Edward.

He was using Abby as a pawn, and there was nothing I could do about it. Not a single thing.

I didn't need Edward to tell me to come home. I planned to return today, but maybe I would check on Abby one last time before I left. I had to know she was okay. I made a huge mistake approaching her, and now I needed time, distance. Edward was right—my feelings were getting in the way, and I knew I could count on my team to keep her safe. When she returned home, I would be ready to protect her at any cost.

Thank you for giving this series a spin!

If you enjoyed this book, consider leaving a review at Amazon, Goodreads, and/or the retailer of your choice to help other readers discover this book.

Stay in touch with
C. M. Boers!
Find out about upcoming releases, giveaways, and chats!

Website: www.cmboers.com
Twitter: @CM_Boers
Facebook: https://www.facebook.com/boerscm
Instagram: CM_Boers

Continue reading for a preview of
Derailed
Book three

DIVULGE

CHAPTER ONE

My feet plodded forward, one right after the other. Our pace remained slow. I watched the dust rise in puffs and settle again with each step we took. Heat rose up my back until I perspired. My lungs felt heavy. As I tried to suck in a deep breath, I felt as if I were underwater. I slid the back of my hand across my forehead to stop the beads of sweat from rolling down my face.

High above my head, trees surrounded me in neat rows. Bursts of sunlight drifted through the spaces between the leaves, casting strange shadows on the ground. Eli trekked ahead of me, close enough for me to touch him, yet he did not respond. Confusion and desperation brimmed at the surface of my patience. Ren seemed to appear out of thin air. He lifted his head toward me in an attempt at a greeting and fell into stride next to Eli, matching Eli's pace. The tree line ended. Eli and Ren continued into the clearing, and I stopped short of it. Someone stepped into view. Who? I couldn't tell.

I squinted as if the sun was causing a glare, but that was far from the problem. Their face was hidden by a gray mist. The mystery person broke into a run and lunged at Ren. Another attacker materialized. Again, his face was obscured. Without warning, his fist connected with Eli's cheekbone. Ren's listless body fell to the ground in a heap. Too much happened at once. My eyes darted back and forth between Ren's attacker and Eli. I stepped back, suppressing a scream. Eli tackled the second man. The grinding of gravel under my feet alerted the unrestrained strong-arm to my presence. My heart thumped in my chest. He rushed toward me, and before I realized what was happening, he stood in front of me, his fist headed for . . .

Jolting from sleep, I tried to reorient myself. *My name is Abby Martin. I am in my room. My dream was not real . . . yet. It will be real at some point, but I have time. Time to figure out what it means. Time to stop it . . . maybe.*

I stretched, letting my heart gradually slow to a normal rhythm. My dreams—nightmares, really—had come true twice, each time leading my friends and me into terrifying situations. A few months ago, I would have laughed at anyone who said their nightmares came true, but I guess the movie directors have to get their ideas from somewhere.

Eli, my boyfriend, came from a line of immortal Protectors—yeah, I know my life is weird—and he was supposed to help me with my nightmares, but after his mom was murdered, he blamed me, and we broke up for awhile. In the meantime, I talked to the elders who governed the Protectors to see if they could explain my dreams. According to the elders, I was gifted but not immortal, which was something they had never seen before. But they thought I'd probably start discovering more 'gifts.' *Well, I don't want them.*

My unique situation, mortal with gifted nature, has given me an in with the elders. One in particular seemed keen on helping me, but from what I could tell, this wasn't normal—, in fact the other two elders seemed perturbed that he had taken such an interest. While I was at it, I made myself available to help catch Eli's mom's killer. The elders put me on a team with four great guys, and once we brought the killers to justice, Eli came back to me. I also gained an ally—the head elder, Edward.

I pushed back the covers, letting the cool air hit my overheated legs. I stretched my arms and sighed. Ah, summer. No school. Free time. Something I had craved for months. Maybe I would settle into normal teenage life again. Maybe. I wouldn't hold my breath.

Lifting myself out of bed, I grabbed the duffle bag that I had yet to unpack from my trip to California and pulled out all the remaining things. I threw my clothes in the laundry before tossing the bag back under my bed. The three little souvenirs I had picked out by the beach made me smile as I laid them on my desk. The first was an ivory seagull wind chime I had bought for my mom. When it spun in the wind, it looked almost like the seagulls were swooping down on the beach. I knew it would remind her of our life in California. The second—a shell necklace—I bought for Bailey. Something about the purple shells made me think of her. And last, for me, a single sand dollar.

Eli was surprised by my choice until I told him about my collection. This would be number four. I only bought sand dollars to mark something special. When I was a baby, my dad bought me one during my first trip to the beach. I still remembered the day he gave it to me, as soon as I was old enough to care for it. I kept it wrapped up in a very safe place—my underwear drawer. Soon after, I got my second one, the day after my dad bought the sporting goods store. We went to the beach to celebrate with our friends and family. I had made sure to bring money with me, and when nobody was paying attention, I snuck off to buy one. I hid it in my waistband until I got home, hoping I wouldn't break it.

The third I bought with Kelly when I told her I was moving. Tears streamed down my face through the whole transaction. I was sure the lady at the store thought I was crazy. It also marked the start of a new journey, though at the time, it had seemed like the worst thing. I bought one for Kelly too, as a memento to remember me.

This one, the fourth and hopefully not the last, marked my first trip to California with Eli. A trip I would never forget.

I mulled it over, remembering the highs and lows as I wrapped up the new sand dollar with the others and nestled them back in the hiding spot I had always used. Two weeks in California had passed in the blink of an eye. Beach trips, sunburns, shopping, and lots of time with Kelly. And the romance. I couldn't forget about that. Eli didn't hold back. My favorite night of the whole trip, he surprised me with my favorite Chinese food and a candlelight dinner by the ocean. He laid out a blanket and buried so many glowing candles in the sand that our picnic area gleamed brightly on the dark and desolate beach. He even made me laugh when he tried to use chopsticks—for his sake I was glad he brought plastic silverware, too. To top it off, he bought the most decadent chocolate cake to finish the evening. There was plenty of star gazing, wave watching, and, of course, a bit of making out. We stayed out until one in the morning. It was the closest I had ever come to wanting to . . . well . . . you know. I still had no idea how he had pulled off such an extravagant gesture. It melted my heart.

Then my mind ventured back to Casey, who had shown up days before the beautiful, romantic evening. What had he been thinking? *Eli isn't who you think he is*, he had said. I had no clue what he was talking about. Eli was the same as he always had been. I wished I had asked him why he had come when I saw him, but I had been too infuriated by his audacity. I just wanted him to leave. In hindsight, that had been stupid. I took the coward's way out instead of pushing to get answers, and then I ran. I didn't see him again during the trip, but that didn't mean he wasn't occupying my thoughts. It boggled my mind. What would have compelled him to speak out so boldly against Eli?

Eli and I went back to work the day after arriving home, and it felt great being there again. The easy banter between our co-workers returned to normal now that Eli had no ax to grind, and the days went by quickly. Late one night, as I stalked up the stairs after work, I realized that even though I missed California all the time, it was no longer my home. Arizona was, and I didn't mind it anymore.

I yawned. After four straight days of eight-hour shifts, I welcomed my day off.

My shiny silver laptop caught my eye from where it sat perched on my desk, beckoning me to open it. Unable to stop myself, I popped it open and typed *car listings* into the search box. I perused auto listings constantly now, and thanks to Eli, I knew a few things to look for and a few things to avoid. Unfortunately, no convertibles had been listed in my price range. I still held out hope though—there was still time. My dad was coming to help me shop, and I was counting down the days until he arrived. I crossed off yet another day on my calendar.

Three more days.

"Abby?"

I spun around to see my mom standing in the doorway, her long brown hair pulled back into a ponytail. Her blue eyes captured my attention.

"Yeah?" I asked.

"Are you going to join me for breakfast? I wanted to talk to you about something."

"Ah, okay. I'll be right down," I said, glancing at her again.

She shut the door as quickly as she had come. I shifted on my feet, hurrying to glance at the newest car listings. When nothing caught my eye, I relented and headed downstairs.

Things between my mom and I had been a little strained. She seemed happy, yet she had become super suspicious about everything I did. Our once-close relationship began to disintegrate, and while I knew it wasn't all my fault, I felt partially responsible. I had to keep secrets. She would never know even half of what I had been dealing with. To her, immortal beings were fiction. Maybe if she knew, she wouldn't be so hard on me, but she would probably lock me in my room and never let me out.

I hopped down the stairs and bounded into the dining room, where the table was already laid out with eggs, bacon, and biscuits. I threw myself into my seat and dished up.

"Are you off work today?" I asked.

"No, I'm going in late." She smiled.

"I see. So, what did you want to talk about?"

"Well, I'd like to have dinner together tonight."

"Uh, I already have plans with Eli."

"Tomorrow, then? With George. Just the three of us."

I had forgotten about George. He had taken up residence in my kitchen before I left for California, but I hadn't seen him since I had gotten back.

I wondered why this was a big deal. I had eaten meals with them before, once even at dinner, but Eli had been there too.

"Okay."

"Good," she said.

She looked pleased, as if she had expected me to put up a fight, and I might have if I hadn't been so confused.

"Dress nice. Make sure you're ready to go at six."

I nodded. I finished eating in silence and went straight up to my room when I finished. I grabbed my phone and sent a quick text.

Good morning.

My phone buzzed to life moments later. Eli's name flashed on the screen.

"Hey," I said into the phone.

"Hey yourself."

"What are you doing?" I asked.

"Laying in bed, staring out the window. The sky is very blue today."

I wandered to the window to look at the sky, which shimmered a brilliant blue I had long since realized was normal for Arizona. Already high in the sky, it cast mirages out in the distance as the heat set in. Our summer temps had already reached the triple digits for weeks. Heat radiated off the glass, so I shut the blinds again to block it out.

"A day off. What are we to do?"

I couldn't help the smile that spread across my face, but I said nothing, knowing he was teasing me.

"Hmm . . . I think something might have gotten my girlfriend's tongue."

I giggled.

"So she is there!" He faked surprise. I could hear him chuckling in the background. "What time am I picking you up?"

"Six?" I asked.

"Okay."

"I'll see you then."

"Bye." He hung up before I could respond.

I held the phone to my chest, smiling to myself like a fool. It had been a month since our explosive reconnection. Before that, Eli had cut off all communication with me as he dealt with—and blamed me for—his mother's death. Thankfully, he had come to his senses. So far, life hadn't slowed down enough for us to just enjoy being together again. But now, without school standing in our way, I anticipated date nights galore. All that started tonight.

My mind drifted back to Casey's accusation that Eli was different. *Different how?* I couldn't stop wondering. I searched for things that were wrong, watching every move he made like I would be able to magically see what Casey was talking about.

I hadn't even told Eli about the conversation with Casey. I felt guilty about it, but I couldn't bring myself to say anything. He already mistrusted Casey as it was, and I didn't need to give him more ammunition.

After lunch, I went outside to stretch my legs and get the mail. The mailbox sat at the end of the block, so I welcomed the exercise and the summer heat, at least for the short walk. I stretched my arms out, letting the sun's rays soak into my skin for a little Vitamin D therapy. After unlocking the box, I pulled out all the mail before locking it again. As I walked back, I browsed through the mail. One piece stopped me dead in my tracks.

A postcard from the Phoenix Zoo—a place that had been the center of good and bad times for me, but few knew it. Five words and I felt like my heart would beat right out of my chest:

See how easy it is . . .

I glanced around, my skin prickling. Pushing the postcard to the bottom of the pile, I rushed the rest of the way home, on edge. I set all the mail on the counter, slipping the postcard out first, and hurried back to my room to mull it over. *How easy what is?*

It didn't make sense. I debated calling Eli right then to tell him about it, but I decided to wait. It didn't seem all that threatening.

As I combed my hair later that afternoon, my mind continued to churn without coming up with any plausible explanation for the note. I threw down the comb with a huff.

Shaking my head, I slid myself into a bright blue maxi dress. It hugged my body in all the right places and flowed down to my ankles. The perfect mix of comfort and sexy. This date also marked the first time I would wear my new necklace, the one Ren had bought me for my birthday. I pulled the delicate chain out of the box and draped the owl pendant around my neck. The owl's blue eyes complemented my dress. I slipped on a pair of white sandals, and I was ready to go.

Eli picked me up a short time later, looking handsome in a button-down shirt. His brilliant blue eyes caught my attention the minute I saw him, just as they had captivated me the first time we met.

"Abby, you look beautiful," he said, taking the time to look me over.

My cheeks warmed under his scrutiny. "Thanks," I said.

"Shall we go?" he asked.

I nodded.

His warm hand rested on my back as we headed to the car, sending shivers down my whole body. Lord, he could set me on fire with just his touch. He opened my car door, and we headed on our way.

I waited until we were in the car to pull out the postcard from my purse and hand it to him. I longed for the night to proceed without complication, but I knew I had to tell him. The note unnerved me.

"What's this?" he asked.

"I don't know. It was in my mail today."

He glanced at it, reading it over. His jaw clenched. Then he slid the note into the crack between the seats.

"Let me know if you get any others," he said.

I sat back and mulled it over.

"What do you think it means?" I asked.

"No idea. Let's just forget about it for tonight, OK?"

"All right."

If Eli said not to worry about it, it was probably nothing. I didn't want to freak out and make this into something it wasn't. I did my best to push it out of my mind and hoped it wouldn't resurface.

"If it makes you feel better, I'll see if I can find out who sent it by the postal stamp."

"Thanks," I said, squeezing his hand.

Fondue was on the menu, and my excitement had been building since we decided to go. I adored fondue. I knew it would be hard for me not to stuff myself before the dessert course came, but that was the absolute best part. Maybe they should switch things around and serve dessert first. Now that would be amazing.

A burgundy curtain closed off our booth from the rest of the restaurant. It felt secluded and romantic. I cuddled up to Eli while we waited for the first course—cheese.

His hand drifted from my fingers to the necklace perched on my throat. He caressed the pendant, inspecting the beautiful gold owl, with its striking blue eyes.

"Where did you get this?" he asked.

"Ren," I whispered, remembering the day he had given it to me. Things had been strained between Ren and me ever since the meeting with the elders. Then he had shown up out of the blue on my birthday. It had been so thoughtful. "For my birthday."

"Your birthday. That's right. I missed it."

I nodded.

"I'm sorry. I can't believe I missed it. I'll have to think of a way to make it up to you," he said.

I smiled to myself, thinking of how he might try. "I'd like that."

"Why an owl?" he asked.

"Ren said tawny owls mate for life. I guess he figured that even though things were bad, you and I would be together again someday. I think it was his way of saying you and I are soul mates."

I opened it, showing him the picture of himself inside. A smile touched the corners of his mouth.

"I love it."

He cradled my neck as he leaned in and kissed me. I reclined back, allowing his lips to brush my neck. My hand gripped his chest as desire filled my body. He pulled me closer. I savored the taste of him on my lips and teased him with my tongue.

A moment later, the curtain slid open, making us jump. I blushed as we pulled away from each other and turned our attention to the steaming metal bowl in front of us. Our waiter prepared it right at the table. I watched closely, hoping to recreate it at home, though I knew it wouldn't be the same.

The waiter poured in the dark beer first and let it warm, explaining that it was of the highest quality. Next, he put in the cheese. Soon it melded together, looking gooey and delicious.

"There you go. The cheese will continue to melt as it warms. Let me know if you need anything else."

"Thanks," I said as he walked away.

I slid the curtain closed again just before we dug into the cheesy scrumptiousness.

I giggled as Eli dripped cheese across the table. A smile crept over his face.

"That funny, huh?"

I nodded, my smile never leaving my face.

"I bet you'll be messier than me!"

"Oh yeah? What's the winner get?" I asked.

"Oh, you want to wager on it?" He grinned.

"Of course."

"All right. How about this—loser gives the winner a massage?"

"You're on!"

It didn't take long for me to dribble a small amount on the table, despite how careful I was being. I looked at him to see if he had noticed, and his eyes were on me. He looked thoroughly amused.

I made a face. "So, my mom wants me to go to dinner with her and George tomorrow night," I said, changing the subject.

"Oh yeah. That won't be so bad, will it?" he asked, taking in my look of doubt.

I groaned. "No, I suppose not. But there's something off about it. My mom's acting weird."

"What do you mean?"

"This morning, she came up to my room to make sure I joined her for breakfast because she wanted to 'talk to me.' I always come down for breakfast. If it was no big deal, why the fuss about it? Normally she would have just said something in passing."

"Hmm . . . I'm sure it's nothing. Maybe you're reading into it."

"Maybe," I said, trying not to be disagreeable, but I knew better. There was something going on, and I wasn't so sure I would like it.

"Don't worry about it," he said.

That was easier said than done.

A few minutes later, I had to admit that Eli knew me well. I had been far messier than he had. I had even tried to hide it a few times without success. Eli just laughed at my misguided attempts. I knew I would lose and end up owing him a massage.

We were halfway through the third course when Eli's phone rang. He checked it and stood up. "I'll be right back."

My eyes followed his back as he walked away, and I couldn't help but wonder who it was. *What would make him leave the table in the middle of our date?*

It was a long time before he returned. My entire plate of meat was gone. I tried to push away my annoyance. *There has to be a good reason.*

"Sorry about that," he said. "Oh, you finished. Ready for dessert?"

"I can wait."

"Nonsense," he said, reaching out of our curtained bubble to flag down the waiter.

"We're ready for the dessert course," he said once the waiter made his way over.

"Absolutely, coming right up," he said.

"You hardly ate any of it," I complained when the waiter had cleared it all away.

"I'm fine," he said.

But I wasn't convinced. He seemed to be trying to speed the night along, making eye contact with the waiter as if to say we were waiting to move on.

Five minutes later, the waiter set the chocolate in front of us, along with a plate filled with strawberries, bananas, pound cake, and rice crispy treats. It was heavenly. I would have gladly devoured a second helping, but my stomach didn't seem to agree. I felt stuffed. The decadence distracted me momentarily from Eli's apparent hurry to end the meal, until we finished, and he again rushed the waiter along by asking for the check while he cleaned up the dessert.

"What's wrong?" I asked.

"What? Why would you think something was wrong?" he asked.

"You seem like you're in a hurry to leave."

"Of course not. I'm having a ton of fun with you here." He flashed a smile at me.

He paid the check the second it came and stood up, holding his hand out to help me out of the booth. We didn't speak during the walk to the car, and when we got there, he didn't stop to open my door for me. His gentlemanly ways had become the norm, so it seemed unusual for him to skip it. I felt frustration rearing its ugly head. *What is with him?*

He drove me straight to my house, even though it was well before my curfew, and walked me to the door.

"Do you want to come in?" I asked when he stopped on the doorstep.

"Nah, I think I'm going to head home. I'm tired."

"Ah, OK. I guess I'll just owe you that massage." I hoped that would bring him back to me from wherever his mind was wandering.

"Uh-huh," he said.

"Don't forget to tie a cowbell on before bed," I said.

"I won't."

He was on autopilot.

"Eli!" I shouted.

His head whipped in my direction. *At least that got his attention.*

"You aren't paying attention to me."

"I'm sorry. I'm tired. I need to go," he said.

"Fine."

He leaned in to hug me and planted a kiss on my cheek. The next moment, he was in his car driving away, leaving me standing on the doorstep, wondering what had just happened.

*   *   *   *

The next afternoon, I stood in front of the mirror, dressed in a knee-length black skirt and a cream-colored top, pondering just what I was in store for. I did my makeup slowly, enjoying that there was no reason to rush. I left my long brown hair down, letting it hang down my back in thick waves.

When I was ready, I waited for my mom in the living room and fingered my pink phone. Other than a few vague texts, I hadn't talked to Eli since he left in a hurry the night before. I knew something must be going on. I wished he wasn't being so distant. I craved his support, even if it was only through text.

Butterflies filled my stomach. The thought of hanging out with my mom and her boyfriend still didn't sit well with me. It felt so strange that she was dating someone who wasn't my dad. Plus, I hated not knowing why I was being asked to dinner. When the doorbell rang, it surprised me. I had never once heard George ring the doorbell before. He always just seemed to be there.

"Can you grab that, Abby? I'll be right down," Mom called down the stairs.

I groaned and marched to the front door. Swinging it open, I found George in black dress slacks, a dark lavender dress shirt, and a black tie. He held a bouquet with a colorful assortment of flowers.

"Hey Abby," he said.

"Hi," I responded, stepping away from the door to allow him to enter.

"I'm so glad you can join us tonight."

I nodded, saying nothing. I still had mixed feelings about him.

"Hey," Mom chimed in behind me.

She glided forward, reaching up around his neck and kissing his cheek.

"These," he gestured toward the flowers, "are for you." He handed my mom the bouquet.

"Aww! That's so sweet. They're beautiful. Thank you." She blushed when she turned back toward me. That's all it took to make her blush? I rolled my eyes.

"Should we go?" George suggested.

"Are you ready?" Mom asked me.

"Yeah."

We piled into George's luxury car, my mom in front next to George. The inside smelled of new leather and looked surprisingly clean. I might have thought it was a rental car if I didn't know any better. I hadn't expected that. Maybe I had envisioned him as a slob.

After my mom settled into her seat, George's hand wandered over to rest on her knee. I gagged. Knowing they were dating was one thing, but seeing such a gesture felt overwhelming. I couldn't help but think of my dad and how, not that long ago, his hand rested there. I shifted my body so I faced out the window instead. This would be a long night.

My phone buzzed in my pocket.

Don't stress. I'm here if you need me.

Eli always seemed to know just what I needed to hear to set myself at ease. I was glad he texted. Maybe he had taken care of whatever had distracted him the night before. I closed my eyes and sucked in a deep breath.

We drove twenty minutes until the streetlights tapered off, and we exited onto a road that weaved upward toward a restaurant that was nestled into the mountain. I found myself pressed up to the window, trying to get a good look around as George searched for a parking place.

"So Abby, has Eli brought you here yet?" George asked as we got out.

I shook my head and mumbled, "No."

"The view is spectacular," he said.

When we walked inside, George grabbed my mom's hand and pulled her forward. They sat on the floor and disappeared. I closed the distance to the spot they had sat down at and found a slide that plummeted into the dining room. My mom and George were at the base, laughing. My mom glanced up at me, smiling. Her face was flushed. It was the happiest I had seen her in months.

"Come on, Abby," she shouted up to me.

I contemplated using the stairs to my right. I hated that someone I didn't know might see me act silly. I hesitated a moment longer, looking around to see if anyone was watching. Feeling satisfied that nobody had their eyes on me, I sat down, crossing my legs to be ladylike, and pushed off. I coasted down fast, faster than I had expected, and slipped off the edge, landing on my butt with my skirt lifted in the air. I clutched my skirt, shoving it back down. My cheeks flushed, and my eyes darted around the room as I scrambled to my feet.

"You all right?" Mom asked through her laughter.

I nodded. This was already shaping up to be a mess. I had just flashed the whole restaurant, my mom, and her boyfriend. *How embarrassing.*

"Right this way," a hostess said. She seemed to appear out of thin air.

We followed her through the maze of tables.

"Graceful landing," a boy said as I walked by. He appeared to be my age and was dining with his parents.

I glared at him and resisted the urge to punch him in the face.

The hostess seated us at a table, handed us our menus, and disappeared. I held the menu in my hand, hiding my face from the rest of the dining room, willing my blush to dissipate. *No one else saw you fall. No one else saw you fall.*

When the waitress ventured back to our table, we ordered and handed her the menus before she left us alone again.

"So Abby, what do you think?" George asked.

I looked at him, perplexed, "Of?"

He chuckled. "The restaurant."

I looked around.

"Oh, it's nice."

"We've come here a few times. The view outside is something you have to see. I know you'll love it," Mom said.

She looked over at George. A moment passed. I fiddled with my hands in my lap and avoided looking at them.

"So, we wanted to have dinner with you tonight because . . ." Mom hesitated, looking unsure. Her eyes shifted from me to George as if she was asking him for help.

"What your mom is trying to say is that we have decided to become exclusive," George said.

"Okay . . ."

Why was this so important for me to know?

"We wanted you to be the first to know." Mom smiled.

I furrowed my brow. *Strange.* To me, they had been exclusive for weeks now. Why else would he have spent so much time at my house?

"I sort of thought you already were exclusive," I said.

"Well, technically we were, I suppose," Mom said, looking at George. "But the thing is . . . we feel like things have moved quickly for us. It wasn't anything either of us expected."

"Abby," George said, pulling my attention back. "We're planning on moving in together."

My eyes went wide. "What?"

"We haven't made any decisions about when," Mom added.

Like that makes it better. "Move in together?" I whispered. My heart thumped in my chest, drowning out all the commotion around us. The waitress moved in front of me, placing three plates on the table and stopping to look at me. After a few seconds, my mom tapped my shoulder. I blinked a few times as I came back to reality.

"What?" I asked the waitress.

"Do you need anything else?" I could tell she was frustrated with me.

"No. I'm fine, thanks."

She moved away from our table, leaving me with my mom and now soon-to-be housemate.

I stared at my food, hoping to escape the stares from both George and my mom.

"Abby?" Mom asked.

"What?" I glared at her, challenging her to push me. I didn't care how I sounded. What I cared about was having to give up part of my house to this man I hardly knew. It hadn't even been a year since we had moved out here. Her divorce was still fresh!

My mom's eyes fell to her plate as she pushed the food around without taking a bite.

"Abby, we brought you to dinner so that you and I could get to know each other better."

"What if I don't want to get to know you?" I spat.

"Abby!"

I glared at my mom. George wrapped his arm around her and mouthed, "It's fine." I rolled my eyes and looked down at my food. I was done with this night. My phone buzzed, but I ignored it. I wolfed down the majority of my food, letting the silence stretch on.

"May I be excused?" I asked out of habit when I finished.

My mom nodded without looking up from her plate. I threw my napkin on the table and stormed out of the dining room, marching straight to the overlook outside. I was fuming. I sat myself on the knee-high wall barrier and pulled my knees to my chest.

How could she do this? Doesn't she know this is too soon? How could she be ready?

I wanted to scream until I caught sight of the lights of the city below. Even in my rage, I had to admit the view was spectacular. I wished I could enjoy it to its full extent. I couldn't see the moon, but I knew it was rising, the brightness on the horizon tinting the sky. Yet it didn't take away from the luminosity of the stars. Up on the mountain, they looked like little night lights glistening by the millions. The sky seemed to stretch on forever.

A breeze swept through my hair, blowing it into my face. I exhaled slowly, trying to get out the pent-up frustration. Closing my eyes, I sucked in another deep breath.

My phone buzzed again. I grabbed it, checking to see who was texting me, though deep down I already knew it was Eli.

I hope everything is going okay. Let me know if you need me.

Knowing he was there for me calmed me a little.

I shoved my phone back in my pocket. I wasn't feeling so angry anymore. Just exhausted and tired of fighting everything.

<u>About the Author</u>

Obscured was C. M.'s debut novel. What began as a way to spend her free time slowly transitioned into a passion for writing. The best is yet to come!

C. M. is a mother of three. She grew up in the sunshine state of Arizona with a love of reading and an ambition to write. But she never took her writing seriously until after the birth of her first child. After that she took up writing more seriously in her spare time and hasn't stopped since.

C. M. BOERS